SUSPICIONS OF A PARLOURMAID AND THE NORFOLK RAILWAY MURDERS

Two cases for DCI Bryce

Peter Zander-Howell

Cover photograph by the late Dr Ian C Allen
© The Transport Treasury

For Orson

CONTENTS

INTRODUCTION

Two more cases for Philip Bryce

1. An affluent elderly lady dies in the leafy London suburb of Dulwich Village. The death certificate cites 'natural causes', but her servants are uncomfortable.

A parlourmaid decides to go to New Scotland Yard, and talk to someone there.

DCI Bryce looks into the matter.

2. Bryce is sent to Norfolk, where two solicitors have been murdered. There are obvious connections between the crimes. First, both men were partners in the same firm. Also, both were found beside railway lines.

However, shortly before these two men were found, a third body was discovered. This victim didn't seem to have any connection to the firm of solicitors – but he too was found beside a railway track.

Which of the three victims was the real target, and which murders were either dry runs or red herrings?

PREFACE

DETECTIVE CHIEF INSPECTOR BRYCE

Philip Bryce is an unusual policeman. A Cambridge-educated barrister, he joined the Metropolitan Police in 1937 under Lord Trenchard's accelerated promotion scheme.

After distinguished army service in WW2, by 1949 he has become Scotland Yard's youngest Detective Chief Inspector.

His fiancée was killed during the war, but he recently married a woman whom he met on another murder case.

Bryce is something of a polymath, and has a number of outside interests – railways and cricket near the top of the list.

SUSPICIONS OF A PARLOURMAID

CHAPTER 1

"I think someone poisoned her!"

The speaker was a woman aged about thirty. Neatly turned out in an inexpensive green two-piece suit, she was addressing the morning desk officer at New Scotland Yard.

Arriving a little after eight o'clock, and without so much as a 'good morning' to the uniformed officer, she had placed a navy-blue leather handbag on the counter between them.

Understandably, Sergeant Bowers had initially assumed the bag was lost property. As he hunted under a pile of papers for the log book, he explained that a full description of the bag and its contents would be recorded. He also gave a date when the woman should return, because if no one came for the bag during the intervening period, it would become hers under the '*finders keepers*' principle.

Slim fingers had twisted together in nervous agitation as the woman listened to the officer's recital. Her wide-set hazel eyes watched impatiently as he found the book and filled in the date. It was only when Bowers looked up and asked for her name and address that she made her blunt declaration.

The Sergeant was not greatly experienced in the running of the Yard's reception desk. In his short tenure, face-to-face contact had mostly been with reporters, agitating either for statements connected to current cases, or for audiences with the investigators involved. Occasionally, he had dealt with a simple road traffic enquiry. But homicide referrals to the Yard, Bowers assumed, were made by telephone and sent via the switchboard to the Criminal Investigation Department. Consequently, he was taken aback by what he heard, and the expression on his face said as much.

Registering his astonished look, and misreading it as dismissive of her, the woman's resolve visibly weakened and she appeared to be on the cusp of running away. Having impulsively set down her handbag when she arrived (a symbolic little anchor, holding her in place as she unburdened herself) she was now reaching out to reclaim it.

Suddenly, she stiffened and withdrew her hand. The bag stayed on the counter as she simultaneously pulled back her shoulders and lifted her chin. Bolstering the determination which had brought her to the country's best-known police station in the first place, she repeated her accusation more loudly:

"I think someone poisoned her!"

Detective Sergeant Alexander Haig,

pausing to tie a loose shoelace as he crossed the foyer, overheard both these assertions, and was struck by the force with which they were made. Curious, he stood up and turned to look at the speaker, just as his uniformed colleague made a beckoning '*Help me!*' gesture at him from behind the counter.

"This gentleman is a detective, Miss. He'll hear you out," said Bowers, as Haig responded to the signalled appeal.

Intrigued by the woman's words and manner, but believing the matter would quickly resolve itself into some sort of misunderstanding, the Sergeant gave her a friendly smile and led her to a nearby interview room. Sitting opposite one another at the small table, the blue handbag once again set down firmly and prominently, Haig introduced himself.

"Tell me who you are please, Miss," he continued in his mild Scottish accent, "and what exactly brings you here today?"

"Effie Williams. I'm Effie Williams."

More twisting of fingers filled a short silence. Miss Williams sat rigidly on her wooden chair, alternately eying Haig and the closed interview room door. Presently she managed:

"Parlourmaid. I'm a parlourmaid."

Wondering if he was to hear everything in duplicate, Haig mentally doubled the time he would need to deal with Miss William's concerns. Looking up, he nodded reassuringly at her, his dark brown eyes their most kindly and encouraging.

Hazel eyes pulled themselves away from the door and stared penetratingly into the detective's own.

"I work for Mrs Eloise Lat'mer."

Perhaps conscious of the contraction in her diction, the maid immediately spelled out her employer's name, "That's L a t i m e r, and the address is 197, Court Lane, Dulwich."

She paused, giving the Sergeant time to record these facts before adding, "And when I say I *work* for her, what I mean is I *did* used to work for her, up until Sat'day gone. That's when she died. And that's why I come."

Noting down the date of death, Haig was pleased that an element of trust had apparently been established after the maid's searching eye contact, and that she felt able to get her recount of events properly underway. "What is it that you think has happened?" he asked.

"Mrs Lat'mer was a widow, a bit over seventy. Her husband died ages ago, long before I arrived in the house – that's eight years come Christmas. He left her ever so rich."

Having carried out investigations at two 'stately homes' – Broughton Place and Mistram Manor – during his time at the Yard, the Sergeant rather doubted if Mrs Latimer's suburban wealth would equal the examples he had seen of the 'ever so rich'. But he smiled again and gave more silent encouragement to the maid.

"Well, she'd been having bad turns over the last few months, see, and the doctor didn't know what it was. He'd come and give her some powders and tonics, and she'd take 'em and get better. Then, a couple of weeks or so later, she'd have all the pains and all the sickness again.

"Sat'day breakfast she was took ever so bad and ever so quick. No time for us to call an ambulance before she'd upped and died."

Haig frowned. "Did the doctor write a death certificate when he came?"

"Yes." A curt little nod accompanied this confirmation, but pursed lips told the Sergeant that the maid didn't think much of the document. She explained, "Yes, he did do that. I never saw it, though. He said I was to telephone Mrs Lat'mer's niece, and he'd give the certificate to her when she came.

"I asked him – straight out – what was wrong with the mistress. He told me gastritis." The lips pursed again, and a disbelieving shake of the head accompanied a withering "But if you arst me, I don't think he really knew what it was. Fobbin' me off, more likely!"

"But why do you think she was poisoned?" questioned Haig. "The doctor obviously didn't, because you say he immediately issued a certificate. Doctors never do that, Miss Williams, if they think there's been anything untoward going on."

Hazel eyes dipped behind dark eyelashes. The maid stared at the table. For a moment, the Sergeant thought she would say no more; that she would instead mumble something about a mistake and get up to leave. He was surprised when her reply came in the same resolute and emphatic voice he had heard in the foyer.

"Because Mrs Lat'mer told me a few weeks ago that she didn't trust her relations. She said she always seemed to get ill after they'd been to see her. She said that to Jenny – the other maid – as well as to me. And it was true; Mrs Lat'mer *did* always get sick after they called on her."

Haig kept his head down over his notes. His first reaction was that a combination of natural process and coincidence could easily explain such turns of events. Elderly people got sick more frequently than younger folk; it was unsurprising. He would have said as much to anyone else raising identical suspicions with him in the circumstances described by Effie Williams. But the maid's obvious determination to speak out, despite her acute nervousness, stayed him from making the point for the time being.

In the short time of their acquaintance the Sergeant had been making all his usual and rapid assessments of the woman before him. He guessed that Effie Williams had not received much formal education; but she struck him as intelligent and sincere. There was also a certain correctness of manner about her that he found persuasive – she had none of the breezy bravado or the sly cunning of the many liars he had met over the years.

Haig followed his instinct and decided there must be more to come. He probed for it: "It's a long way from Dulwich to Scotland Yard. And several police stations in between. Why not go to your local police station? Or any station closer than here?"

Stiffness instantly returned to Effie Williams' posture and manner. She replied defensively. "Doctor Acres is very friendly with the police. Very. I think he works for them sometimes. Me and Jenny thought we should come here – to the best police station there is. Monday's my day off, so I come."

Without any visible reaction, Haig absorbed the clear implication that Effie Williams didn't trust the late Mrs Latimer's doctor, or the local police. It wasn't much of a leap for him to conclude that she was probably not inclined to trust him fully, either. He picked his words carefully and accompanied them with another kindly smile.

"I understand. I expect Dr Acres is a police surgeon. If that's his connection to the Force I can tell you I've never come across him in my work. I've never even heard of him before today. Is there anything else you'd like to tell me, Miss

Williams?"

"Yes!"

The maid's voice was at its strongest and most determined. She was a simple working woman, and when measured against a qualified professional man she knew she was of no particular consequence in most people's estimation. She also knew that she had crossed an extremely sensitive threshold in suggesting that because the doctor was closely acquainted with the local police, they would either not listen to what she said; or that if they listened, they would not believe her. Having spoken out, there was absolutely no point in holding anything back from the Sergeant now.

"Since the mistress died, her nephews and niece have been all through the house taking whatever they fancied; just carted it all off." Her features became severe as she recalled how paintings, jewellery, and the contents of the small wine cellar had been loaded into waiting cars. "Lootin', I'd call it. They're proper unpleasant, that family. Every last one of 'em.

"I spoke up about it to Mrs Wade yesterday – she's the niece. I told her that it didn't seem right. Well, I got a complete earful for my trouble. Told me it was none of my business and that she'd thank me to '*...know your proper place, Effie'.*"

Pale cheeks turned pink at the memory. "Well, being concerned to see things done proper and the way your mistress wanted, isn't getting above yourself. Leastways, not in my book!

"So, then she goes on to tell me, still all hoity-toity, that the mistress had willed the house and her belongings '*...to her family, naturally.*'

"That'd be her and her brother, Donald Pilkington, and their two cousins, Henry and Spencer Ogilvie.

"And, she said she'd already spoken to the solicitor on Sat'day morning – soon as he arrived in his office – and told him her aunt had died."

Haig noted the simmering annoyance in the maid as she recalled the exchange with Mrs Latimer's niece. But even so, it was hardly a police matter. This time he said so.

"I can see it would be upsetting for you to have the family swarming all over the house, and removing Mrs Latimer's possessions so soon after she died. And there's plenty of people who would say the four relations were premature, and that what they did wasn't nice," he smiled sympathetically, "I'd be one of them myself, actually.

"But if the will leaves the house and belongings to the family – and from what you say it sounds like Mrs Wade had an opportunity to check that fact with the solicitor when she telephoned him – then she and her relations are entitled to claim their inheritances. And if what they took is all recorded for probate, then there's nothing wrong with that behaviour in law, Miss Williams."

The Sergeant was about to explain that failing to fully declare assets for probate would not, initially anyway, be a criminal matter for the police. The Estate Duty Office would be the correct authority to investigate, if necessary.

The maid forestalled him.

"No; that's exactly it! That's why I'm here. Jenny and me, we *don't* think they're entitled. Not at all!"

Effie Williams leaned forwards earnestly, elbowing her handbag to one side. Bringing the palms of her hands down on the table in front of the Sergeant, she delivered a sharp slapping sound with both.

"Two weeks ago, the mistress told us she'd been to another solicitor to create a new will. She was all riled up on the day, *'I'll teach them to assume they're getting my money'*. That's what she said; her exact words."

Hearing this, Sergeant Haig knew there was definitely something to be investigated if what he had just learned was all true. He closed his pocketbook and stood up.

"All right, Miss Williams, you sit tight for a bit while I go and talk to my boss," he said. "I'll not be long, and I'll send someone in with a cup of tea for you in the meantime."

First arranging the promised brew, Haig went up the three floors to Detective Chief

Inspector Philip Bryce's door, gave it a loud rap, and let himself in.

"Good morning, Sergeant," came the warm greeting. "And I can tell you it's a long time since I had such a good start to a morning! No serious ongoing cases; a silent telephone; and time to properly catch up on all my paperwork." Bryce leaned back in his chair, clasped his hands behind his head and looked quizzically at his subordinate. "But will that happy state of affairs change, I wonder, when you tell me what brings you here?"

Haig returned his chief's smile as he took his customary seat. "I believe it might, sir." He outlined Effie William's story and added, "She strikes me as completely honest, sir, and she says that another maid was told the same by Mrs Latimer; so it looks like there's corroboration."

Bryce's response was serious. "I absolutely agree it needs to be looked at. Is she still here?"

"Yes, sir."

"Good. Go back, and see if she knows the names or the firms of the two solicitors – the original one and this new one." Almost before he had finished speaking he held up a hand. "No; on second thoughts, I'll come too. I'd like to speak to her myself."

Returning to the interview room, Haig introduced the Chief Inspector. Handshakes exchanged, Bryce sat down beside his colleague to face the young woman.

"Effie, the sergeant has told me about your mistress. I'd like to ask you a few more questions. "Do you know the name of the solicitors who drew up Mrs Latimer's old and new wills?"

"Not the new will, sir, no. But Mr Fisher, of Fisher and Holden, was involved with the old will. He's been to the house several times over the years that I've been there."

"You'll appreciate we must somehow find the second solicitor. So, on the day your mistress went to make her new will, do you know if she walked, or took a bus, or what?

This was an easy question for the maid and she answered confidently about Mrs Latimer's travel preferences. "She never took a bus, sir; not ever. She took a taxi if she had to go anywhere far; and of course a train if it was an even longer journey. Sometimes she got me to call for a taxi. But if her business was around Dulwich Village, she always walked.

"That day, she didn't arst me to call a taxi for her. And I don't believe she called for one herself, because I know me and Jenny didn't answer the door to a cabbie – and they always ring the bell."

"Good, that's helpful, and will certainly narrow things down for us a little. You say Mrs Latimer died two days ago, on Saturday. Have any funeral arrangements been made that you know of?"

"Mrs Wade told us that there would be a

service and a cremation as soon as possible, sir, but I haven't heard a date has been fixed. She said me, Jenny, and Cook could all attend; but after that was sorted out, we're to leave the house and she'll give us all a month's pay instead of notice."

"I see. Who are the undertakers?"

"Harbin and Sons; they come and took the mistress away."

"Thank you, that's all very useful. Might you know which bank Mrs Latimer used?"

"Martins." Effie Williams smiled for the first time as a memory came back to her. "And because she was so rich she always used to say she had '*an appointment with my bank manager*' – she was never just 'going to the bank'."

"Excellent. Now, we need to talk to Jenny as soon as possible, and Cook, too. With the relations all milling around, when would be best, do you think?"

"There's nobody from the family has said they're coming today, so any time today, perhaps. Or, tomorrow is Jenny's day off, so she could come here to you like I have today, no bother.

"Cook is free to leave the house any morning for up to an hour, so's she can get odds and ends of shopping done – things that aren't regularly delivered to the house."

The Chief Inspector nodded. "All right, let's try today. Are you happy to go back to Dulwich with Sergeant Haig, and get Jenny and Cook to come out, one at a time, to talk to him?"

This was immediately agreed.

"And you say you used to call for taxis sometimes; I assume there's a telephone in the house?"

"Yes, sir; the number's TOW7859."

Fishing into his jacket breast pocket, the DCI produced a small white rectangle. "Take my card. If anything happens that you think we should know, call the number and ask for me or Sergeant Haig."

Effie accepted the card with thanks. Releasing the clasp on her handbag, she carefully stowed the little slip away.

"Now, this is what I want you both to do. Sergeant, first take Miss Williams' statement. When she's signed that, take her back to Dulwich, but not right up to the house. Park at a distance, just in case any of the family turn up unexpectedly.

"Whilst Sergeant Haig waits in the car, you walk the rest of the way home, Effie, and bring Jenny out to the car. After Jenny returns, Cook should be brought out, if she's available." Bryce looked at Haig, "Statements from both of them, too, Sergeant. We'll sort out what's admissible and what isn't, later."

Turning back to the maid, Bryce emphasised the need for confidentiality. "It's extremely important that all three of you carry on as normal. Say nothing to anyone; not to

Mrs Latimer's family, not to tradesmen or the postman, not even to your own family or close friends. Sergeant Haig will reinforce that with Jenny and Cook as well. Can you do that?"

"Yes, sir. I can and I will!"

The vehemence of this response brought a smile to the Chief Inspector's lips. The maid had obviously tackled her most difficult task in coming to the Yard; everything else would be easy in comparison.

"Good. I'll just have a quick chat with the Sergeant outside, and then I'll leave you with him. I may see you again another day, Effie. You did absolutely right to come and report to us."

In the corridor, Bryce outlined further details of his plan. "Whilst you're in Dulwich, I'll find out whether there are any likely solicitors in the vicinity, and see if anyone knows about a new will. Then I'll probably talk to the coroner's office.

"When you've finished taking the statements, Haig, I suggest you use a call box, rather than Dulwich police station, to contact me here. It may be that I'll have further instructions for you."

"Aye, to all of that," acknowledged Haig. "What do you think of Miss Williams, sir?"

"She's definitely telling us what she believes to be true and, as you said, the new will – if it exists – is potentially the crux of the matter. If that testament shows the family have been disinherited, then subject to other factors we may well have a fresh murder investigation on our hands.

"There is an oddity that jumps out of all this, though, Sergeant, and we may as well have it to the forefront of our minds until we can clear it up. We're told that an elderly lady confided in her staff that she falls ill after her family visit – but apparently didn't do anything about it."

Haig was thoughtful. "Because she didn't forbid her niece and nephews from visiting, or report them herself, do you mean?"

"Exactly. Still, I'm going to take it up to the Chief Super. I think he'll be quite happy that we take this preliminary look."

Haig returned to Effie in the interview room as Bryce took the stairs to the first floor to speak to his boss. As expected, that gentleman was quite willing to allow the DCI to "poke around a bit", and asked to be kept informed.

Back in his office, Bryce picked up the telephone and asked the Yard operator to connect him to the Law Society's offices in Chancery Lane. Reaching the institute's switchboard, he explained who he was and what he wanted. He was quickly put through to a helpful lady who provided the details of four solicitors in and around Dulwich, including Fisher and Holden.

With an 'A to Z' map in front of him, Bryce located Fisher and Holden and ignored the firm, pinpointing instead the addresses of the three other firms he had been given. Selecting the one nearest to Mrs Latimer's house, he placed another telephone call and struck lucky with his first choice.

The receptionist at Carstairs and Prendergast was very helpful. "Oh yes, we had a Mrs Latimer come in a couple of weeks ago and enquire about making a new will. She didn't have an appointment, and normally there'd be at least a few days' wait – sometimes quite a bit longer. But I knew Mr Prendergast was free, and he agreed to see her at once. He's here now, if you'd like to speak to him?"

"Yes please; and thank you very much," replied Bryce, delighted to receive such a pleasant and accommodating response – something which was, as he had often found, by no means a given.

Seconds later, he was speaking to Mr Prendergast and explaining the reason for his call.

"Very interesting, Chief Inspector," said the solicitor. "The key thing for me is that Mrs Latimer is dead. I had no knowledge of her death, but I'm happy to take your word for it as I know of you by repute, and I heard you on the radio recently. I agreed with everything you said, incidentally."

This was a reference to a broadcast in which Bryce had been told to participate some weeks before. The Commissioner had been invited to speak, but had not wished to do so himself. To Bryce's astonishment, the order to present himself at the recording studio had come to him directly from the supreme chief, apparently bypassing other more senior officers.

"I'm absolutely open to discussing our dealings with Mrs Latimer," continued Prendergast, "and I suspect that I may have something of additional interest for you."

"I'm all ears," said Bryce, and drew a clean sheet of foolscap towards him.

"Well, let me say at once that I never actually had sight of any earlier will. When Mrs Latimer came in, she brought only the draft of the new will with her. However, as we ran through it together, she gave me a précis of what the previous will contained.

"The old document had four principal beneficiaries – a niece and three nephews. She said they were her only blood relations, and they would have shared what promises to be an enormous estate compared with most I've handled. There was also a generous bequest to her doctor, plus bequests to three members of her domestic staff.

"As I mentioned, Mrs Latimer had already drafted her new will and brought it with her for us to tidy up and type. None of the relations got a mention, and she gave me no explanation as to why they had been dropped as a body.

"You'll appreciate that it's not uncommon for an elderly person to remove one or more beneficiaries as time passes. Sometimes a beneficiary has pre-deceased the testator and left no issue of their own. Irrevocably falling out with a relative isn't unheard of; and a lapse in contact over many years can also precipitate removal. I've even seen a couple of cases where one child has prospered under their own steam rather better than their siblings have managed, and has been removed from a will for that reason alone.

"But to disinherit the entire living cohort of one's blood relations, that's a most unusual and drastic action. It's not something that I've ever been involved with before – blood really is thicker than water in these matters.

"The niece and nephews weren't the only ones to be jettisoned. Mrs Latimer's doctor got the old heave-ho as well. Bequests to her staff, on the other hand, she'd apparently increased very substantially, and she'd added a gardener to the list, too. After probate, her estate was to be realised and the proceeds sent to reduce the national debt.

"We prepared the document as requested, and the testatrix, a most charming lady, incidentally, came in a few days later to sign it. Two of our clerks were witnesses and I am appointed as sole executor."

Michael Prendergast paused. Realising he

had been speaking at some length, and all without hearing any sort of response, he worried that the line had been disconnected and he was talking to himself. "Are you with me so far, Chief Inspector?" he asked.

"Very much so," replied Bryce. "What you tell me concurs exactly with what a member of Mrs Latimer's staff believes. And, off the record, it seems that some of the original beneficiaries may have been counting chickens ahead of time!"

Prendergast chuckled. "Even with my limited knowledge of Mrs Latimer's assets, I think it would take a very long time to count all the chickens. However, that's not all, and I believe what I tell you next may be significant.

"When Mrs Latimer returned to execute the will, she brought with her a sealed envelope, which she entrusted to me with specific instructions. I am directed to post this envelope on her death. The addressee is the local Coroner.

"I have absolutely no idea of the contents, so I can't help you there. I did ask her if she wanted me to know what the letter contained, but she declined, '*It will be sufficient for you to forward it*,' was what she said.

"Frankly, at the time I thought she was perhaps contemplating taking her own life. Although I was entirely satisfied that she was fully *compos mentis,* she didn't strike me as a well woman.

"You wouldn't need to speak to many

solicitors to find one with a client who, when given a diagnosis without any hope, wanted to ensure that no one else would be wrongly implicated if they decided to call time on their own innings, so to speak. As I'm sure you know, a letter outlining their intention, lodged with a solicitor, is an accepted way of protecting everyone else who might otherwise be suspected of criminal involvement.

"But in view of what you've told me, Chief Inspector, I can see how Mrs Latimer's letter may actually say something quite different."

"I'm grateful to you, Mr Prendergast," said Bryce, "and I wish I could simply thank you, bid you good day, and leave the matter there.

"Instead, I must ask you to think about something else. It seems pretty certain that you are indeed the executor of Mrs Latimer's last will. As I've explained, certain others believe that they are her beneficiaries – when in fact they aren't.

"Beyond what the family wrongly believes, I can also tell you that someone at Fisher and Holden was promptly informed of Mrs Latimer's death on Saturday morning, and doubtless thinks that *he* is the executor, empowered to act under the previous will.

"I know you must, of course, speak to that firm to explain the situation. My question is: for how long would you agree to delay that conversation?"

"Yes, well, you haven't taken me

completely by surprise, Chief Inspector. It occurred to me a few minutes ago that your question might be coming," replied Prendergast. "I really can't delay my duty for any great length of time – and I'm sure you wouldn't expect me to. But what I can do is this: I'll get the letter hand-delivered to the Coroner immediately, with a covering note explaining my involvement as executor.

"As for Fisher and Holden, I'll delay contacting them until late this afternoon – roundabout when they're shutting up shop for the day. All I shall tell them is that I believe we hold Mrs Latimer's last will, and I'll give them its date. I'm sure they will want to satisfy themselves regarding the new will, but I shall say that a meeting isn't possible tomorrow and suggest Wednesday instead. I'll hint, but obviously can't insist, that it might be better if they don't contact the family until after they've viewed the will. All in all, that's the best I can do for you."

"Extremely helpful, thank you," said Bryce. "If I decide to fix up a meeting at Mrs Latimer's house on Wednesday with someone from Fisher and Holden, and as many relatives and beneficiaries as can be assembled, would you agree to preside?"

"Oh, most definitely," replied Prendergast, "just let me check."

The sound of the solicitor thumbing

through his diary reached the DCI.

"Late morning would suit me best, but I could shift appointments around and make it the afternoon, if required."

"Excellent – I shall be in touch. Oh, and can you give me the name and – if you have it – the telephone number for your local coroner?"

"His name is Atkinson, but I don't have his number; sorry.

"Anyway, I wish you joy with the other part of your investigations, Chief Inspector," said the solicitor. "If there have been any dirty dealings, someone must be apprehended and held to account."

Bryce thanked Prendergast again, adding that he looked forward to meeting him before long.

CHAPTER 2

The DCI asked the telephone operator for the Coroner's office covering Dulwich, and was quickly connected. He had never met this particular coroner, but after giving his name and rank to the telephonist, he was pleased to be put through to the man himself. Bryce explained the situation, and the Coroner quickly grasped the salient details.

"All right, Chief Inspector. It certainly sounds a bit fishy. I'll order an immediate *post mortem*. We lose nothing by that, and it may provide something for your investigation sooner, rather than later.

"I take your point about the Police Surgeon, so I'll ask the Home Office for one of their pathologists – Teare or Camps or someone.

"You say the body is with Harbins; I'll arrange removal at once. No promises, but I'd expect the PM to be done tonight or first thing tomorrow.

"When this mysterious letter arrives, I'll let you know what it says. And I'll tell the pathologist to let you have his findings direct. You'll keep me informed of your investigations, I assume?"

Bryce gave the necessary assurance. Thanks and farewells concluded his second highly satisfactory conversation of the morning.

The proven existence of a new will had already justified the quite limited investigation so far. And the outcome with the coroner – an immediate post mortem by an independent pathologist – was far better than Bryce had expected. With no other leads for him to pursue, he returned to his paperwork.

An hour later, Sergeant Haig telephoned. "All done, sir," he reported. "Another two honest and sensible women, in my opinion. No love lost between them and the four relations is putting it politely. Do you have anything more for me now, or shall I come back to the Yard?"

The DCI relayed the information regarding the will, the timescale for informing the original solicitors, and the Coroner's interest.

"I have a gut feeling that Effie has brought us an interesting case, Sergeant. I'm going to chance my arm a bit here, and proceed on the basis that the pathologist will find something sinister.

"So, you go back to the house, Haig. We'll have to hope that no family member turns up while you're there. Don't mention the will, or the *post mortem*. Ask the staff to find addresses and telephone numbers for all the relatives, Dr Acres too. Telephone those details through to me while you're in the house, if possible. I'm going to try to broker a meeting for all the interested parties on Wednesday morning.

"When you've done that, go and see the undertakers. Explain that there's to be a PM, and that nothing should be done with the body until the coroner's officer has been in contact. They shouldn't have done anything anyway, until a second doctor has approved the cremation – I just hope that hasn't been organised yet, but the intervening weekend may help us there.

"I'm sure that as soon as you've introduced yourself Harbin's will realise that this is a suspicious death we're investigating. But persuade them, if you can, to say nothing to the family or anyone else at this stage, although there's not much we can actually do to stop them talking, of course.

"Take fingerprints whilst you're at the undertakers. They might come in useful for exclusion purposes. I know we could probably find hundreds of Mrs Latimer's prints around her house, regardless of how conscientious the maids are; but it's easier to take them from the body now, rather than hunt around the house if we realise we need them later.

"After you've done all that, come back to the Yard."

Bryce returned to his paperwork and put in a productive hour before the Dulwich coroner rang.

"Two things, Chief Inspector. First, the autopsy will start at seven o'clock this evening, but the full report probably won't be with you before tomorrow afternoon.

"Second, Mrs Latimer's letter. It's exactly as expected, someone is trying to kill her and she always falls ill after her family visit. She writes that the fact that I am reading her letter means they have now succeeded. She wants me to investigate, but everything in the letter is conjecture; not a shred of evidence is provided. Almost as an afterthought, she accuses the doctor of gross incompetence. I'll send it on to you at the Yard, such as it is."

"Oh," said Bryce, disappointed. "I confess I was hoping for something incriminating. Pity she didn't at least give some of the dates when she was taken ill; and how her bouts of sickness tied in with visits from her nearest but apparently not-so-dearest. Still, until the PM results come in I've got nothing cast iron to question anyone with, so I have to hang fire anyway."

Bryce thanked the Coroner and had barely replaced the receiver when the instrument rang again. This time it was Haig. The list of family addresses with telephone numbers was soon recorded on his desk pad. Bryce thanked his Sergeant, returned the handset to its cradle, and sat back to think.

He didn't want to tell the family that

the meeting he was planning for Wednesday morning involved the police – much less that the police had actually instigated it. He decided that, in the circumstances, a departure from his usual direct approach would be justified. He resolved to action his alternative plan after first reporting to Tommy Burrell, the Chief Superintendent.

Taking the stairs down to the first floor at a jog trot, he found his boss eating lunch from a greaseproof paper bag. Recognising this as a police canteen offering, Bryce realised his superior was probably every bit as snowed-under as the rest of his Force were, if he was too busy to stop for a better meal.

A cheese and pickle sandwich was offered.

"More bread and pickle than cheese, as usual, but you're welcome just the same," said the Chief Super.

Bryce, who got on very well with his senior officer, smiled broadly and declined. "Cheese is still too hard to come by in any quantity, sir. I wouldn't dream of depriving you!"

"So, in here twice in one day, Philip? Must be something serious with your new case?"

Bryce gave his Chief a concise review.

"I see. Well, Haig was right to bring this to you; it certainly looks like a police matter." Tommy Burrell swished some stray crumbs off his jacket and into his wastepaper basket before remarking, "Seems to be shaping up well, your Sergeant."

Bryce was quick to agree. He had appreciated his subordinate's potential from their first case together, and that initial impression had been repeatedly reinforced. When the time was right, he intended to use the fullest extent of his own influence to help Alex Haig achieve promotion.

"Rhetorical question now, Philip, I assume you want to hang on to this case, since it was dropped into your lap and you've made a good start?"

"Absolutely, sir."

"Very well; I'll clear it with the local Super. Keep me informed."

The Chief Superintendent returned to his sandwich and Bryce returned to his office. Picking up the telephone, he placed another call to Michael Prendergast. He first gave the solicitor the gist of Mrs Latimer's letter, and confirmed that the meeting would go ahead on Wednesday.

"When you contact Fisher and Holden later today, could I prevail upon you to also tell them about the meeting yourself, and get them to nominate a representative to attend?

"And if it isn't too much of an imposition, I'd appreciate it if you would get someone to telephone the four relations and Dr Acres." Bryce quickly explained this special request. "I only ask because, if at all possible, I should like no one else apart from you to be aware of the Yard's involvement at this time.

"My intention is that Sergeant Haig and I will arrive first and sit in the meeting without any introduction. The family and representative from Fishers' can initially make any assumptions they like as to who we are – additional members of your firm, for example; or pretty much anyone other than Scotland Yard detectives. Be assured there will be absolutely no deception, Mr Prendergast, because if anyone should question our presence before I'm ready to declare it, I shall tell them who we are without hesitation."

The solicitor didn't take long to give his answer. "Yes, in view of the potentially criminal aspects, I don't see any reason why I can't oblige you in all of that, Chief Inspector.

"Let me have those telephone numbers. I'll deal with Fisher and Holden myself, and pass the family and the doctor to my secretary to contact. Much easier for her to deflect any questions which may arise by honestly stating she has no details – which I assure you she won't have. Beyond the date and time of the meeting, and the fact that she's ringing on behalf of Mrs. Latimer's executor, there's probably no need for her to say any more."

Bryce was highly satisfied with this; Prendergast's proposal sounded the best way to maintain the small and temporary withholding of information he planned. It was more than likely that when the family and the doctor picked up their telephones and heard the words *'I'm ringing you to arrange a meeting regarding the late Mrs Eloise Latimer's will'* they would – entirely of their own volition – conclude it was a secretary at Fisher and Holden calling.

Prendergast had another helpful suggestion: "And I shall arrange for two extra copies of the will on Wednesday. I imagine that if you and your Sergeant each sit with a copy on the table in front of you, it will go some way to establishing your *bona fides*."

Bryce made a couple of points regarding the conduct of the meeting, before ending the call with further warm thanks for the solicitor's generous assistance.

The sight of his boss's sandwich had awakened Bryce's own appetite, and he wandered out of the building to find sustenance. One of his favourite locations for a quick bite was the cabmen's shelter at Embankment Place. Only licensed taxi drivers could sit down inside, but the vendor did a good trade in providing decent simple fare for a few other Londoners – mostly regular clients – to eat outside.

He enjoyed a bacon roll and a cup of tea. The shelter had a number of convenient objects on which to stand one's beverage, and he was able to relax surprisingly well as he refreshed himself.

Internally recharged, he returned to the Yard and met his Sergeant in the foyer. Climbing the stairs to the third floor together, Bryce told Haig what the Coroner had said.

"Very efficient, that Coroner must be, sir," said Haig as he settled himself once again into the chair opposite his boss. "When I got to the undertaker, his officer was already there. It didn't need the two of us to persuade Mr Harbin to keep what we told him to himself – he was helpful from the outset.

"He said the family displayed little interest in the arrangements, other than everything should take place without delay. It's been left to him to organise a date for the cremation and so on. The only other stipulation from Mrs Wade was that Harbins should trim all the costs as far as possible. He wasn't expecting to contact Mrs Wade again before Thursday.

"I took Mrs Latimer's prints before she was taken to Guy's for the PM."

"Good. Whilst you've been busy, I've set the arrangements for Wednesday's meeting in train." Bryce explained his requests to the solicitor. "As for Mrs Latimer's letter, it falls short of what we were hoping for. Allegations against the relatives are no more than a vague '*I think my family may be poisoning me*', no more substantiated than the allegations from Effie Williams.

"Dr Acres was described as incompetent – but she made no suggestion that he was killing her, or had any involvement. However, if the *post mortem* does show anything in the way of poison, he'll definitely go on the list of suspects. I've asked Prendergast to invite him as well.

"Anyway, nothing more we can do now until the pathologist reports tomorrow."

Bryce changed the subject. "Are you and Kittow fully prepared for the Oxford Assizes?" he asked, referring to a case which had recently taken the three detectives to a country mansion in that city's shire.

"Oh, aye, sir. Kittow is in two minds about it. On the one hand he knows it's good to get experience of going into the witness box in front of a red judge and a jury. On the other hand, he's a bit nervous – apart from a couple of cases before magistrates he's never given evidence in court before."

"I'm expecting him to give a good account of himself," said the Chief Inspector. He was confident about the junior detective's abilities, and had provisionally decided that if ever another case needed a larger team, DC Kittow would be his first choice.

Bryce's thoughts reverted to matters closer to home. "When you were in the Latimer house, Sergeant, did you happen to see a room which would be suitable for about twelve people?

"More than one, sir, it's a big house. I passed a large sitting room which would accommodate that number; and the dining room could easily seat twelve – with more chairs around the walls."

"Good. Contact Effie Williams again. Tell her there will be visitors at, or a little before, eleven thirty on Wednesday morning, and that I'd be grateful if she could arrange for coffee in the dining room for up to a dozen people. You can also tell her that she, and Jenny and Cook, are expected to be present throughout the meeting.

"Added to which, the servants are to pretend that they don't know who we are. May be a waste of time, but I'd like us both to observe faces when the various *denouements* occur."

Haig returned downstairs to his own office, and Bryce pulled his 'in' tray a little nearer. He spent the rest of his Monday afternoon dictating letters to his secretary and processing a mountain of paper.

***

At two-twenty the following afternoon Bryce's telephone rang. Picking up the handset he was pleased to hear the voice of a Home Office pathologist whom he had met several times before. After exchanging pleasantries, the voice told him:

"Your Eloise Latimer, Philip. Arsenic, and stacks of it. Smaller quantities over a period of roughly three months, and a larger, fatal dose, ingested either via food or drink a couple of hours before death. The stomach contained the remnants of a light breakfast – porridge, toast, tea. I'll let you have my full report by five o'clock."

"Thanks, Keith. Off the record, what would you think of gastritis as a stated cause of death, given that the doctor in question had attended Mrs Latimer during previous bouts of sickness, and issued the certificate after she died?"

A thunderous snort escaped from the telephone. "Gross incompetence; possibly worse – but don't quote me! Nothing wrong with her digestive system whatsoever, aside from the arsenic, of course."

The autopsy report arrived by motorcycle messenger as the DCI was preparing to go home on Tuesday evening. He quickly scanned its contents, then telephoned Haig on the internal line and invited him to come up and read it.

One low whistle was the Sergeant's first reaction.

He pushed the report back to his boss and wryly remarked, "We've definitely not been wasting police time ourselves, then, sir!"

CHAPTER 3

On Wednesday morning, the two Yard detectives set off for Dulwich.

"I've told Prendergast I want us to look as though we're simply junior colleagues. It may not work, but I'd like to give it a try," said the DCI as he steered the police Wolseley.

As agreed with the solicitor, the detectives arrived at the Court Lane house well before the appointed time to ensure they were first. Effie Williams opened the door to them, and even though there was no one to observe the maid was politely indifferent. She gave them a formal "Good morning, sirs," then led the way to the dining room.

To one side of the room, a blank-looking Jenny and an equally expressionless Cook stood behind a beautifully ornate silver and enamel samovar on a large trolley. Fine china cups and saucers were arranged in readiness, together with all the other necessaries for coffee.

"There are seats for you gentlemen here and here," said Effie to the policemen, as she and Jenny put down their cups and saucers opposite one another at the far end of the table, either side of an imposing carver chair. Two sealed envelopes, each proclaiming 'Carstairs and Prendergast' in large bold font but otherwise unaddressed, were waiting for them.

"A Mr Prendergast came earlier and introduced himself. He placed those envelopes himself, and said you two gentlemen should arrive first and be shown to these seats," Effie told them, before leaving the room to wait in the hallway for the next visitors.

The detectives seated themselves and savoured their excellent coffee in silence for a few minutes. Bryce looked around the room with interest. The samovar was of Middle Eastern origin, he thought, possibly Persian. Evidence of a Middle Eastern connection was to be seen all around the room, in the fabric of the curtains, the huge rug beneath the table and chairs, and the designs of the Iznik ceramics on the side boards. He idly wondered if these artefacts had been collected on holidays before the war, or whether the late Mr and Mrs Latimer had business connections in that region.

The doorbell pealed again, and Jenny and Cook readied themselves by the samovar as Effie returned with two men.

A more closely matched Tweedle Dee and Tweedle Dum would have been hard to find. Both were very rotund men in their early forties. Each wore a black, pinstripe suit, with a white shirt and dark tie; each had thinning fair hair.

Their facial expressions, however, were totally different. One was smiling and appeared at ease; the other looked very unhappy indeed.

The more relaxed man took the carver at the head of the table and waved at the chair next to Haig, telling his companion, “Suggest you park yourself there, Holden old chap.”

Coffee almost instantly materialised in front of both men. Before anyone had a chance to speak, Effie came back into the room again accompanied by a woman and three men. Settling themselves into seats, two on either side of the table as indicated by more waving from Prendergast, the four were quickly attended to by Jenny and Effie. Both women made a point of clearly addressing each of the new arrivals by name as they set down their coffee.

Bryce silently admired the commonsense of the two maids in identifying each of the relations so inconspicuously, at the same time noticing that not one of the family responded with a ‘thank you’.

Mrs Wade had taken the chair next to Mr Holden. She was smiling at him and about to engage him in conversation when she realised that the three members of staff were drawing back chairs at the other end of the table, preparatory to sitting down. Her incredulous expression almost shrieked ‘*How dare you*!’ at the sight of this liberty.

Her annoyance had no chance to form

itself into words. During his earlier visit, Michael Prendergast had instructed the staff to take their seats at exactly half past eleven. This they had done as the dining room clock chimed its first musical notes to mark the half hour. Seeing Mrs Wade's horrified expression, the solicitor leapt up and took charge, pre-empting any censure or question from her. In a most authoritative manner, he signalled that the meeting had begun.

"Ladies and gentlemen, it is half past eleven and I intend to save time and dispense with unnecessary protocol. Every one of us has cause to be here, and all questions will be answered as we proceed – including who's who.

"I shall begin by saying that there are representatives from two firms of solicitors here this morning." He accompanied this statement with a small upwards gesture of both hands, similar to that made by vicars when welcoming their congregants to a service. Whilst not in any way specifically indicating the detectives sitting either side of him, it was nevertheless an all-encompassing movement, easily taken to mean that everyone at the table who was not family or staff, was a solicitor.

"Some of you may have met Anthony Holden, of Fisher and Holden." He waved towards his fellow-solicitor.

"I am Michael Prendergast, of Carstairs and Prendergast. The reason for the involvement of two solicitor firms will become clear very shortly. The three indoor staff have been invited to join us, because they too have an interest in the late Mrs Latimer's final testament, and it is right that they should be here. Doctor Acres has also been invited, but he is late and we will start without him.

"Mrs Latimer, as some of you know, made a will about a year ago. She had made several earlier wills, in fact, but last year's was properly signed and witnessed and lodged with Fisher and Holden. Mr Holden is here today regarding that will. I believe some of you have either seen that document, or have perhaps been told what it contains."

Bryce noticed the smirk which played around Mrs Wade's mouth at the mention of the will. She was a proud-looking woman in her early forties, tastefully dressed in a dark blue dress and matching coat, a fussy little hat completing her ensemble. A large gold brooch, shaped into a spray of flowers, was pinned to her lapel, its sapphires and diamonds matching an impressive dress ring on her right hand. Bryce wondered if these gems had been amongst the haul of valuables removed over the weekend. She sat, relaxed and expectant. Her brother, Donald Pilkington, sat beside her and looked every bit as smug and comfortable.

Prendergast delivered his first news. "That version of the will, however, is no longer Mrs

Latimer's last will and testament. She came to my firm a little over two weeks ago, and made a fresh will, which was duly signed and witnessed a few days later. I am appointed as the sole executor .

"It follows, therefore, that the last will and testament in the possession of Fisher and Holden, and of which Mr Fisher was sole executor, has been superseded and is no longer valid."

Sergeant Haig had expected the family to receive this announcement like an incoming grenade. Instead, all four relations appeared something between surprised and startled – but not at all disconcerted. It quickly dawned on him that having not the slightest inkling of what the new will contained, much less the contents of their relative's letter, as yet not one of the four realised they had any cause for consternation.

This was indeed the case. Privately, all four were assuming that their aunt had recently discovered more assets to distribute, and that instead of altering her previous testament, she had decided to start afresh. Consequently, each avaricious individual was anticipating that their own share of their aunt's wealth was to be increased in this last iteration of her will.

"I shall deal with the more minor bequests first," Prendergast announced. "The three indoor staff were, as I understand it, beneficiaries, under the earlier will. They remain so under the new will, but their legacies are now increased.

"Jennifer Cass, Euphemia Williams, and Pearl Maria Winter, will each receive one thousand pounds. Geoffrey Webster, a gardener, and not present here today, receives the same.

The three women looked stunned.

As did the four family members.

Henry Ogilvie's astonished expression was also one of irritation. He was an accountant in a small private firm, and thus had a reasonable facility for numbers and mental arithmetic. He made some swift calculations. One thousand pounds to each of *four* staff, when considered against the original twenty-five pound legacies previously left to only *three* staff, corresponded to over nine hundred and eighty pounds lost to himself (and as much again to his brother and cousins).

True, this would not amount to more than a tiny fraction of his aunt's total estate – he still anticipated he would be a very rich man for the rest of his life. But even so, this missing money would have paid the lion's share of the brand-new Rover P4 he anticipated buying. He begrudged the additional bequests.

The front door bell cut across the "Good heavens above!" and "Absurdly generous, if you ask me!" mutterings of the family to one another.

Jenny, seated nearest the dining room door, shot up and ran off.

During her absence, the relations

continued to speak in low voices. Bryce caught a few words, and realised that Sebastian Ogilvie was completely convinced his aunt had found more money and assets to bequeath, on the grounds that '...the bally skivvies'... legacies had been so substantially increased. Bryce looked forward to seeing reactions when more details were revealed.

The maid returned with a man for whom she poured coffee, identifying him as Dr Acres in the process. He pulled back the chair between Donald Pilkington and the Cook, sending a disdainful glance towards the three staff at the table as he did so, and apologised for being late.

"Not at all; not at all, doctor. You arrive most opportunely," said Prendergast, introducing himself to the newcomer. "I was just explaining to the company that Mrs Latimer created a more recent will, which differed from her earlier one."

The solicitor paused for a moment to ensure he had everyone's attention again, before delivering his bombshell.

"Under the latest will, the four blood relatives present here are to receive nothing. Nor, doctor, do you. Mrs Latimer told me that she did not wish for the original bequest of £1000 in your favour to be included in the newer will."

Shocked silence from the family was quickly replaced by pandemonium.

Donald Pilkington stood up and shouted,

"This is preposterous!" His sister and cousins remained seated but reacted equally forcefully. Cries of "Undue influence!" and "We shall contest it!" were discernible, together with more than one expletive.

Prendergast banged down hard on the table with his fist, causing several nearby cups to rattle in their saucers.

"There is little point in talking about undue influence until you hear what Mrs Latimer intended to happen to her very extensive estate."

Bryce smiled inwardly as the solicitor spoke. He thought Prendergast was handling the meeting very well indeed.

"This house and all its contents, three further properties currently let, several thousand acres of managed woodland and numerous portfolios of preferential stocks, debentures, bonds and securities, are all to be sold. There are also some substantial bank deposit accounts."

"Other than the bequests to the three servants present here, and to Mr Webster, there is only one other beneficiary. Mrs Latimer wished for the national debt to be reduced. So, lady and gentlemen, I believe you would struggle to accuse anyone in His Majesty's Treasury of exercising undue influence."

Mrs Wade snarled, small flecks of spittle reaching the polished surface of the table as she spat out, "Perhaps not undue influence, then. But Aunt Eloise was obviously *non compos mentis*. The family will challenge the will on that basis!"

Her brother and cousins all gave voluble endorsement to this promise.

Prendergast's response was cool. "Naturally, you may take whatever action you choose, individually or in concert. As executor, beyond saying that legal representation will certainly be needed, I obviously cannot advise you.

"I can tell you, however, that when Mrs Latimer came to my office, she brought with her a handwritten draft of what she wanted to say, which my firm retains on file. It was very well composed, and there was nothing whatsoever in her manner, or in the draft, which caused me think that she didn't know what she was doing."

Prendergast pushed home his point. "She was perfectly in control of herself, both on that day and on her second visit, when she came in to read and sign the new document. If necessary, my receptionist, together with the two clerks who witnessed her signature, will all attest to the fact that she presented as thoroughly capable in all her dealings with us. I shall certainly attest to the same, if required."

Doctor Acres, silent until now, looked contemptuously at Prendergast and addressed him with sarcastic disparagement. "She was extremely unwell, man! And that's not the uninformed speculation of a solicitor-Johnny like you!"

He continued in the same unpleasant tone. "That Eloise was extremely unwell is my opinion as her medical adviser of many years. I daresay she might have appeared normal enough to *you*, on what was obviously a very short acquaintance. But you'd never met her before to know any different, *had you*?"

It was a rhetorical question, given in the accusatory manner of someone who is extremely sure of his own ground, and wishes to thoroughly demolish that on which his opponent stands. But even if it had not been a rhetorical question, Prendergast could not have contradicted the medic, and so he remained silent.

Acres hadn't finished. "And who are you to say what unseen affliction may have been warping her brain, man? Hmmm? Have you medical qualifications? Have you medical experience and expertise?"

This sustained assault on the solicitor's competence to assess mental capacity went down extremely well with the family.

Mrs Wade picked up the doctor's verbal cudgel and scathingly applied it. "And I rather doubt your office staff are any better qualified than you are, Mr Prendergast, for all your high-handed guarantees of them attesting to Aunt Eloise's state of mind!"

Spencer Ogilvie tapped his forehead and mocked the solicitor by pulling a gormless face at him. "Ruddy obvious to anyone with a brain cell, I should think, that the old trout had something badly wrong 'upstairs'. She must have been completely cuckoo!"

His brother agreed. "Absolutely puddled; there can't be any doubt about it!"

"Well," continued Prendergast, still surprisingly calm, "those uncalled for remarks lead me to another point. Mrs Latimer didn't only instruct me regarding her will. She gave me an additional duty to discharge in the form of a sealed envelope, with instructions to post it to the Coroner in the event of her death."

The room was now silent. Nine people stared at the solicitor in astonishment. Bryce and Haig, seated opposite one another and with a good view down the table, watched only five of them.

"The envelope was delivered to that gentleman by hand on Monday, as soon as I heard of Mrs Latimer's death."

"The Coroner? Why on Earth would the batty old fruitcake write to the Coroner?" thundered Donald Pilkington. "Completely proves our point that she was right off her chump – and how!"

Bryce decided to intervene.

"Thank you for your excellent handling of matters so far, Mr Prendergast. I think it's time for me to answer Mr Pilkington, and respond to some of the other points which have been made.

"I am Detective Chief Inspector Bryce, and the gentleman next to Mr Holden is Detective Sergeant Haig. We are from Scotland Yard."

Once again there was a babble of family voices trying to be heard. This time, it was Bryce who rapped on the table for silence.

"Why the letter to the Coroner? Because your late aunt makes certain allegations. She believed she was being poisoned. She accuses you, Doctor Acres, of failing to spot that this was happening.

"As she never said anything to Mr Prendergast about this when she was alive, we can only surmise. But it would seem probable that her belief was the catalyst for the dramatic changes to her will."

There was further uproar, as the relatives again all started shouting at once, to each other, to Bryce, and to the solicitors.

"That proves it!" shouted Henry Ogilvie above the commotion as he threw his arms up into the air. "She was completely insane!"

Doctor Acres was outraged. "I demand to see this letter! I won't have my professional reputation impugned in this way. And all before a gaggle of gossipy underlings as well," he added, waving arrogantly at the servants, "it's an utter, utter disgrace!"

Mr Holden, with nothing to contribute to

the meeting so far, now made an observation during a lull in the noise. "A few minutes ago, Chief Inspector, before you identified yourself, it dawned on me I'd seen a picture of you in the papers not so long ago, and I was wondering why you were here. I take it there is something rather more solid than Mrs Latimer's letter which interests you?"

All voices in the room were now completely silent, and all faces turned towards Bryce.

"You're quite right Mr Holden. A *post mortem* examination was carried out on Monday evening by a senior Home Office pathologist. I won't go into detail, but the basic fact is absolutely clear – Mrs Latimer died of arsenic poisoning."

Effie started to cry. "I knew it; I just knew it," she said quietly to herself as Jenny nodded and patted her friend's arm.

"So," continued Bryce, "The suggestion that Mrs Latimer wasn't in possession of her faculties has been dismissed. It would seem to me – and I believe the prosecution will have no difficulty in presenting the same to a judge – that even if she wasn't as mentally acute as she might have been without the effects of the poison, she was more than sufficiently sane to make the allegations that she did. And to change her will in the way that she did."

"Balderdash!" cried Donald Pilkington,

his face contorted and flushed. "Are you really suggesting a sane woman would, in the first instance, knowingly allow herself to be poisoned? And in the second instance, continue with a doctor whom she thought was incompetent? Stuff and nonsense, I tell you! Complete and utter piffle!"

The Chief Inspector was indifferent to both the criticism and the vehemence with which it was delivered. "Regardless of what you think, Mr Pilkington, I am conducting a murder investigation. And I can assure you I intend to find an explanation for what, I concede, looks like an anomaly at present.

"Mrs Latimer was not specific in her accusation, and in many ways that is unfortunate. But it doesn't alter the facts of the *post mortem*. Everyone in this room will be investigated, together with anyone else who may have had the opportunity to poison her."

The three members of staff looked alarmed as they realised they must be included in the 'opportunity' category. Jenny also began to cry.

"Sergeant Haig and I will be interviewing all of you over the next day or so. This house will be treated as the scene of a crime. It will be searched from top to bottom."

Nobody spoke.

The cook, who had been dumbfounded twice already – once when she learned that a thousand pounds was to be hers, and then again when she heard the confirmation that her mistress had been poisoned – sat very still but shed no tears. She was decades older than the two younger women, and had spent all her spare time during the war in the WVS. After that experience, she had felt there could be nothing left in life to shock her ever again. As the morning's events had unfolded, however, she realised she had been wrong, but she was now certain that she really had 'lived to see it all'. A formal police interview therefore held no terrors for her; especially not if the Scottish detective, who had taken her statement on Monday, was involved.

Bryce continued, "Correct me if I'm wrong, Mr Prendergast, but I believe the family members have no standing in this matter now?"

The solicitor nodded. Contrary to his usually impeccable professionalism, he took obvious pleasure in stating with firm emphasis: "Absolutely correct, Chief Inspector. *These people have no standing whatsoever*!"

Bryce turned to the four relations and addressed them in a detached and commanding voice, "You will all leave the house immediately, collecting nothing but your hats and coats on the way out."

Prendergast added his own warning. "And if any one of you has already removed anything – anything at all – from the premises, you will need to make arrangements for it to be returned within forty-eight hours. I'm sure Mrs Latimer's staff will be able to tell me what has been taken. And by whom."

The two maids were both nodding vigorously, Jenny helpfully informing the solicitor, "We made a list, sir, Effie and me, best as we could."

Scowling and evidently in a filthy frame of mind, the four relations shoved back their chairs and filed out of the room under Haig's eye. The three staff also stood, undecided as to what they should do next, but Bryce motioned them to sit down again.

"A tricky job, Mr Prendergast. Thank you and well done," said Bryce extending his hand. "You'll apply for probate now, I take it?"

"Yes, I'll crack on with that as soon as I get back to the office."

"I'm sorry that your firm has lost out through no fault of its own, Mr Holden," said Bryce, extending his hand again, "and thank you for coming."

The representative of the deposed firm had recovered much of his customary good humour, and managed a smile. "My senior partner is fuming over the will business. You'll appreciate there would have been a considerable amount of work – and a considerable fee – for us in winding up Mrs Latimer's affairs. But when Bob Fisher hears about the rest of the circus here today, he'll wish he'd come himself instead of sending me!"

The two solicitors departed as they had arrived, together.

Doctor Acres was still seated, staring blindly at the table. With an unsteady hand he took a sip of his coffee.

"We'll need to interview you in due course, Doctor. And given what I've read in the PM report, I expect the General Medical Council will have a few questions for you, too. You'll be able to see the PM report later. But I'll tell you now that a top pathologist has reassured me that Mrs Latimer's digestive system was absolutely fine – apart from the effects of arsenic, of course."

Acres gave no sign that he had even heard what the DCI had said. He rose and made his way out of the room without uttering a word. When he had gone, Bryce took a seat at the end of the table near the three servants.

"I've only met Effie before," he said to Jenny and the cook, "but I'm pleased to meet you two ladies as well. As you've learned this morning, your suspicions were shared by your mistress. And all of you were absolutely right for deciding to come forward.

"You've probably realised that your concerns about the will led to the new one being found. That might not have happened for weeks, unless Mr Prendergast happened to learn of Mrs Latimer's death via another source. But any delay might have been catastrophic – once your mistress was cremated, the arsenic couldn't be found. So your actions have been vital. Thank you.

"Now, as I said a few minutes ago, we have to look into every possibility, and that does mean that we'll have to interview you, and search your rooms, and so on. Don't worry about it – in a murder case we have to go through the procedures. Do you understand?"

The three nodded, displaying a mix of emotions.

Haig returned after supervising the family and Dr Acres out of the house.

"Before we do the interviews, Sergeant Haig and I need to make our inspection of the property," said the DCI. "We'll need some help from each of you, but otherwise you should all stay here in the dining room. It won't take long.

"Let's start with you, Effie. Take the Sergeant and show him your room, please, and then come back downstairs and wait in here with Cook while he carries out a search.

"Jenny, I've seen a garage beside the house. Is there also a garden shed, or something like that?"

"Yes, sir, there's a shed and a garage. I've never been in them though. And Mrs Latimer hasn't had a car all the time I've been here. There's keys in the scullery for those places, sir."

"Excellent; show me please."

The maid led Bryce through the house

and into the scullery on the lower ground floor, where a large scrubbed pine dresser stood against the wall between the sink and the back door. A variety of hooks were fixed to the upper side of the dresser by the sink. Looped over these hooks were wire baskets containing different sizes of scrubbing brushes, cleaning preparations, and cloths, all conveniently to hand for anyone busy at the sink. A row of smaller hooks above the baskets held only keys, each with a parcel label tied on to identify it. Reaching for two of these, Jenny handed them to the Chief Inspector. “Those are for the shed and the back door of the garage, sir.”

Bryce took the keys and let himself out of the back door, climbing the few steps up to a large terrace. He saw a beautifully tended garden beyond; someone who took pride in their work was clearly involved in its upkeep.

A gazebo was situated a little way down the garden, and the shed that Jenny had mentioned was almost hidden away behind some fruit trees at the far end. Bryce wandered down the path running through the lawn. The house was big for a London suburban dwelling – probably six bedrooms plus servants’ rooms, he thought – but the garden was large even for a house of this size.

Selecting the key for the shed padlock, he opened the door and stepped inside. A pre-war petrol-engined Atco lawnmower sat in one corner, and beside it a smaller hand-operated mower, presumably kept as back-up. Next to those was a wooden wheelbarrow with detachable high sides. An array of well-cleaned spades, rakes, forks and hoes, together with other long-handled implements, were hung neatly on one wall, with smaller tools like trowels arranged beneath. Stacked on the floor against another wall was a collection of terracotta pots of various sizes, and beside these three watering cans and a pair of buckets. All these items were quickly noted by Bryce, before he crossed the shed to a small workbench. There was nothing on this, but a bag of bone meal rested against it. Above the workbench was a shelf, on which stood a number of bottles, tins, and jars.

Bryce first looked at, and then peered hopefully into, all of these. There was no sign of any arsenic. The poison was not a declared ingredient of any of the commercial preparations on the shelf, and there was nothing hidden inside any of the larger receptacles. In fact, the most dangerous item was a tin of sodium chlorate, which he knew was not only an indiscriminate weed killer, but was also – if mixed with a common kitchen commodity – potentially explosive.

Satisfied he had searched the shed thoroughly he re-locked it, and walked back to the house. He looked at the back door of the garage. The window beside it was so dirty and filled with cobwebs on the inside that he couldn't see anything through it. Inserting his remaining key, he unlocked the door, and was surprised that the key turned very easily, given the unused look of the building. He stood back and eyed the round metal door knob, then turned and went back into the house. He passed through the kitchen, and called up the stairs: "Sergeant, leave what you're doing for the moment, and bring the print kit to me. I'm just going out to look at the front of the garage."

The garage was attached to the house. It was immediately evident that the front doors had not been opened for many years.

Haig joined his boss, and the DCI indicated that they should walk around to the rear garden.

At the back door of the garage, Bryce said, "the door lock seems to have been well oiled, Sergeant, which rather contradicts first impressions that this garage isn't opened up very often, if you go by the state of that window."

He pointed to the eight-foot boundary wall with the neighbouring house, against which the garage had been built. "The door is quite well protected by the roof overhang, and that high wall also helps. So I'd like you to check that door knob and see if there are any prints on it. The inside knob, too."

Haig quickly dusted the knob, and reported some reasonably clear prints. This done, he opened the door, and repeated the procedure on the inner knob. A minute later he reported that there were apparently identical prints on the inside door knob.

While Haig was packing his kit away, Bryce looked around the garage. As the maid had reported, there was no car, and it looked as though nobody had been in the garage for many years. An old-fashioned lady's bicycle rested against a wall. Both tyres were flat, and the wicker basket was green with decay. Against the opposite wall was a workbench, similar to the one in the shed. Here, however, there were no garden tools, but a neat rack above the bench held hammers, screwdrivers, and a brace-and-bit.

On a long shelf above the tools were a number of jars containing screws and nails, old tins of paint, and some distemper. These also looked to have been undisturbed for a very long time.

But at the end of the shelf, beside an oil can, was a tin. The label was almost facing the front, and although also obviously old, the print was designed to be eye-catching and clear:

ARSENIC TRIOXIDE AS_2O_3

POISON

CHAPTER 4

The two policemen eyed the tin for several seconds.

"Looks like a lot less dust on that than on anything else in here," remarked Haig, "and the spiders haven't been anywhere near it, either."

Bryce, who was tall enough to look directly at the surface of the shelf, agreed. "You're right – the marks in the dust on the shelf suggest it's been picked up and put down quite recently. Let's get it down carefully, and see what you can find on it."

This exercise proved fruitless. Whoever had been handling the tin had taken the precaution of either cleaning it when they had used it last, or they had worn gloves.

"Hardly surprising," said Bryce when Haig confirmed the absence of prints, "but it all leads to a good chance that it's the contents of this tin which caused Mrs Latimer's demise, so I think we can claim we're moving forwards."

"Aye, we must be in with a chance with the prints off the door knobs as well, sir," said Haig. "Hopefully, whoever it was thought about prints on the tin but didn't think the door was important."

"We can certainly hope for that, Sergeant. But it's also possible that someone else had to come in here – perhaps a tradesman working on the house arrived without a necessary tool and asked to look in here. Or Mrs Latimer herself. You'll need to use the prints you took from the body to exclude her.

"It's also possible that the gardener came in here occasionally to get some arsenic to deal with dandelions in the lawn. A usage which Armstrong proposed in his own defence, if you recall. Still, we can check that with Mr Webster soon enough.

"In the meantime, get that tin safely locked away in the car, and we'll make a start with interviewing the staff."

***

Back in the dining room, the three women were talking quietly together. Bryce asked Effie to come along to the sitting room for a chat. Haig joined them as they sat down.

"Well, Effie, you look just a bit happier now," said the DCI.

"Yes, sir. I know it's wrong of me, but really I've got to look out for myself now – nothin' I can do will bring the mistress back. And I can't help thinkin' that the money'll make my life so much easier in the future. My fiancé and me, well, maybe we can afford to marry now. Although I'm not raisin' my hopes too high yet, sir, not 'til the money comes through."

"Very sensible," replied Bryce. "Now I won't keep you long, we've just got a few routine questions for you.

"First, though, we need to take your fingerprints. There's nothing sinister about asking – if we find anything of interest we need to be able to eliminate the prints of other people. We've taken the late Mrs Latimer's prints already."

Effie obediently allowed Haig to take her prints, after which she wiped her fingers on the clean piece of rag he handed to her.

Sergeant Haig had a very good memory, and although he didn't have the garage doorknob prints to hand, he knew the owner had prints of the 'whorl' type. Effie's were of the 'loop' pattern. He caught Bryce's eye and shook his head firmly.

Effie turned back to look at the DCI.

"Now, about the garage. Have you ever been in there?"

"Never, sir. I don't even remember ever seeing the doors open. The mistress didn't have a car. She told me once that her late husband had a car. He could fly, too. He was killed in an aeroplane accident."

"I see. Have you ever seen anyone else go inside?"

The maid thought a little and then shook her head.

"This morning, we met the doctor, and the four relatives. You told us that they, and the doctor, and a solicitor who wasn't here this morning – Mr Fisher – used to visit. Were there any other visitors in the last few months? I'm particularly interested in ones who might have come several times?"

"Not in the last few months, sir, no. The mistress used to have three friends who called quite often – they'd come for lunch or high tea usually, or sometimes dinner. They'd play whist or rummy. But one of them died in the last year, and both the other two are very poorly and haven't been able to come for months. The mistress used to visit them though; she told me one was bedridden and the other housebound. They couldn't get here to see her, and she was very sad about that. There's nobody else I know of who's come more than once."

"What do you know about the gardener?"

"Geoff Webster comes two full days a week, usually Mondays and Fridays. But it rained here all day Monday, so he didn't come. Don't know if anyone's told him about the mistress being dead yet.

"He might come tomorrow to make up for missing Monday, but if not he'll come on Friday. Geoff wouldn't harm the mistress, sir. He was injured in the war, and you won't find anyone more grateful for their job than he is."

"No, no, Effie, I don't suspect him any more

than I do you! But we do need to talk to everyone who's been around this house over the last few months. Do you have his address?"

"No, but Cook might have it, sir. If not, it's likely in the mistress's address book in her study. That's where we found the relatives' addresses for the Sergeant here. I know she put all sorts in that, not just friends and relations, 'cos I saw her get it out one day to find the number for the butcher."

"Good. Do you know if she also kept a diary?"

"I'm not sure sir. But once when I was dusting in her bedroom one day I did see a leather book with a little lock on it, on the dressing table. That might have been a diary, but I never heard her mention keeping one. Perhaps she put it in a drawer out of sight – I know I would if I kept one!"

"That's useful, Effie. You see, it might help if we knew exactly which dates Mrs Latimer fell ill – and whether any visitors were also here around those times."

"Oh yes, I see that, sir. Well, Cook makes a list about the meals for everyone every week, so she would've planned for any visitors. But I don't know if she keeps her lists when the week's over."

"We'll check that with her. In fact, perhaps you'd ask her to come along and have a chat now. You stay with Jenny for just a little longer."

"Don't really matter how long you take

with us now, sir," said Effie as she stood up. "Cook only has to do our meals, and of course we don't have to answer to Mrs Wade and the family any more – you and the new solicitor really put that lot in their place!" the parlourmaid beamed happily at the memory.

Bryce didn't comment on the statement. He thanked her and said, "We may need to talk to you again, Effie, but that's all for now."

To Haig, he said, "Nip into the study, Sergeant, and get the address book. Then go up to Mrs Latimer's bedroom and see if you can find a diary. I believe lovelorn young ladies keep theirs, together with their secret dreams and so on, hidden among their underwear. That may still apply to widows in their seventies, for all I know."

Haig grinned, and departed.

A few minutes later, the Cook came into the sitting room and Bryce stood to greet her and shake her hand. A trifle flustered by so much courtesy, she smiled when the DCI said, "We didn't get to do things earlier in the way I normally do them, and I'm sorry we weren't properly introduced. But as you'll realise, I was concentrating on letting people have the information about the new will before anyone knew who I was – so the Sergeant and I could observe reactions.

"Anyway, how long have you worked here, Mrs Winter?"

"A few months before the end of the war, sir. Before that I was in a house in Kensington, until one night the Germans came over and it was bombed to bits. It was my evening off, by good fortune, and I was doing my WVS work, but my mistress, her husband and a maid were all killed. I was also very lucky finding this position – Mrs Latimer put an advertisement in 'The Lady' the day after the raid, as her previous cook was retiring. She'd been with Mrs Latimer for forty years, and I was told later she'd not lived even six months into her retirement, poor woman. The mistress has certainly been good to us servants in her will, considering none of us has come near forty years' service – even if you add all our years together."

Sergeant Haig came in unobtrusively, and sat down. He held up three items for Bryce to see.

"We've already asked Effie this question and she couldn't help. Do you happen to know where Mr Webster lives?"

"Can't say that I do, sir. I think he lodges somewhere in the village. He'll be here on Friday, though. He's very reliable, and a really nice young man. Injured in the war, like so many, but they patched him up pretty good and his limp doesn't stop him doing most things."

Bryce nodded. "The garage. Do you ever have any reason to go in there?"

Mrs Winter looked at him in surprise, the question 'what on Earth has that got to do with this murder' very obviously on the tip of her tongue. Bryce said nothing, and after a few seconds the cook said:

"No, sir, never had any call to. I don't know what might be in there, but whatever it is it's no use to me in the kitchen."

"Fair enough. Have you ever seen anyone else go in the garage? Or borrow the key hanging in the scullery?"

"No to both, sir."

"Right, last question. Effie told us that you draw up menus for each week, showing what meals are to be prepared and so on. I don't suppose you keep old copies, do you?"

"Sorry, sir, no. I think I see what you want, though, and maybe the mistress would have that sort of information. She kept all the household books, and you might see from those what extras were bought and when – so perhaps you could tell when visitors came for meals or stayed over."

"That's right," intervened Haig; "I've found that book, sir."

"Good. Well, there's just one more thing." He explained the need for fingerprints, and Mrs Winter gave hers without protest.

Once again, Haig shook his head.

Thank you Mrs Winter. Unless the Sergeant has a question, or you want to tell us anything, that's it for the moment."

Both Haig and Cook shook their heads, and Bryce stood up to see the latter out.

"Please ask Jenny to spare us a few minutes, Mrs Winter, and then you and Effie can carry on."

"You were right about the diary, sir," said Haig when the cook had gone. Hidden away under a pile of unmentionables. I saw the household accounts book while I was looking for the address book – both in the top drawer of her desk. Thought the accounts might be helpful."

Haig was silent for a minute. "I think you made a good call to spring the various bits of news onto unsuspecting people without warning, sir. If whoever it is had had even a bit of notice, or even a bit more time, the arsenic would have disappeared, and perhaps the diary and accounts too, if they contain any incriminating facts. When you as good as threw them out of what they thought was going to be their property I nearly cheered. As, I think, did Effie."

Bryce smiled.

"Yes; if the killer is someone who was here today, then for a start he or she has been most remiss in not getting rid of the arsenic straight away.

"I can't say I warmed to any of the relatives, but did you get a feeling about any of them?"

"No; at least no feeling that a particular one is a murderer, sir. I thought they were all equally unpleasant, so my money is on one of them doing the dirty deed, rather than on one of the servants."

"Agreed. Ah, here's Jenny."

The interview with Jenny elicited no new information. Her fingerprints were also dissimilar to those on the garage door knob, and she soon left the room again.

Bryce looked at his watch "Good lord," he muttered, "it's coming up to three o'clock, and we haven't eaten. You should have kicked me!"

The Sergeant didn't say that he thought that kicking a DCI was a bad idea, given that it would not only be a criminal assault but also a sackable offence, and Bryce continued:

"Tell you what. If you can survive another hour, we'll take a quick look in the address book and see if we can locate the gardener. If so, we try to find him. Then, we'll call it a day and see if our wives can double the size of our evening meal, or something."

Haig nodded his agreement, and Bryce pushed the address book over to him, picking up the diary himself. It was, as Effie had suggested, a locked book. Rather than waste time searching for a key he felt no compunction in forcing the lock, which had never been designed to be more than a token barrier. He quickly scanned through the more recent entries, and uttered a mild profanity – not something he was in the habit of doing.

"Mrs Latimer has recorded in detail who came visiting and when; and also how her own health has allegedly been affected by the visits. It will need carefully going through and all the dates and names set out on one sheet. I'm glad we got to it first because it's certainly something else that the murderer would have wanted to find and destroy – assuming he or she knew Mrs L kept a diary, of course.

"Anyway, how are you doing?"

"Got it, sir. There's an address, no telephone number. Also a note that Webster works for people called Baxter on Wednesdays. Ah, and Mrs L has an address for some Baxters, and a phone number. Might be worth calling them, and if he's there they could ask him to hang on until we arrive? Save missing him between addresses that way."

"Yes, go and do that, will you? Just explain to the Baxters that this is a routine enquiry – he might be a potential witness – and that the matter is urgent."

Haig left the room taking the address book, and Bryce went back to the diary and accounts.

The Sergeant returned inside five minutes.

"Webster's there now, sir. I spoke to Mrs Baxter, who was very helpful. I emphasised that we needed to talk to Mr Webster as a potential witness, and she didn't ask any questions. She undertook to tell him to stay on site until we arrived, and that we could interview him in the summerhouse, if that was convenient."

"Well done. Let's get going. Do you know where to go?"

"Yes, sir, I've glanced at the A to Z. It's less than half a mile away."

CHAPTER 5

Haig parked the car outside the Baxter residence. It was a tad smaller than Mrs Latimer's, but of similar standing. Bryce mentally debated whether to walk straight round to the rear garden, but decided that would be rather discourteous to the householder, and rang the front door bell instead. It was opened by a lady in her mid-fifties who clearly wasn't a servant.

"Good afternoon, gentlemen. I'm Emmeline Baxter. I understand you need to speak to Webster."

"Yes, madam. I'm Chief Inspector Bryce, and this is Sergeant Haig – you spoke to him a few minutes ago. I'm very sorry to trouble you. I'll emphasise what you were told – there is no problem with Mr Webster – we think he may be an unwitting witness to a crime which he almost certainly doesn't even know has been committed. Perhaps if we just go around to the back garden?"

Mrs Baxter looked at the officers for a moment, and then said:

"I think you should come inside first, and talk to me for a minute."

She led the way to a study.

"Do please sit down. This is my husband's room, but he's out at present. Now, I'm not entirely stupid, Chief Inspector – I was one of the first female solicitors, although I no longer practise. Eloise Latimer died a few days ago. She and I were colleagues on a couple of committees. Not intimate friends, you understand – I was a good few years younger, and we'd never been in one another's houses – but we'd worked together for some years. Now, I telephoned her first thing this morning, and that was when her maid told me that she had died.

"Now, I put two and two together here. Webster works for Eloise as well as for me. She is dead. People of your rank don't come to interview someone who might possibly have seen a road accident. My guess is that you are looking into a possible case of murder, and you think Webster may be able to help."

Bryce smiled faintly, and nodded.

"Very astute of you, Mrs Baxter. Yes, the late Mrs Latimer was, without doubt, poisoned with arsenic. That will probably be in the newspapers tomorrow."

"Oh dear – poor Eloise. Well, I'm sure Webster isn't responsible, but I'll fetch him in here so you can ask your questions – I assume you aren't arresting him?"

"Certainly not, Mrs Baxter. And although it's unusual, I am perfectly happy for you to be present during the interview. Not that I have any reason to suppose that he might require the services of a solicitor!"

"That's very understanding of you, Chief Inspector. I'll fetch Webster. I was going to tell him about Eloise when he came to be paid at five o'clock, but I'll say nothing now except that you want to talk to him and that – if he has no objections – I'll 'sit in', as it were."

A few minutes later Mrs Baxter returned, accompanied by a blonde-haired clean-shaven young man of medium height, walking with a slight limp.

"This is Geoffrey Webster, gentlemen. He is happy for me to observe. Please treat the room as yours, and act as though I'm not here."

"Thank you, Mrs Baxter." Bryce offered his hand to the gardener. "Do sit down, Mr Webster. Now, this must seem very odd to you, but I assure you it's just a routine enquiry. I'm Detective Chief Inspector Bryce, and this is Detective Sergeant Haig. We're from Scotland Yard.

"I have a couple of questions, but let me just give you a few bits of information first. I fear this may come as a shock.

"First, Mrs Latimer died on Saturday. I understand it rained all day on Monday, so of course you didn't go to the house and therefore didn't learn of her death.

"Second, she didn't die of natural causes – she died from arsenic poisoning. We are investigating her murder.

"Third, in the fortnight before her death, she made a new will. You – and Mrs Latimer's three house servants – all benefit from that will, to the tune of one thousand pounds each.

"Fourth, her niece and nephews, who expected to inherit under the terms of a previous will, no longer receive anything at all.

"Finally, Mrs Latimer left a letter to the coroner, accusing her relatives of poisoning her."

Webster, as he sat listening to Bryce's list, appeared more and more astonished. When the DCI stopped talking, the gardener just sat staring at him, with his mouth open.

Eventually, he spoke for the first time:

"I hope you don't think I did it, sir. Mrs Latimer was very good to me. If she's really left us workers some money, I suppose that gives us motive. But I've lost a job, and with it an employer who accepted my limitations – like Mr and Mrs Baxter do here." He half-turned to acknowledge his mistress sitting behind him.

He sat, shaking his head, still clearly upset and bemused.

"I have absolutely no reason to suspect you, Mr Webster, so please don't be concerned. Nor the house staff either, for that matter. But in a case of murder, we follow procedures even more rigidly than usual. Now, my questions.

"First, have you ever been inside Mrs Latimer's garage?"

“The garage? No, sir, never. I go in the shed, of course; that's where the garden tools are kept. And I go into the scullery and kitchen for breaks. I don’t even know what’s in the garage.”

“Fair enough. Now, when you get dandelions or daisies in the lawn, or something like that, what do you do?”

Webster smiled for the first time.

“I’ve got a daisy grubber, he said. It’s like a special narrow fork...”

“That’s all right, Mr Webster,” interrupted Bryce, “I’m familiar with that implement, and I saw yours in the shed earlier.

“But what if you get a bigger patch of weeds?”

“There’s some sodium chlorate in the shed, sir, but since I’ve worked for Mrs Latimer I’ve only needed to use it once – and that was over a year ago.”

“So you wouldn’t use arsenic?”

“No, I certainly wouldn’t,” said the gardener emphatically. “I’ve no experience of using it, and even if I knew where to get some I’d be very nervous about sprinkling the stuff about. There’s cats come through the garden, for a start.”

“I ask,” said Bryce, “because there was a tin of arsenic trioxide – white arsenic – in the garage.”

Webster stared at him again.

“I see,” he said. “Well, there’s never been

any in my shed, and like I say, I've never ever been in the garage."

"Good enough," replied Bryce. "Now, we have fingerprints from the garage. Are you willing to allow us to take yours for comparison purposes?"

Mrs Baxter stirred, but remained silent.

Webster immediately agreed to give his prints. Bryce signalled to Haig, who pulled out his little 'bag of tricks' that his boss had told him to bring in from the car. Five minutes later, the job was done, and Webster was wiping his fingers on a rag which Mrs Baxter had fetched, as Haig had run out of cloths in his bag.

For the fourth time, Haig looked at the DCI and shook his head firmly. Mrs Baxter, seeing the signal, smiled to herself.

"Thanks for providing those, Mr Webster," said Bryce. I assure you that your prints will be destroyed as soon as the case is solved.

"Just one further question. You heard me say that Mrs Latimer wrote to the Coroner about her suspicions that her relatives were trying to kill her. We also understand that she spoke to at least one of the domestic staff about the same thing.

"Did she ever say anything to you on those lines?"

"Not that specific, sir, no, although Jenny and Effie told me she'd talked about it to them."

"Unfortunately that's hearsay, and not

evidence that can be used."

"Yes, I understand, sir. But Mrs Latimer did tell me that she didn't like and didn't trust her nephews. She said they didn't love her, only her money. She told me this a couple of months ago, and then again about a month later."

"Just the nephews? What about the niece?"

"I don't remember that she was mentioned. But, and I see this isn't evidence either, the niece is a horrible woman. In the last few months she's taken to coming out while I'm working, and giving me instructions as though it was her garden. Not just telling me what to do, but the way she speaks – she treats me like I was the lowest of the low. And three or four times when I thought her orders were stupid, and I checked later with Mrs Latimer, the mistress got very cross and said to take no notice of what Mrs Wade had told me to do."

"I see," said Bryce. "All very helpful Mr Webster – we always need to build a picture of everyone involved in a case, and you've painted an interesting one of Mrs Wade. Did you also have any dealings with the three nephews?"

"No, sir. I worked for Mrs Latimer for three years, and for the first two of those I never saw hair nor hide of any of them. But then they started coming, and more and more frequently of late. They never spoke to me. I saw them around, but they took no interest in what I was doing."

"Last question. Did you ever see anyone go into garage via the back door? Any of the relatives, or a servant, or Mrs Latimer herself, or anyone at all?"

"Sorry, sir, I never did."

"No matter, Mr Webster. Thank you very much for talking to us. Now, as I said earlier, assuming there isn't yet another will lurking around somewhere – which I think is extremely unlikely – I believe Mr Prendergast will be contacting you in due course about the will. He is the solicitor from Carstairs and Prendergast, and is Mrs Latimer's executor. I suggest that you take the opportunity of gently suggesting to him that you might continue to maintain the garden for the time being. He will be aware that a well-kept garden will certainly make the house more attractive when it comes to be sold – and he could pay you out of the estate funds, although don't say I suggested that! And it may be that a new owner, seeing the good job you've been doing, might want to take you on."

"Thank you, sir, that's very considerate of you. I'll certainly try to find an opportunity to suggest that to the solicitor."

Webster, seeing that the interview was over, stood up to go, and Bryce and Haig followed suit.

"I'll come and find you in five minutes, Webster, and pay you," said Mrs Baxter.

"I appreciate your allowing me to sit in for

that interview, Chief Inspector," she continued when the gardener had left. "I'm glad his weren't the suspicious prints – he's a really good man. But I have a question of my own." She stared piercingly at Bryce for some seconds.

"Do you have a twin brother, Chief Inspector?"

Bryce looked at her in surprise. He shook his head. "I don't have any sort of brother," he replied.

"I've seen your picture in the newspapers – the Pimlico case – but I'm sure I've also seen you in person. A long time ago, before the war. I don't forget a face."

She continued to stare at the DCI, almost rudely. Suddenly, she smiled.

"Got it – but I guess my memory must be failing me, because the person I'm thinking of was in the West London County Court, and he was a 'white wig'. I wasn't involved in his case, which was a landlord and tenant matter as I recall. I do remember that he won."

Sergeant Haig was trying not to laugh, and Mrs Baxter noticed this.

"Come on, Sergeant, what is it? Is the joke on me?" she enquired.

Bryce took pity on his subordinate.

"No, Mrs Baxter; I see I'll have to explain. Your memory, far from failing, is actually quite remarkable. The man you saw that day, thirteen years ago, was me. That was almost the first time

I'd been allowed out of chambers with a brief of my own. And an extremely boring case it was too.

"But, as you can see, I later decided to take up a career in the police rather than at the Bar. Perhaps if my brief that day had been for a murder case at the Old Bailey – a very unlikely possibility – my life might have been very different now!"

CHAPTER 6

Back in the car, Bryce told Haig to drop him at his house, and then to take the car on to his own home.

As they went along, Haig explained the differences between the door knob prints and those of Webster.

"I'm quite glad they're not his, sir – he seems a decent chap making the best of his circumstances."

"Agreed, although we can't completely eliminate him just yet. We mustn't assume that the prints on the knob are necessarily those of the murderer.

"Tomorrow, we somehow need to get the prints of the relations and the doctor. Frankly, if we don't find a match for the door prints amongst that lot, I'm not sure what we'll do!

"You got the various addresses and telephone numbers. The letter to the Coroner helpfully confirms those addresses. The relatives all live north of the river – and in any case I can hardly ask them to go back to Court Lane for their interviews. That would really be putting the boot in. I think we'll invite them to the Yard, one at a time.

"I'll make my own way in to the Yard in the morning as usual. I want you to go straight out to Dulwich. I'll ring from home tonight to tell them you're coming. Do a more detailed search among her papers. I can't think there's anything more to find – but in her letter she didn't think to mention her diary, so I suppose it's possible there's still something else which might be useful hidden away somewhere.

"But your principal job is this. Ask all three of the staff to describe – in detail – what happened when one or more of the visitors came. Particularly at mealtimes. It seems very unlikely, but did the niece, for example, have anything to do with preparing the food? What is rather more probable is that tea or coffee was left for the family to pour – that would seem to be a better way of doing it. So ask if that did happen.

"There's always the possibility that something was inserted into some item that only she would touch, so there would be no risk that one of the servants would sample it later – maybe something like a Lapsang Souchong tea that the servants would be unlikely to use. Difficult to ask suitable questions about that sort of thing, but see what you can do. If you can identify anything that might fit the bill, bring it away, of course.

"I'll go through the diary this evening, and draw up some sort of chart to see if there's any correlation between visits from relatives and bouts of sickness – Mrs Latimer clearly believed that there is."

"What about the Doctor, sir?"

"Yes; he must remain on the list of suspects. We'll have him in for a chat in due course. The old girl didn't suspect him of anything other than incompetence, but he had something of a motive. And, I suppose, the means. However, it would seem that Mrs L was already ill each time he was called, so it doesn't look as though he had an obvious opportunity.

"It would be interesting to see exactly what treatments he gave her. We can ask him, but can't compel him to divulge that information. And at this stage we don't have grounds for asking for a court order to seize his records.

"Poke around the bedroom and bathroom – medicine cabinet if there is one – and see if there's any sign of the powders and tonics mentioned by the staff.

"The diary appears to be very detailed, so it'll probably tell us if he was there for meals. But ask the staff about his visits anyway. Do they know if he gave her any powders, for example, from his own bag rather than via a prescription dispensed by a pharmacist?"

"Okay, sir, all understood. If I get to Dulwich by eight o'clock, I should be back in the office soon after two."

"Yes; I'll try to persuade the niece and nephews to come along during the afternoon. If that isn't possible for one or more of them, then we'll have to make other arrangements. I anticipate that they may refuse to have their fingerprints taken. Before they have that opportunity, we'll use a tried and tested method that I employed some years ago – give them a sheet of paper to read, and a beaker of tea to hold."

The two officers discussed other departmental matters for the rest of the journey, before Haig dropped the DCI at his house.

***

Veronica was very surprised – although delighted – to see her husband home by half past four. When he explained that he had eaten no lunch, she proposed that she should bring dinner forward to half past five, and then they could have a sort of late supper if they became peckish again at about ten thirty.

"If you're not going out again, my love, I'll open a bottle of Beaujolais to have with dinner."

She brought him a cup of tea, and he settled down with it beside the telephone. He spent the next half hour making calls.

He was successful in contacting all three nephews, but was unable to get hold of the niece. The men all agreed, albeit with considerable reluctance, to come to the Yard at various times the next day. Bryce knew that they would probably talk to each other before the interviews, but there was nothing he could do about that. In fact, he asked Mr Pilkington if he would try to contact his sister later, and invite her to come along as well.

He then started to draw up a schedule, using Mrs Latimer's diary to show who visited her, and when; and when she had been sick. She had first recorded what appeared to be the symptoms of poison some three months ago, although at that time she didn't seem to have any suspicions, merely later recording in her diary 'acute biliousness'. That time scale corresponded with the Pathologist's view as to when the chronic poisoning had started. He noted that the last diary entry had been made early in the morning of the day she died. He had not completed his task when Veronica called him to come and eat.

His wife had experience of helping her husband with two cases – one before their marriage, and another on their quite recent honeymoon. He had already given her the gist of the current case, and now, over the meal, he gave her an update. She was fascinated to hear how the meeting had gone.

"It sounds as though you could have charged for seats," she said. "I'd have paid to see the faces of the disinherited people.

"Actually, I suppose the revocation of the

original will is a sort of comeuppance for whoever did it, assuming it was indeed one of the family. A bit unfair on the other three, though," she remarked as she deftly removed the central bone from her salmon.

"Yes. If the original will was still extant, and if one of them were to be convicted, then under an old Common Law rule he or she wouldn't be able to inherit anything anyway. You could certainly say that would be fairer to the innocent parties. But I rather think Mrs Latimer had reason to dislike all of them, murderer or not."

"But how very fortunate that Alex was in the foyer just when the maid was blurting out her suspicions," continued Veronica. "I bet the matter would have been brushed aside otherwise.

"Anyway, you've got a nice lot of suspects. Looks like the gardener is out of it, and from what you say the servants don't seem very likely. Pity there isn't a butler!"

Bryce grinned. "Come on, Vee – we've discussed that old chestnut before!"

"Oh, I know," laughed his wife. "Do you have a favourite suspect yet?"

"Not at all. I haven't interviewed the four principal ones yet – haven't even spoken to them other than as a group at the meeting. I've just arranged to see at least three of them tomorrow.

"I'm rather banking on finding a match for

the print on the garage door. Anyway, Alex is going back in the morning to see if he can find anything in the house – particularly the kitchen – which might have been used to deliver the arsenic, but it's probably a forlorn hope. Lovely meal, by the way."

"You remembered to say that in the nick of time," she giggled. "I'll allow you some dessert, now.

"I often think how fortunate we are that you have use of a staff canteen, and that we can afford to buy meals at cafés. It makes such a difference to be able to save our ration coupons for our main evening meal."

After dinner, Bryce returned to his chart, taking with him the last glass of wine. He spent only ten minutes more, and then sat back to contemplate the result.

Prima facie, it certainly appeared that every bout of sickness occurred during or very shortly after a visit. Unfortunately, from Bryce's point of view, this proved nothing either way, because on every occasion when sickness did arise, all four suspects had been visiting at the same time, occasionally staying overnight. Each individual had also made solo visits, when no sickness resulted.

If a relative was involved, he or she was being very circumspect, thought Bryce.

But then, who else could have been introducing the poison over such a long period?

Veronica came to sit with him at this point, and he explained to her what the chart indicated – and what it didn't indicate. He voiced his question – who else?

"Surely you can eliminate the possibility of anyone you don't already know about?" his wife replied. "A one-off, perhaps; but not regularly over a period. And I suggest the fact that every known attack occurred at the same time as a group visit can't possibly be coincidental.

"I still think one or perhaps more of the family must be involved. But I suppose you'll have to consider the three servants too. Very easy for one of them to time the non-fatal doses for when all the family members are present. And for the final fatal dose, too."

"The same argument holds for Mrs L to have organised this herself, if she wanted to incriminate her relatives," remarked Bryce.

"But no," he continued, rejecting the hypothesis, "I really don't think anybody contemplating suicide would willingly put themselves through the agonies of several preliminary poisonings. Also, the container would surely have been found after she was taken fatally ill."

The two sat in companionable silence for a few minutes. When the conversation restarted, it was on domestic topics. An hour or so later, though, Veronica returned to the crime.

"I agree with you that this wasn't suicide,"

she said. "Of course, the killer was really unlucky. Given what the GP had diagnosed on all the previous occasions, he or she would have every reason to expect that he would give a certificate on the same basis. Get the body cremated, and that's that.

"Nor, of course, could they know that the victim had already voiced her suspicions to the staff. The new will and the coroner's letter couldn't possibly have been foreseen either.

"I think what I'm trying to say is that the murderer may have been a tad over-confident, and that it's possible that a mistake has been made – but that mistake hasn't been found yet."

"Apart from the prints on the door knob," said Bryce. "But I take your point."

CHAPTER 7

The next morning, Bryce refused to let Veronica drive him into Westminster, and made the tedious journey in by tube. He was sitting at his desk when the telephone rang.

"Haig here, sir," he heard when he picked up the handset. "News. I'd only been here an hour when the doorbell rang. I was going through the victim's desk when Effie came in. She said a man had come in a taxi, and she thought I'd better speak to him. She said 'he tells me he is Mrs Latimer's son'. So I told her to bring him into the study.

"Well, she shows this man in. He's a pleasant-looking chap, in his late forties I thought; very well-dressed. Before I can even invite him to sit down, or even introduce myself, he says: 'Have I come to the wrong house? I understood Mrs Eloise Latimer still lived here, but that maid behaved very oddly just now.'

"I sat him down, and told him who I am, and why I'm there. I asked him to explain his own presence – given that we've never heard of a son. He was silent for a minute.

"Then he told me that he was indeed Mrs

L's son. His name is Paul James Latimer, born in 1902. It seems that for some years before his father died – that was in 1923 – he was on bad terms with his parents, and when the father was killed she apparently irrationally blamed the son for her husband's death in the plane crash. They became completely estranged, and allegedly her parting shot was to inform him that he no longer existed as far as she was concerned. Fortunately for him, he had just graduated from Oxford, and was able to find employment. Later, he emigrated to South Africa, and from the look of him clearly made good over there.

"He says he's sold his business interests in South Africa. He arrived back in this country about six months ago, and intends to start up another business here.

"Would you like to see him, sir? He's still here, walking round the garden."

"Yes; I certainly should. How long before you're ready to leave?"

"About half an hour, sir, I reckon."

"Okay. Ask him to accompany you to the Yard. If he doesn't want to come, find out where he is staying – and if you aren't satisfied with that information arrest him on suspicion of murder and bring him in anyway."

The call finished, Bryce sat thinking. The last thing he wanted was an addition to the list of suspects. He shrugged his shoulders and returned to his paperwork.

***

At five minutes past one, a knock on his door produced Sergeant Haig.

"I've put him in an interview room, sir. Seems a nice co-operative chap, actually. He accepted that I wouldn't talk about the case at all, and spent most of the journey talking about his life in South Africa."

"Okay. Have you had lunch?" queried the DCI.

"No, sir."

"Right – very unorthodox, but let's take him to the canteen and have a bite to eat. The first of his cousins arrives at two-fifteen, so we'll interview Latimer over some food. Bring him through, please, and I'll meet you in there."

At the canteen door, Haig performed the introductions. Bryce shook hands, apologised in advance for the limited range of food, and the three chose their meals and sat down.

"First of all, Mr Latimer, my condolences on the loss of your mother."

"You can abandon the conventions, Chief Inspector. My mother and I had a rocky relationship as I grew up, and I've not seen or even been in contact with her for over twenty-five years.

"Just tell me, if you will, what has happened. Your strong silent Sergeant here won't enlighten me, apart from saying that my mother is dead. You'll forgive my saying this, but the involvement of a senior Scotland Yard officer suggests that something stinks."

"A reasonable deduction," replied Bryce, pausing while he chewed on a sausage.

"First, though, you really need to convince us that you are who you say you are."

"That's easy. I don't have a British ID card, but I carry my passport instead. I'm still a British subject. Here..." he took the document from his pocket and pushed it across the table.

"Okay," said Bryce, passing it on to Haig, who glanced through it and returned it to Latimer. "Tell us something of what happened back in 1923."

"I went up to Oxford in 1920. I was already on fairly bad terms with both my parents. Father had wanted me to read either law or medicine, and when I chose Greats he was incandescent with rage. 'Total waste of time and money', he shouted at me more than once. Mother took his side, as always.

"Things were very unpleasant during holidays, and I took to staying with friends, or travelling, instead of going home. At that stage, I was still in receipt of a fairly generous allowance from father, and I also had a small income from a bequest from a grandparent which was independent of my parents. Incidentally, we'd moved into the Court Lane house immediately after the Great War.

"Things went from bad to worse. Looking back, I don't entirely blame my parents; I was probably an obnoxious prig at that time. One day, during a blazing row, I said openly what I'd believed for years – that father was a war profiteer, with no moral scruples whatsoever. I knew it rankled that Lloyd George had only thought him worthy of a CBE, and when I said that given the amount of money he'd made he could have given a bigger bribe to obtain a knighthood it really made him furious.

"Anyway, a couple of days later he was killed in a flying accident. Mother blamed me completely; said I'd shaken him up to such an extent that he made a mistake. She basically disowned me – cut me dead at the funeral service, and I haven't seen her since.

"But I used my degree – and the contacts I'd cultivated at Oxford – to get on in life. First here, and later in South Africa. In a nutshell, I 'made good' – very good as it happens. When I came home I wanted to see mother to show her that 'Greats' had been an excellent choice."

There was a silence for a couple of minutes, while Latimer caught up with his eating. Then Bryce spoke:

"I have to tell you that your mother was murdered. A hefty dose of arsenic, which actually followed up some earlier lower doses. That, as you surmised, is the reason we are involved."

"I see," said Latimer. "Who's 'in the frame', as the Americans would say? I suppose I've just jumped to the top of the list."

"Well, we'll certainly want to look into your movements over the last few months. Have you been in the house at any time between your leaving in 1923 and today?"

"Not once. A few months ago, I drove past the house in a taxi, and asked the driver to stop outside for a while. I didn't see anybody. I'd been thinking, you see, of making some sort of approach to mother, to see if after all these years she might like to see her only son. Today, I decided to take the bull by the horns, and call on her. I didn't give notice, because I thought it would be less easy for her to refuse to see me if I was actually on the doorstep."

"I see," said Bryce. "Are you willing to let us take your fingerprints for exclusion purposes – we have some prints that we want to identify."

"Sure, whenever you like. I suppose, depending how competent the servants are, that there may still be a few of my prints lingering around the house – but there's no way they'll be on any incriminating object."

"Thank you. Now, is there anything else you'd like to know, Mr Latimer?"

"I don't think so, Chief Inspector. I assume you haven't released the body yet, so no funeral has been arranged? I'm not sure if I'll attend, but I'd like to be informed about it, if you wouldn't mind. I'm leasing a house in St John's Wood – here's my card."

"You haven't asked about your mother's will," remarked Haig.

"No; I can't imagine that I'll benefit from it. She made that very clear at the time. Dad left everything to her, of course. In any case, I'm a rich man in my own right. Her will is of minimal interest." Latimer hesitated, and then added, "Hang it all, I actually wanted to tell her I could buy and sell her several times over now!"

"As you'll appreciate, the will is of considerable interest to us. Even if you hadn't been a classics scholar, you would understand the expression *cui bono?* In any murder case, that's the first question the police always ask."

Latimer smiled for the first time, as he took the last sip of the coffee.

"Don't tell me – my weaselly cousins have been sniffing around the old girl. Dreadful shower. A couple of them are older than I am, and a couple younger, although there's not many years between any of us. But none of them has ever attempted to contact me since the estrangement – even all those years ago I bet they all realised that it was to their benefit if I just vanished."

"It's a bit more complicated than that, Mr Latimer. You see, they were the principal beneficiaries up to a fortnight ago. But then your mother changed her will, and they were completely written out. They were not aware of this change before she died."

Latimer started to chortle.

"Oh dear; how very sad for them. Couldn't have happened to a nicer bunch of cretins. So you asked *cui bono?* and the answer was my cousins – even though in fact they aren't going to benefit."

"Indeed. Now, I suggest you contact Mr Prendergast, of Carstairs and Prendergast, solicitors in Dulwich, to keep you informed. He is your mother's executor. Go along with the Sergeant, and he'll take your prints. We have the pleasure of interviewing your cousins this afternoon." Bryce grinned at Latimer. "Shall I pass on your regards?" he asked.

Latimer laughed again.

"Please don't," he replied, "but you can tell them I found the fact that their expectations have been dashed most amusing."

The DCI stood and tucked his chair under the table. "When you've finished with Mr Latimer, Sergeant, come back to my office. Keep the fingerprint paraphernalia with you – we'll be needing it again."

Bryce returned to his room and rang down to tell the desk officer to let him know when Mr Henry Ogilvie arrived.

CHAPTER 8

Haig returned just as the call came from the front desk, and the two officers went downstairs to meet the first of Mrs Latimer's nephews. Bryce asked the desk man to organise some tea – in beakers rather than cups.

Paul Latimer's adjective 'weaselly' had probably been intended to describe character rather than appearance. But if he had meant the appearance as it had been twenty-five years earlier, then – in this cousin's case at least – it certainly remained appropriate now.

After shaking hands – somewhat reluctantly – with the officers, Ogilvie sat down in the chair indicated by Bryce. He glared at the DCI, and immediately went on the attack.

"Why have I been summoned here? If it's true my aunt was poisoned, it's obvious that one of the servants did it. It's disgraceful that you suspect people like us. I know nothing about her death. Should I have a solicitor?"

"Slow down, Mr Ogilvie. We're investigating a murder. You can surely appreciate that we must interview every possible person involved in any way. As it turned out, you didn't gain by your aunt's death – but you can also see that at the time of her murder, you expected to do so. To put it very bluntly, not to have you, your brother, and your cousins on the list of suspects would be a clear dereliction of duty on my part.

"This interview will be what is called 'under caution'. Whether or not you want a solicitor present is entirely up to you. You can stop us at any time and ask for one. Carry on, please, Sergeant."

Haig issued the formal caution, and sat ready to take notes.

"Were you close to your aunt, Mr Ogilvie?"

"We got along all right."

"In the last five years, say, how often did you visit her? Remember we can ask the servants for corroboration."

"I don't remember. Occasionally."

"You see, Mr Ogilvie, our information is that you'd hardly been seen in your aunt's house until a few months ago – since when you have been in the house almost every week. Why the change in habits?"

"Well, she was getting elderly, and I wanted to keep an eye on her."

"She was seventy, Mr Ogilvie, and in good health. Surely that frequency of visiting – often all four of you at the same time – wasn't necessary? And it must have been very inconvenient – all of you live some distance away. Couldn't you have organised some sort of rota between yourselves?"

"I don't think the idea was ever discussed."

"I see. When did you learn that your aunt intended to leave some of her very substantial estate to you?"

"She wrote to me – to all of us, I gather – about eighteen months ago, and said so."

"Do you still have that letter, Mr Ogilvie?"

"I doubt it; I don't keep unnecessary correspondence."

"Would you be surprised to hear that I can tell you exactly the date on that letter? It was in fact only five months ago – about the time your visits started in earnest."

"I don't see how you know that. I think it was far longer ago."

"Ah, well, unless you can show us the letter to prove otherwise, I think we'll have to accept your aunt's diary entry of five months ago, where she specifically states that she has just written to each of you to inform you of her will. And according to her diary – and according to the evidence of the domestic staff – your visits started very shortly afterwards."

Ogilvie was silent.

"Let's move on. During your visits, what did you do, apart from have a chat with your aunt about her health?"

"I don't know what you mean – and I'm finding your insinuations quite offensive."

"Really? That's rather unfortunate, because I haven't begun in earnest yet. You must see how this situation looks to an outsider. You don't have significant contact with your aunt for years. Then you learn that you are to gain a hefty inheritance. You start to make more and more visits. Not long after, your aunt dies. Before probate is granted – indeed before your aunt is buried – you and your brother and cousins swarm over the house in anticipation of your inheritance. Unfortunately, it then emerges that your aunt was poisoned. Worse, she has accused one or more of you of killing her. And from your point of view perhaps worse still, you find you have been disinherited.

"Anyway, I'll rephrase my question. During your visits, did you go into the garden?"

"Sometimes, I expect. I'm not really interested in gardening."

"Did you ever go into the garden shed?"

"No."

"What about the garage?"

"The garage? No, never."

"Did you spend any time in the kitchen, talking to the staff, or perhaps getting some food for yourself when they weren't present?"

"No. I might have passed through on the way out to the garden, but I didn't chat to the staff. Why on earth would I?"

Ogilvie drank some of his tea, and remarked that it tasted like bilge water. The DCI didn't comment, although he privately thought that the man had a point. He continued:

"Now, as you know, your aunt wrote a letter making a serious accusation against you and your relatives. This is a transcript of that letter." He passed a paper across the table. "Would you like to make any comment about what she said?"

Ogilvie took the paper and read it. Pushing it back, he said:

"Foul calumnies. She produces no evidence against any one of us. It's just a lunatic rant by a deranged woman."

"So you all said yesterday. But whether or not she was correct in her targets, she was quite correct about being poisoned."

Once again Ogilvie sat silent.

"What do you know about the uses of arsenic in the garden, Mr Ogilvie."

"As I said earlier, I'm not a gardener. I know nothing about arsenic, except that it's poisonous, of course."

"Would you mind allowing us to take your fingerprints?" asked Bryce.

"I jolly well would mind," expostulated Ogilvie. "I'm sure you can't force me to do that unless you charge me, or arrest me, or something."

"Very well, Mr Ogilvie. Clearly you prefer to stand on your rights, rather than help us find your aunt's murderer by providing exclusion prints. No matter.

"Just one last thing. Yesterday, as Doctor Acres was arriving, the four of you were discussing what Mr Prendergast had already said, and I caught a reference to 'Paul'. Would you care to explain the mention of that name?"

Ogilvie hesitated. "I can't," he replied, "perhaps you misheard."

"You really aren't helping yourself by dissembling, Mr Ogilvie. A few minutes ago, we interviewed Paul Latimer – the son of your Aunt Eloise. You are perfectly aware that you had a cousin. At the moment I'm talking about, you had just learned that the will had been revoked, but didn't know the new dispositions. I suggest that you all feared that the prodigal had returned and might be the principal beneficiary after all. Am I right?"

Ogilvie glowered but said nothing.

Bryce allowed the silence to develop before closing the file in front of him and standing up. Looking down at Henry Ogilvie he said, "Very well. I don't want to speak to you anymore. For the moment. Good afternoon."

Haig held the door open for the man to leave.

"He doesn't come across too well, sir. But whether he has it in him to kill, I don't know."

"I agree. We'll keep an open mind on him. Now, his brother Spencer is due next in about fifteen minutes.

"Get Yapp to come down and take the letter and Ogilvie's beaker. He should be able to get decent prints off one or the other. Give him the door knob prints and he can do the comparison. I'll get the desk to bring in more tea for the next Ogilvie. I have three more identical transcripts of the letter, so he can have a fresh one."

Within five minutes, Yapp had been and gone. Bryce and Haig waited in the interview room. Right on time, the desk sergeant brought in Spencer Ogilvie. He arrived at the same time as a constable with the tea. After the usual formalities, the DCI invited Ogilvie to take a seat.

"Thank you for coming to see us, Mr Ogilvie," he started. We've just been having the pleasure of a chat with your brother Henry. Did you see him outside, by any chance?"

"No – in fact I haven't spoken to him or my cousins since that awful meeting yesterday. After you threw us out, we had a bit of a family spat outside, and all went our separate ways afterwards. I don't think any of us will be on speaking terms with the others for some time."

"I see; well, we have a few questions for all of you, but this won't take very long."

The interview questions almost duplicated those posed earlier, but Spencer Ogilvie appeared less affronted and rather more savvy than his brother. He maintained that none of the family members would dream of shortening their aunt's life, although he agreed that the circumstances might look a little 'fishy'. He suggested, again, that a disgruntled servant must have been responsible. However, he was unable to think of any occasion where one of the servants had appeared anything other than content. Realising that he wasn't helping the defence of his family or himself in his responses, he changed tack and suggested the gardener might be the culprit. He then had to admit that he had no idea how the man got on with his mistress.

When shown the transcript of his aunt's letter, he screwed up his face in disgust.

"It's all supposition and contains no facts at all. If she were alive, we could sue her for libel."

"Quite true, Mr Ogilvie; beliefs are not evidence. However, your aunt did provide a lot more facts, via very detailed entries in her diary."

Ogilvie looked surprised. "I didn't know she kept a diary," he said.

"Ah, well, no doubt some significant entries will be produced in evidence at the appropriate time."

"Do you mean at someone's trial, Chief Inspector?"

"That's a distinct possibility, of course, and one that we're working towards; but I really meant at the inquest into your aunt's death."

Ogilvie denied ever going into the garage. When asked to give his fingerprints, he asked if it was compulsory. On being told that it wasn't, he declined.

"I don't know on what object you may have found some fingerprints, Chief Inspector, but my prints must be on hundreds of items around the house. I'd prefer not to provide any more, for the moment at least."

Bryce asked him about the mention of 'Paul'. Ogilvie sat silently for a minute, looking at him.

"Well, you're quite right that Paul was mentioned yesterday. Paul Latimer is Aunt Eloise's son. Or at least he was – he hasn't been heard of for many years and may well be dead.

"When we heard the will had been altered, someone – I think it was Gwendolyn – wondered if he had returned and got back into our aunt's favour. But that idea was soon shot down, of course, when we were told about the new terms."

"Yes, thank you. It may or may not be of interest to you, Mr Ogilvie, but your cousin Paul is very much alive. In fact he was in this building not an hour ago."

"Good Lord," exclaimed Ogilvie. "Is he a suspect too?"

"You can hardly expect me to answer that question."

"No, I suppose not. But can you tell me if he intends to contest the will?"

"I can't tell you because I don't know. However, I very much doubt it," replied Bryce.

"In the first place, I believe he is already very prosperous. In the second, he has in no sense been dependent on his mother since he came down from university – hasn't even spoken to her in twenty-five years – so I don't think he could have any standing to dispute his mother's wishes now."

Spencer Ogilvie departed. Haig went to arrange for DC Yapp to repeat the exercise with beaker and paper. The beaker was still full, both officers having noted that Ogilvie had merely toyed with it, but had not actually tasted the anaemic-looking brew.

CHAPTER 9

Returning to the interview room Haig found the DCI starting blankly at a wall.

"Come up to my office," said Bryce. "I can't think in this miserable windowless little room."

Once in his rather brighter surroundings, Bryce motioned the Sergeant to take a seat. He himself sat back in his chair, and put his feet up on the desk – something Haig had never seen him do before.

"Right; apart from the unexpected appearance of Paul Latimer, is there anything else to report from Dulwich?"

"No, sir. The servants say that what with rationing and so on, there's practically nothing that Mrs Latimer had that was different to what they all had. She had no special tea. She didn't have a bedtime drink. Nor, apart from when she was already taken ill, did she have any medicines – powders for instance.

"Anyway, sir, the women all believe the poisoner is a member of the family, of course, and they think the arsenic was put in tea or coffee somehow. They don't see that the poison could be in food from the kitchen because when family members came they ate formally in the dining room and there was always at least one of the servants present doing a sort of silver service.

"The maids were never present in the room while Dr Acres was examining their mistress, so they can't actually say whether he administered an interim dose of something from his bag. However, on each occasion he prescribed powders, and one of the women was sent round to a nearby pharmacy to collect them."

"Okay. The PM shows that the time that Mrs L died, and the quantity of poison ingested indicates that she took the fatal dose at or certainly very close to breakfast time. We'll have to find out how that was done.

"I've drawn up a sort of chart, based on Mrs Latimer's diary. You can look at it – and the original diary – yourself later. But in essence, it suggests her suspicions were well founded. She had four distinct bouts of sickness over about three months – and the onset of each coincided exactly with the arrival of the family. All four members, unfortunately. When only one or two were present, she was never taken ill."

"I suppose defence counsel would admit – as he'd have to – that she disliked and mistrusted her relatives, and suggest that she appeared to become ill simply because of the presence of those people. There's a medical word for it, I think, sir."

"Psychosomatic, Sergeant. Yes, that's certainly a potential problem. We'll need to get rather more definite evidence than apparent correlation between visits and sickness.

"It's been known since Aristotle's time that correlation doesn't necessarily mean causation. Or, as the mathematicians put it, *post hoc, ergo propter hoc* is a fallacy.

"There also remains the possibility of suicide – again an option which any defence team could hardly fail to put forward."

"I just can't see it as suicide, sir. There's no evidence that Mrs Latimer had any such thoughts. Three servants, Mr Prendergast and his staff, the gardener, and Mrs Baxter as well – all say she was normal and reasonable. No suggestion from any of them that she was depressed or anything. Just as importantly, the doctor, who's seen her quite often, says nothing to suggest that either. Then there's the matter of the earlier doses of arsenic, which must have been excruciatingly painful. I just don't buy it, sir."

"Nor do I, Sergeant; nor do I. Actually, I'm very surprised that neither of the Ogilvie's suggested it. Perhaps the next two will. In any event, if one of these people is tried, I'll bet that the suggestion is made very rapidly – probably with a litany of occasions when Mrs Latimer allegedly expressed threats to kill herself."

The telephone rang. Bryce picked it up,

listened for a moment, and said "Thank you, we'll come down."

"It seems Gwendolyn Wade has arrived. Evidently her brother did manage to contact her, despite everyone apparently not being on speaking terms."

Mrs Wade had been taken to the same interview room, and as they passed the desk Bryce indicated that the tea routine should be repeated. The detectives sat down with Mrs Wade. She was a well-built but good-looking woman in her early forties.

"Your brother managed to contact you, then, to say we'd like to talk to you?"

"Yes, he called me an hour or so ago. I'd been out. I thought I'd come along straight away; get it over. I gather he's coming to see you at five o'clock."

Bryce went through the same routine as with the previous two suspects, and got precisely nowhere.

Mrs Wade looked as though she would like to tear up the transcript of her aunt's letter, and made similar comments to that of her cousin regarding the libellous nature of the document.

She too denied going into the garage, and nominated the gardener ('an insolent oaf') as the likely killer.

Like her cousin Spencer, she hesitated over whether to admit that Paul's name had been mentioned, but eventually agreed that it had.

She looked flabbergasted when informed that Paul was not only alive but was living in London, and had already been interviewed.

She unwittingly followed the example of both her cousins, and declined to provide her fingerprints.

After she had gone, and Yapp had collected the items for the third time, Bryce went out and spoke to the desk officer:

"Last one, name of Donald Pilkington, will be coming in about five, Dickson. We'll wait here this time. Tea again when Pilkington arrives, please. I have to say that I've never had so many cups of such awful tea in such a short time."

Sergeant Dickson grinned. He was a habitual tea-drinker, but he had to agree with the DCI – indeed, he sometimes doubted if the infusion generally found in the Yard was sourced from tea plants at all.

A few minutes later, Donald Pilkington was shown in. Facially and in build, he closely resembled his sister, but owned to being four years older. As far as facial looks were concerned, Latimer's reference to 'weaselly' didn't apply here, any more than it did for the sister. If on the other hand the expression referred to character – well, that was not yet apparent.

This interview differed slightly from the previous three. Mr Pilkington denied having ever been inside the garage, but when asked agreed immediately to have his fingerprints taken. Bryce wished he hadn't ordered the tea. However, he continued with the handing over of the transcript, in case the suspects subsequently compared notes and saw through the subterfuge.

Pilkington readily agreed that Paul's name had been mentioned, and that for a few minutes they thought he had probably re-appeared and that their aunt had decided to make her son the principal beneficiary after all. When told that the man was alive and well, he said:

"I always thought he'd make good. A couple of our Oxford years coincided, and I got to know him quite well then – nothing to do with being family. He was right in a way, all those years ago. Uncle Silas wasn't much better than a crook. Aunt Eloise could be very sweet, but her husband could do no wrong in her eyes. No criticism of him – not even from her son – was ever to be permitted."

"Thank you for coming in, Mr Pilkington. I'll leave you with Sergeant Haig to take your prints. Then you're free to go, of course. It may be that you'll be required to give evidence at the inquest. Good evening."

Bryce returned to his room, but within seconds there was a rapid knock on the door, and DC Yapp burst in.

"Sorry, sir, but I thought this was urgent. The prints of the woman, sir, Mrs Wade – hers are the ones on both door knobs."

"You're sure?"

"No doubt whatsoever. If Fred Cherrill himself – begging your pardon, sir – if Detective Chief Superintendent Cherrill were somehow giving expert evidence for the defence, he'd have to accept that the prints are identical."

Bryce smiled at the constable's enthusiasm, and appreciated the reference to the greatest fingerprint expert in the Yard – in the world, probably.

"Well done, Yapp. You'll have one more set to check on in a few minutes, but these are properly provided ones. Of course, if they match the ones on the door knob as well, the whole basis of the fingerprint system will have to be abandoned!"

Sergeant Haig arrived, and the DCI told Yapp to repeat everything he had said.

Haig also grinned at the reference to the legendary forensics man. Bryce thanked Yapp, and told him to take the prints Haig was holding, but not to come back unless the impossible happened.

"Well, sir, that's all to the good," said the Sergeant. Mrs Wade denied entering the garage, but we now know she did."

"It's a step forward, certainly. But it's nowhere near enough. She can say that she just forgot that she looked into the garage one day. Maybe a jury wouldn't believe that, but no jury could convict on that alone. In fact, if that was all we had, the judge wouldn't even let it get to the jury. We have no evidence that she took any arsenic out of that tin. Indeed, there's no evidence that the arsenic used even came from that tin. Nor is there any remaining evidence as to how she administered arsenic to Mrs Latimer."

Haig looked crestfallen, but he recognised that the DCI was right. The two sat in silence for a few minutes.

"Let's go home," said Bryce at last. We'll recharge our batteries and come back to this a bit fresher in the morning.

Haig got home just in time to see his daughter before she was packed off to bed, and then spent a quiet evening with Fiona, his wife.

Bryce, who hoped for a child of his own one day, spent a similarly happy evening with Veronica. He gave his wife an update on the case.

"I'm a bit disappointed, Philip. As there isn't a butler to have as my preferred suspect, I'd plumped for the doctor. Very suspicious character. For it to be the niece is a bit of an anti-climax."

Bryce laughed, and the conversation moved onto other topics.

But the thoughts of both officers returned to the case at intervals during the evening, and again while they waited to fall asleep – but neither had a 'Eureka moment'.

CHAPTER 10

The next morning, Haig came up to Bryce's room. He found the DCI in the same position as the day before, feet up on the desk, staring into space. Bryce waved him to a seat without speaking. Several minutes passed. At last, Bryce stirred.

"I'm stumped, Sergeant. We'll have to bring Mrs Wade in again, but I'm not at all confident of getting a confession. She's not stupid, and apart from the garage print which no doubt will be explained away somehow, the woman will be aware that steadfast denial will be enough. Basically, we have no real evidence. The situation here isn't like one of our other cases, where someone goes out and buys poison. I'll bet that tin in the garage had been there since before the husband died. So there's no point in even going on a trawl around pharmacies."

"I see that, sir. But you never know – maybe she'll break down."

"I doubt it. Still, I can't for the life of me think of what other route to pursue.

"Although the diary tells us a lot, it doesn't detail things like who poured the coffee, or who handed the cups round in the drawing room. In fact, it doesn't seem to take us much further.

"Take the diary, and my chart, and examine them for an hour while I do some other paperwork. See if you can spot something that I haven't been able to see. Come back up here at ten o'clock, and we'll go out to Dulwich – look around again, talk to the staff. Call the house, please, and tell them we're coming between ten-thirty and eleven."

Haig returned to the CID office, and Bryce settled down to routine paperwork. His mind kept wandering, however, and several times he put down his pen and stared out of the window. He was just sufficiently senior to have an office which he didn't have to share, and a view – albeit restricted – of the Thames.

The comment Veronica had made about Doctor Acres kept coming back into mind – 'a very suspicious character'. Shrugging this off for the time being, he resolved to discuss it with Haig as they travelled to south London.

It occurred to him that it would be courteous to inform Prendergast about Paul Latimer. Picking up the telephone, he was fortunate to find the solicitor at his desk and free to talk.

"It seems the late Mrs Latimer had a son, Paul. They had been estranged for something like twenty-five years, but he turned up yesterday – apparently ignorant of his mother's death. He's been 'making good' in South Africa since the

1920s. I'm inclined to believe him, incidentally, although the timing of his arrival does stretch one's belief in 'coincidence'.

"He may contact you, but I think not to discuss the will. He hasn't decided whether to attend the funeral, and I told him that by the time the coroner releases the body the police are still unlikely to have any information. Apologies, but I thought you as executor were the best person for him."

"That's quite all right, Chief Inspector. You don't think he'll try to contest the will, then?"

"No, I don't. I'm sure you would see him off anyway if he tried it, and he'd have to find a pretty dodgy solicitor to pursue such a case."

Bryce heard Prendergast laughing. "I learned a bit more about you from Holden after the meeting yesterday. So I can take it that counsel's opinion is that Latimer has no grounds?"

"Shall I ever live down the fact that I was once a barrister?" sighed Bryce. "I'll give you one piece of advice that you can take. If you really want counsel's opinion on this – and I'm quite certain that you don't – find yourself someone with recent expertise in probate. I found the topic slightly less interesting than Roman Law!

"Anyway, can you give me an update on the status of the three indoor staff? I want to talk to them and go over the house again this morning. Oh, and by the way, I took the liberty of telling the gardener – who works there two days a week – that he might suggest to you that you keep him on, so that the property remains attractive to would-be purchasers. And that he might be kept on by a new owner, of course. He is a deserving cause, if I may put it like that."

"All of the staff are still in post," said Prendergast. "I haven't had time to think about the matter, actually. When you tell me that I can get people in to start valuing for probate, then I can decide what to do with them. For the time being, the estate can certainly afford to keep them on, and I have very wide powers as executor.

"I agree with you about the gardener. If you're going there today, perhaps you can get one of the servants to tell him to contact me as soon as possible."

"I'll do that, thanks. Actually, I see no reason why you shouldn't get valuers in now. After an initial search, we haven't restricted the movements of the three women. We'll look around again today, but I don't think there is anything else for us to find. You might as well carry on."

"Many thanks, Chief Inspector. I'm negotiating with the tenants in Mrs Latimer's other properties to give us access, but it would be good to move ahead with Court Lane right away."

Bryce didn't pass on any details of his progress, and Prendergast knew better than to ask.

***

Haig took the wheel for the journey to Dulwich. As they crossed Westminster Bridge, dodging a pair of trams, Bryce told him about the conversation with the solicitor.

The Sergeant admitted that he hadn't gleaned any additional useful information from the diary or the DCI's chart.

"I suppose we have to assume that the earlier bouts of sickness were caused by doses of arsenic, sir. That being so, the fact that all four relatives were present every time can't be coincidence. And it also implies that the murderer deliberately smudged the trail. After all, each of them was also present alone or in a pair at times when there was no sickness.

"And if one of the servants was responsible, surely she would have been bright enough to have chosen to target a particular relative, and chosen dates when that person was the only visitor?"

"Yes, that's a fair point, and one of the reasons why I don't seriously suspect any of them," replied Bryce.

"But whoever was responsible, why not finish the woman off in one go – why go to the rigmarole of giving her lower doses on several occasions? Each time you do that you're facing additional risk.

"As you know, Veronica takes an interest in these things. She had decided – with no logical basis whatsoever – that Doctor Acres was a suspicious character, and last night when I told her that the prints on the door knob were Mrs Wade's, she was most disappointed. However, I can't seem to get Acres out of my mind.

"Could the prints on the door actually be irrelevant? Could he have done the deed himself?"

Haig didn't answer for a minute, partly to give himself time to think, and partly because he was negotiating a busy junction beside the Imperial War Museum.

"Several things against picking him, sir. Why would he use a crude poison like arsenic? Doctors must have access to lots of things that could be used more easily.

"If the stuff came from the tin in the garage, how did he know it was there? And how could he creep around outside to take some? If it didn't come from that tin, he'd have to buy the stuff elsewhere. Even more risk.

"Then there's the motive. Doctors are rarely poor, and he certainly very well-dressed when we saw him on Wednesday. I don't see that the possibility of inheriting £1000 would be enough for a man in his position to risk the gallows.

"But surely the most important thing in his favour, sir, is that he only ever arrived after the sickness had started?"

"All very true, Sergeant. Unarguable, in fact – which is why I haven't even bothered to interview him. However...Veronica has these moments of intuition, and I can't shake off the thought."

For the rest of the journey, the two men continued talking about the case. But whichever suspect they chose to evaluate, the apparently insuperable problem recurred – the lack of any evidence as to how the arsenic had been administered.

On arrival in Court Lane, they were admitted by Jenny.

"If it's convenient, Jenny, we'd like to sit down with all three of you over a cup of coffee, and just have a chat."

"No problem, sir," replied the girl. "As there's only five of us perhaps we could go into the drawing room – it's a bit more comfortable. I'll sort some coffee and fetch the others.

Ten minutes later, they were all seated in the drawing room. As Jenny had said, it was certainly very comfortable – plush armchairs, and a nice view out over the well-maintained garden. Low tables allowed each person to have their cup conveniently to hand.

The three women sat together on a long sofa. All appeared tense and watchful. Bryce surmised they assumed they were all under greater suspicion, and he quickly squashed that fear.

"First, I can tell you that although we haven't completely eliminated anyone from our enquiries, you three and Mr Webster are not under serious consideration. I can't tell you much more that you don't already know," he continued. "An old tin of arsenic was found in the garage, and appeared to have been opened quite recently. We have to assume that the arsenic used to kill your mistress came from that tin. What we don't know is how the poison was given to her, and in a few minutes I'd like to hear your thoughts on that.

"Yesterday, Jenny saw a man who said he is Mrs Latimer's son. I can confirm that he is exactly who he claims to be – Paul Latimer, who left this house in 1923 and hasn't spoken to his mother since. I doubt if he'll come here again – he isn't a beneficiary under his mother's will. You may or may not see him at the funeral. He isn't under suspicion either, incidentally.

"The funeral can't be arranged until the Coroner releases the body, and that won't be until he's held an inquest – which also hasn't been fixed yet. It's likely that you'll all be called to give evidence at the inquest, and the Coroner's Officer will tell you if you are required to attend and everything else you need to know.

"Over the next few days, someone may come to value the house and contents – that has to be done before probate is obtained, after which the estate can be sold. No doubt Mr Prendergast will also keep you informed about that."

Bryce took a sip of coffee, and resumed.

"I don't know if you are all aware of this, but Mrs Latimer kept a diary, quite a detailed one. That has given us very useful information about the dates and times when she fell ill, and which relations were visiting at the time.

"Unfortunately, by itself, it isn't enough to prove that any individual is guilty. You all know that Mrs Latimer's had suspicions about her relations. However, suspicions are not evidence – although clearly her belief that she was being poisoned was absolutely correct.

"What we would really like is for one of you to have a flash of inspiration, and tell me how someone might have managed to get arsenic into her food or drink.

The three women looked at each other. The Cook spoke first:

"Well, sir, we've talked a lot about this; last few days we've not had much else to talk about. Best if one of the others tells you 'cos I'm not near the family when they eat and drink. You say, Effie."

"We reckon it couldn't have been put in the food at breakfast or lunch or dinner, sir. Here, even breakfast is served by us – not like some houses where you go to a sideboard and help yourself. We can't see how anyone could have put poison in the mistress's food without anyone seeing. Jenny and me, for a start."

The Cook nodded. "And it wouldn't be any easier for someone to come into the kitchen and start interfering with food."

"Even drink at meals would be difficult," continued Effie. "All those meals with the family, we'd leave the teapot, or a coffee jug, by the mistress. She always poured for everyone else. She didn't drink wine herself, although she often provided some at dinner when there were guests."

"That's very helpful, Effie; carry on please."

"Well, drinks at other times, that might be different, sir. So in the middle of the morning, she might ring for coffee. That'd happen whether there were visitors here or not.

"What Jenny or me would do then is bring the coffee and cups and so on and set them out on a table. Then one of us would pour and serve a cup each. But there was always plenty in the jugs for second or even third cups. We think that maybe the mistress didn't get up to serve others, but they did it for themselves – and maybe brought her a cup that they'd poured. We weren't there to see, but they must have had second cups most times.

"Same thing happened with afternoon tea. We'd give each person tea and a plate, and then offer them sandwiches and so on. But then we'd leave, and people might have got up and helped themselves after that. It would've been easy to give the mistress something with poison on it – or put something in her second cup of tea.

"I hope that makes sense, sir?" she finished.

"Yes it does, Effie. The problem is that the fatal dose of arsenic was almost certainly in Mrs Latimer's last breakfast. But she didn't drink coffee with that meal – she drank tea. With only porridge and toast on the morning she died, it's difficult to see how she could have ingested arsenic that morning without noticing it – tea probably wouldn't disguise the taste like strong coffee might." Bryce was about to say something else when the Cook suddenly let out an exclamation.

"I've just remembered something else, sir – I don't know how I haven't thought about it before. Mrs Latimer was very fond of this concoction called '*patum peperium*' – not sure if I've said that right. She used to spread it on her toast at breakfast time, and occasionally for supper too."

"That's right," said Effie.

"I've never heard of this stuff, sir; what is it?" asked Haig.

"It's usually called 'gentleman's relish', Sergeant, and it is very much a love-it-or-loathe-it food. I don't like it myself. Although I like the main ingredient, anchovies, I dislike some of the herbs and spices in it. Carry on please, Mrs

Winter."

"Well, sir, when the war broke out, apparently Mrs Latimer realised it would become scarce, anchovies not being native to our shores, I suppose. So she went to Fortnum's, and bought a case – thirty-six jars, she told me. Lovely decorative pots, they were. There are still some empty ones around the house. But apparently the relish only lasts a couple of years or so, even if it's unopened, and the mistress said that by about 1943 each time she opened one it was 'off'. What was left of her original stock had to be thrown out. Then, she said she found a few jars in various little shops over the next few years, but some of them also were also 'off'. Anyway, about the time I came here, she couldn't find any more. But she found a recipe, and asked me to make some for her myself. I've done that four or five times over the last three years or so. But it hasn't been easy to make either. Anchovies are hard enough to get, and the butter ration is so small that even though the mistress allocated all her own ration of both butter and margarine to the making of this relish, supplies of the stuff have been a bit limited. And we found that homemade doesn't last nearly as long as the shop stuff seems to. It's still impossible to buy any."

"Sergeant, go to the kitchen with Mrs Winter, and find this relish, please."

Bryce chatted quietly to the two girls while the others were out of the room. It was ten minutes before they returned.

"The jar isn't in the pantry, sir," reported the Cook. Nor anywhere else around the kitchen. We've even looked in the dining room cupboards, but it's not there either. I remember there was plenty in the jar when I sent it up to the dining room on Saturday, so there would have been a good bit left after that breakfast. The jar certainly wasn't empty, so it should be somewhere."

"I tipped out the dustbin, sir, and it isn't in there either," said Haig.

"No – if the relish was the medium, the jar almost certainly left the house the same day. Effie, Jenny – I don't suppose either of you can remember clearing it off the breakfast table that morning?"

The maids shook their heads.

"All right, let's change tack for a minute. All of you said you've never seen anyone go into the garage. Fair enough. But what about people going out into the garden? Anyone in the garden could easily go into the back door of the garage without, I think, being seen from anywhere in the house."

The Cook spoke again:

"You can get into the garden through the French doors in the drawing room, as well as through the kitchen. I can see a good bit of the garden from my kitchen, though until now I didn't have much time to stand admiring it.

"Anyway, of the four relatives, the only one I ever saw go out through the kitchen was Mrs Wade, and she did that many times over the last couple of months.

"Any of them might have gone into the garden from the drawing room, but all I can say is I never saw one of the men out there. Geoff saw them arrive sometimes when he was working in the front, so he knew them all by sight. You can ask him for yourselves, but he said only a few days ago that he'd only ever seen one of the nephews in the back garden – and he didn't speak."

"I gather Mrs Wade did speak to him, though," said Haig.

"Oh yes," giggled Effie. "Every time they were here on the same day. He said he'd never met such a bossy woman – and she knew nothing about gardening."

"When Mrs Latimer was taken ill on various occasions, we know that the relatives were here in the house. Who actually called Doctor Acres? Did someone ask you to do it, or did one of the family make the call?"

The three women looked at each other, and each shook her head.

"None of us ever called him, sir," said Effie. "I heard Mrs Wade call him once. The telephone's in the hall."

"Interesting," said Bryce. "I saw the telephone as we came in, but I didn't see a directory. Is the doctor's number written up near the telephone, or did she ask one of you for his name and number?"

There was more shaking of heads.

"The mistress prob'ly had the Doctor's number in her address book in the study," said Jenny. "She kept the telephone direct'ry in that room, too. As you say, the little telephone table in the hall has nothing on it – there's no shelf or anything to hold a direct'ry."

"I see," said the DCI. "Effie, when you heard Mrs Wade call the Doctor, did you hear any of the conversation?"

"No, sir, I'm very sorry; I was sent away to fetch something."

The Cook looked uncomfortable at the mention of Mrs Wade calling the Doctor. Now, she hesitantly said:

"I'm not sure if I should tell you this – I've never even mentioned it to Effie and Jenny, because it was none of my business at the time, and it just seemed like gossip for gossip's sake."

Sergeant Haig's pencil was primed and ready to take down what he instinctively felt would be an important piece of information.

Mrs Winter continued, "About a month ago I was with a friend in Battersea Park. I saw Doctor Acres and Mrs Wade walking together – they were arm-in-arm, sir, very close...very lover-like, I thought. I'm sure it was them. They didn't see me. I thought it wasn't my business, and like

I said I never even told Jenny and Effie here."

Bryce looked at her kindly. "You're quite right to tell us now, Mrs Winter. It may mean nothing, of course, but every little scrap of information helps us to build up a picture." He stood up. "Thank you ladies; you get back to whatever you have to do."

With the room to themselves, the officers looked at each other.

"Are you thinking what I'm thinking, Sergeant?"

"Probably, sir. You're thinking that Wade did the deed, and that Acres' role was simply to supply a misleading diagnosis."

"Yes – and ultimately a death certificate, stating a cause which was apparently consistent with his earlier diagnoses. It would explain why it was thought necessary to have stages in administering the arsenic, rather than giving the Mrs Latimer one fatal dose."

"We're still short on proof, though," remarked Haig. "Who do you reckon would be the more likely to break down?"

"I've been trying to decide that very question. I think it might be better if we tackle Acres first. We can't offer a specific inducement to turn King's Evidence, but we can point out that a conviction for being an accessory after the fact would be preferable to a conviction on a capital charge."

"True, sir. Although isn't it also likely that

he was an accessory before the fact; and that the two of them conspired to commit murder?"

"Oh, yes; almost certain. But offering the lesser charge might persuade him to talk. Anyway, let's get back to the Yard.

"Assuming Acres and Wade are in some sort of relationship, I don't want to telephone Acres to ask him to come in – that would give him the chance to contact her. They may have done that already, of course. We'll get a couple of DCs to bring him in."

CHAPTER 11

Back in his office, Bryce called down to the CID room, enquired who was there, and instructed Yapp and Barker to come up.

Yapp already knew a little about the case, but Haig gave both men an up-to-date outline. Then the DCI took over:

"Go and find Acres. We have his address from the copy of the original will we've been given, and almost certainly his surgery will be in the house." He passed a slip of paper to Yapp.

"He may well be out on his rounds, or doing something else, but I guess that he'll have a surgery between about four and six. So aim to get there a bit before four, but keep out of sight as best you can. Assuming he is there seeing patients, watch to see when the last patient leaves, if you can. I don't want to inconvenience any of them more than necessary. Then go in, and invite him to come in for questioning. Do not allow him to make a telephone call.

"If he refuses to attend, arrest him on suspicion of the murder of Eloise Latimer, and bring him in anyway. If you do have to arrest him, caution him. Don't talk about the case with him at all. Also, I think he is the local police surgeon, so don't mention this to any other police officer.

"If he isn't there, and there's no indication that there will be a surgery today, then just one of you should go the house door and enquire if you can see the doctor. Try not to look like a policeman! If he is there, then you both go in, but if he isn't, you should be able to find out when he will be home without anyone realising who you are. Off you go."

With the detective constables gone, Bryce looked at Haig. "Lunch?"

Both stood up, and Haig said:

"What about your favourite cabbies' shelter, today, sir? I fancy one of their bacon butties – well tidy scran, as they say north of the border."

"Excellent suggestion, Sergeant. Let's go."

***

At twenty past four, Bryce's telephone rang.

"DC Yapp here, sir," said the voice. We've stopped at a police box just to say that we've got Doctor Acres, and we're on the way back. Had to arrest him, sir. He ranted quite a bit. His housekeeper witnessed the arrest, so she probably knows how to find a locum for any overnight call or for tomorrow's surgery."

"Well done Yapp. Book him in when you get here; I'll explain to the desk officer before you arrive. Then park him in an interview room."

After giving the desk man some instructions, Bryce went off to brief his boss.

"I'm not sure if there is any precedent for arresting a police surgeon," said the Chief Superintendent. "I hope you can make this stick."

"I don't expect to actually charge him with the murder, sir; I'm just hoping that he'll squeal on Mrs Wade."

"Yes; well, good luck. You've managed to keep this out of the papers so far, I see. And I assume the Coroner hasn't been pressing you about an inquest. Anyway, I think the Assistant Commissioner will want to know about this development, so I'll seek an appointment."

Shortly after five, Bryce was informed that the suspect had arrived. He went downstairs, collecting Haig on the way.

In the interview room, he thanked Yapp and Barker, and sent them back to their desks. He and Haig sat down opposite the doctor.

Acres looked white, but whether that was in fear or anger wasn't yet clear. He sat staring at the DCI, but didn't immediately speak. Bryce let him stew for a full minute, and then said:

"You've been arrested on suspicion of murder, doctor. You have already been cautioned. Do you wish to have a solicitor present?"

Acres hesitated. then said:

"I haven't murdered anyone. Just get on

with it."

"As you wish. Note the Doctor's choice to be unrepresented, Sergeant. Now, on the fifth of July this year, you were called to one hundred and ninety-seven Court Lane, to attend Mrs Eloise Latimer, who had been taken ill."

"That's correct, although without my notes I can't swear as to the exact date. And, as must be obvious, she was ill before I got there."

"Indeed. But then she was taken ill again on three other occasions after that, and you were summoned each time."

"Yes."

"On each occasion you diagnosed gastric trouble, and prescribed some form of treatment?"

"Yes."

"Finally, last Saturday, you were called again, and this time Mrs Latimer succumbed to her illness. You certified her death as being due to gastritis."

"Correct. With hindsight, I have to admit that I was in error there, but I suggest it was a reasonable mistake, given her earlier problems which had similar symptoms."

"Who telephoned you to ask you to call on these various occasions?"

Acres hesitated again. "I'm not sure; it certainly wasn't Mrs Latimer herself, so probably one of the servants."

"No, it wasn't, doctor. Think again."

"Well, my receptionist might have taken the calls. I really don't remember."

"Please don't dissemble. We can always check what your receptionist remembers. But the last occasion was a Saturday. Does your receptionist work at weekends?

"A half-day on Saturday; but my housekeeper might also have taken that call."

"I see; well, we can ask them. Are you married, doctor?"

"Not any more. My wife died a few years ago. I live alone apart from three servants. I really can't see how that is any of your business."

"Can you not, doctor? I think you can. I think you know who telephoned you on each of the five occasions – and it was the same person every time."

Acres said nothing.

"Your silence is noted, doctor. I'll remind you who called you – it was Gwendolyn Wade. Do you remember now?"

"It's possible that she called me on one or two of the occasions. She was certainly present sometimes."

"Oh, she was present on every occasion, doctor, as you very well know."

Acres sat silently staring down at the table.

"There is an interesting question for us. The only telephone in the house was in the hall. The GPO directory was in a drawer in the study, as was Mrs Latimer's own address book. Mrs Wade doesn't seem to have consulted either of them at any time.

"So how did she know what number to call?"

"I have no idea, Chief Inspector. Are you intending to keep me here much longer?"

"Oh yes, Doctor, much longer. In fact, you won't be leaving here tonight, except perhaps to be transferred to a cell in another police station.

"Would you like to reconsider your answer about the number?"

Acres sat back, closed his eyes, and remained silent.

"Very well," continued Bryce. "I'll help you out. Mrs Wade didn't need to look up your number, because she already knew it well. That's because the two of you know each other. Do you deny that?"

Acres looked discomfited. "I met her at Mrs Latimer's when I was called there before these more recent incidents."

"You're dissembling again, doctor. That's the third time I've had to use that word in two days, and I can tell you that I don't appreciate people wasting my time.

"Why would she have your telephone number?"

"I don't know."

"That isn't dissembling, doctor – that's a simple lie. You know her very well indeed. In fact you are on close enough terms to walk arm-in-arm through the park. Why didn't you tell us that at the outset?"

Acres, looking even more discomfited, hesitated again. "I don't know. I suppose I should have said."

"So, you are more than casual acquaintances. Are you lovers?"

"I won't answer that question, Chief Inspector; it's most improper."

"Perhaps not quite so improper as colluding in the murder of an elderly lady," said Bryce sharply.

Yet again, Acres said nothing.

"Let's go back to the earlier instances of what you called 'gastritis'."

"There's no 'what I called it' about it. She had gastritis," interrupted the doctor.

"No she didn't, doctor, as you are very well aware. At the meeting when you received the news about your disinheritance, I didn't give you all the full details of the PM. In fact, it is very clear that Mrs Latimer had been systematically poisoned with non-fatal doses of arsenic for several months. Your diagnosis wasn't just erroneous at the end; it was wrong on the other four occasions too.

"Oh, God," said Acres.

"I'll help you out here, Doctor, since your memory seems to be failing, and remind you what actually happened.

"Your paramour discovered that she was going to inherit a substantial sum of money – it seems the estate may be worth well over a million pounds, so even after duties her share might be a quarter of a million. A very tidy sum – and a far greater incentive to hasten her demise than the few hundreds which Mrs Latimer had promised you.

"So she, or perhaps the two of you, hatched a plan. Mrs Wade would administer some arsenic, and your task was to muddy the waters by diagnosing a completely innocent complaint. When you'd done that a few times, the scene was set for the fatal dose. Neither the rest of the family, nor the servants, would question the stated cause of death following the recent history."

The DCI turned to Haig.

"I don't think I've made any mistakes in that summary, Sergeant, do you?"

Haig looked straight at Acres as he replied to his chief:

"Oh no, sir. I think you've got it exactly right."

Acres sat still, now holding his head on his hands with his elbows on the table.

After a minute, he muttered, "I didn't kill her."

"Well, that may be a matter for a jury, Doctor. What I have to decide now is whether to simply charge you with being an accessory after the fact; or before the fact; or with murder.

"One of those is inevitable, and the last two carry the death penalty. Which would you suggest, doctor?"

Without looking up, Acres repeated:

"I didn't kill her. Gwendolyn planned it all. She explained it all to me. I went along with it. You're right, we are close, and I suppose I'm besotted. She's a very persuasive lady. I wish now I'd never met her."

"I expect you do, doctor. I'm going to leave you with Sergeant Haig, and he'll take a written statement from you. When you've signed that, I'll see how we can proceed. I make no promises – in fact in this case the Attorney General may well take an interest in you – precedent suggests he'll be prosecuting Mrs Wade himself."

Bryce went along to the CID room, and found Yapp and Barker still at work. He explained briefly what had transpired, and asked if the two would mind earning a bit of overtime and carry out another task. They were enthusiastic.

"Right, come up to my office, and collect an address. I want you to go to Hampstead, and arrest Mrs Gwendolyn Wade on suspicion of the murder of Mrs Eloise Latimer. If she isn't at home, wait. Don't bring her here, take her to the local police station, and book her in on my authority. Tell the Custody Sergeant to hold her there overnight, and I'll come out to see her in the morning. If she asks for a solicitor, of course she can have one. I'll explain the situation to the local DDI."

Half an hour later, Haig returned, and handed some sheets of paper to his boss.

"All signed and sealed, sir. To use colloquial parlance, he's coughed it, and well and truly dobbed her in. They've put him in the holding cells."

Bryce quickly read through the statement.

"Well, that's pretty comprehensive; well done. On the basis of this statement, there's clearly a common intent.

"At this stage, to hold him I'm only going to charge him with being an accessory after the fact. But, as I said before, the AG may well instruct us to up the charge. if so, Acres will likely hang.

"Anyway, I'm going to leave charging him until first thing in the morning. I've sent Yapp and Barker out to arrest Wade. Assuming they find her, they'll take her to Hampstead first, as it's convenient, and we'll go and see her there in the morning. Then I think the easiest thing will be to transfer both of them to East Dulwich nick after they've been charged, and they can appear before a local magistrate. A good day's work, Sergeant. Let's go home."

CHAPTER 12

That evening, Bryce said nothing to Veronica about the case until they had finished their dinner, washed up together, and were relaxing in the lounge – this time each enjoying a glass of claret.

"Well, my angel," said Bryce, you were partly right. The doctor was indeed heavily involved. Not the prime mover, probably, but a willing dupe. Please don't say 'I told you so', Vee!"

He gave his wife an outline of what had happened during the day.

"We still have a potential problem. The defence will undoubtedly say that it's unbelievable that a woman would willingly continue to allow herself to be poisoned. In fact, Donald Pilkington made that very point during the first meeting."

Veronica thought about this for a minute.

"It does seem strange, certainly. But I don't see it as anything more than a red herring. It can't be denied that the old lady was poisoned. The doctor admits conspiring with the niece. The arsenic was in the garage, and you can prove that the niece went in there. The timings of the visits all fit in.

"It is a fact that, despite her suppositions, she continued to allow her suspects to come and visit. I don't see that what seems to be irrational behaviour detracts in any way from the evidence. And this juror thinks you have plenty of that, and votes for a finding of guilty."

Bryce grinned. "I can't help thinking that any defence counsel would object to your presence on the jury! Anyway, I hope you're right."

"Actually, Philip, I can think of a possible explanation for her conduct, although there's no evidence for this, of course. You said Mrs Latimer was upset about her close friends either dying or being too ill to visit. You also mentioned that the solicitor wondered if she was intending to take her own life. It may be that, in a sense, she was. Perhaps she was content to die, and was even prepared to suffer in doing so because she thought – probably correctly – that her dying would result in a better chance of her relatives being convicted."

"Interesting theory, Vee. You may well be right, although we'll never know for sure.

"By the way, to be honest, it was your other theory a couple of days ago which made me think about whether the doctor could possibly be involved after all, and caused me to push the staff to describe how he had been called in. So you can take most of the credit.

"When the AC gets to hear this, I'll be demoted, and the Yard will probably pay you a retainer to teach chief inspectors how to do their jobs!"

Veronica laughed. "Thanks, but no thanks. As a matter of fact, I've been thinking about a different job. Doing something which brought in an income, wasn't so time-consuming that I couldn't look after you and the house, and didn't conflict with your own job. Also, one where, if we were to have a baby, I might not necessarily have to give it up."

She looked at her husband. "What do you think so far, Philip? Are you strongly against that?"

"On the contrary, my love, I think you need something to exercise your most excellent brain. You'll have my full support in whatever you choose to do."

"I thought you'd say that, and I really should have discussed it with you before. However, I've realised that there just aren't many jobs for women which meet my criteria – not ones requiring any brainpower, or earning much money, anyway."

Bryce smiled. "I think I can see what's coming. You want to go into business for yourself?"

"I see why you're a detective," she laughed. "Yes, absolutely right. You met Fenella Jacobs at our wedding – I worked with her during the war, if you remember. Well, a year or so ago she took over her father's business when he retired. It's an import/export agency, really, mostly dealing in antiques. It was very profitable in the twenties and thirties, but was obviously moribund during the war. Fenella joined the firm in 1945, just as it was picking up again. Now, her husband's firm wants him to move to the United States for at least three years, and she wants to sell the business. She's been kind enough to give me first refusal. I have two weeks to decide.

"I've got the books and the annual returns to Companies House, and so on. I wondered if you..." And of course it requires an investment..." Her voice tailed off.

"I don't know why you are looking so sheepish, Vee," he said, smiling. You seem a bit reluctant to name a specific figure for the purchase, but you have quite a bit of money, and I should certainly be willing to back you up and put some in too, if you didn't have enough."

Veronica came across and gave Philip a huge hug. "Thank you so much," she said. "I knew you'd be very positive about it, but I have been nervous – still am actually, but now about the enormity of the project rather than worry about how you'd react.

"On her father's advice, Fenella is asking twenty-six thousand pounds. It sounds an awful lot, but when you see the accounts..."

"Okay. What we'll do is this. I'll look

through the accounts tomorrow evening, but we need a professional to do it properly. I know an accountant who'll take on that task. Business owners always overvalue their own companies when it comes to selling, and I guess that the asking price is optimistic. We'll probably be able to acquire the business for a good bit less, but we'll see. Then, I suggest you and I go together and visit the office, or whatever they've got. I don't suppose you know if they own the freehold? Or how many staff are employed? Or whether all their eggs are in one basket because they only have a single client?"

"I can answer all those questions, Philip. But I suggest you read the papers when you can, and then we should pay a visit. I've been to look round already, but of course it's going to be up to you."

Her husband smiled. "Sorry to contradict you, Vee; no, it isn't. It's entirely your decision. If you decide to go ahead, I'll back you to the hilt in any way I can."

Both Bryces sat happily for the rest of the evening. Veronica had never really doubted that she would get her husband's full support, but was nevertheless delighted to actually have it confirmed. Philip was very pleased that his wife had made these positive moves on her own initiative.

But every few minutes, his thoughts strayed from his wife, and he wondered how the interview with Mrs Wade might go in the morning.

A little after eight o'clock, the telephone rang, and Yapp reported the successful arrest of Mrs Wade.

"We've parked her in Hampstead, as you instructed, sir. She said absolutely nothing until she was being booked in, when she asked for a solicitor. The local boys contacted the man she requested, and he agreed to come at nine in the morning."

"Well done, Yapp, and thank you. I'll deal with it from now on."

Bryce then rang Haig's number. To Fiona, who answered, he apologised if the call might have woken her daughter.

"Och, not to worry, Mr Bryce," she replied. "It'd take the crack of doom to rouse her. Alex is having a bath – can I get him to call you back?"

"No – just pass a message, please, Fiona. Alex took the car last night, as you know. He was going to pick me up at seven thirty and take me in to the Yard, but he can have a bit more sleep now – if Rosie allows it. Ask him to pick me up from my house at nine o'clock instead, and then we'll be going straight out to Hampstead."

CHAPTER 13

The next morning, Sergeant Haig arrived almost exactly on time, and Bryce climbed into the front passenger seat.

After the usual 'good mornings', Haig said:

"Thanks for giving me a lie-in, sir. Fee managed to keep Rosie quiet until a quarter to eight, and I was about to get up anyway when she came charging in.

"I take it the lads found the Wade woman, then?"

"Yes; she's safely in the cells at Hampstead. Said nothing on arrest, apparently. Her solicitor is coming in at nine, so I thought I'd give him half an hour with his client before we start on her."

Haig certainly didn't have 'the knowledge' of London streets that a taxi driver was required to learn – nobody other than a cabbie could approach anywhere near that standard – but he was pretty good at getting from one borough to another along the more major thoroughfares. On reaching Hampstead, he spotted a policeman at the side of the road, just removing his white sleeves after finishing a period on point duty as traffic thinned towards the end of the rush hour. Haig slowed so that Bryce could enquire the location of the police station. Within two minutes, they arrived. The Sergeant found a convenient space to park, and the two men went into the building.

The Custody Sergeant was expecting the DCI, so even though he had never seen him before, he realised who he must be, and snapped to attention.

"I've taken Mrs Wade out of the cells, sir, and put her in an interview room with her solicitor. He's a Mr Jones, sir. Haven't come across him before – and I'm not sure how much criminal work he's done anyway. There's a constable outside the door, sir." He pointed along a corridor. "I thought I'd wait until you came before offering them a cup of tea."

"Thanks, Sergeant, quite right. However, we'll skip the refreshments this time."

Bryce nodded to the officer guarding the door, identified himself and the Sergeant, and told the man he could disappear while they were inside. He tapped on the door, and went in, Haig following.

The solicitor was standing up, facing them, and facing his client who was seated with her back to the door.

"Good morning," said Bryce, holding out his hand. "I'm DCI Bryce, and this is Sergeant Haig."

"Brandon Jones, Chief Inspector – how

do you do. You've met my client already, I understand."

Bryce nodded towards Mrs Wade.

"Let's all sit down, Mr Jones, unless you prefer to remain standing. I hope your client is ready to be interviewed?"

"Yes; she has apprised me of her position. I was informed last night that she has been arrested on suspicion of the murder of her aunt."

"That's correct. I don't know how much detail she's given you, but I suggest we start the interview. If at any time you want to ask me a question, then of course you must do so. If you want to take further instructions, or to advise your client, and you wish to do that in private, just say and we'll withdraw for a few minutes."

"Thank you, Chief Inspector. I was just saying to my client that I normally handle only civil matters, and that she might prefer to consult a solicitor who regularly practises criminal law. She has known me for some years, though, and she wants me to stay. But should she change her mind, I trust that you will stay the interview until a replacement can be found?"

"Certainly, Mr Jones; that's very fair.

"Let's start. Mrs Wade, you were cautioned by the arresting officer last night, but we'll just do it again. Sergeant..."

Haig went through the formal caution once more.

"For your information, Mr Jones, your

client said absolutely nothing on arrest last night, apart from requesting your presence, so we start from scratch this morning.

"Your aunt died on Saturday, from a massive dose of arsenic. Do you have any knowledge as to how that poison was administered?"

"No knowledge whatsoever. It was obviously one of the servants, or the gardener, or perhaps my aunt actually committed suicide."

"I am quite satisfied that you do know, and that in fact you personally obtained the poison, and administered it yourself to Mrs Latimer."

"You cannot prove anything of the kind."

"Oh, I think we can. You haven't been entirely truthful, you see. Also, you've failed to pass on a piece of information which a jury might think is suspicious. And there are other people who have information to assist us.

"You often went into the garden, during your visits, did you not? And spoke to Geoffrey Webster, the gardener?"

"Yes, I did, what of it?"

"Nothing much. Did you go into his shed?"

"Yes, I did, once or twice. There was very little in there other than garden tools – I certainly didn't see any arsenic, if that's what you're getting at."

"No, there was none there, Mrs Wade. Webster, very wisely, doesn't use the stuff. But there is a tin of white arsenic in the garage."

"I take your word, Chief Inspector, but I have no knowledge of that."

"Yes. You told us before that you had never even been inside the garage. It's certainly had very few visitors in the last twenty or more years."

"I wouldn't know – but I've not been one of them."

"We'll leave that for the moment, then. Now, something I didn't disclose at the meeting in the late Mrs Latimer's dining room on Wednesday. The Home Office pathologist found that not only had Mrs Latimer been given a fatal dose of arsenic on the day she died, she had also received non-fatal doses on a number of earlier occasions. Actually, anyone reading Mrs Latimer's letter to the coroner might infer that she believed that to be the case, but as I've said to some of your relatives already, her suspicions are not evidence.

"So, let's think about why someone would administer several non-fatal doses, and then ultimately a fatal one. Each incident was risky, of course – and the cumulative risk would seem to be pointless. But it wasn't pointless, Mrs Wade, as you know."

Jones stirred. "You keep implying that my client knows something about this, but so far you've provided nothing to support that hypothesis."

"Bear with me, Mr Jones. I think you'll

be satisfied in a few minutes – or more likely dissatisfied.

"Let's talk about Doctor Acres for a minute. He was called in to treat Mrs Latimer on a number of occasions, when she was – in his professional opinion – suffering from gastritis. Incidentally, and perhaps this was not known to you, your aunt kept a diary, in which she recorded in great detail her bouts of illness, the attendance of her doctor, and the presence of various of her relatives."

Mrs Wade didn't speak, but surprise registered on her face as the DCI disclosed the existence of a diary. He continued:

"Now your aunt believed that Acres was merely incompetent. I don't think that at all. I believe that he was there for the sole purpose of providing a history of gastric trouble, so that eventually he could certify a death – which he knew to be from arsenical poisoning – as being from the same cause."

Mrs Wade had listened attentively but with no expression on her face. She hesitated, and then spoke, her tone and manner composed.

"Even if that's correct, which I doubt, the poisoner could be any one of several others – or even the doctor himself."

"Ah – I wondered if you'd throw Acres under a bus. How well do you know him?"

"Hardly at all. I'd seen him at my aunt's house when he came to treat her. And I knew, because Aunt Eloise told me, that he was to receive a small bequest in her will. In the will which she later changed, she added bitterly."

"Yes, that must have come as a great shock. The loss of what might be a quarter of a million pounds must be just a little disappointing."

Mrs Wade scowled, but didn't reply.

"You see, Mrs Wade, as any intelligent person knows, in cases like this one the police always look to see who benefits. And at the time of this murder, there were four runners, as it were, who were well clear of the field. The whole business was very suspicious. We know exactly when Mrs Latimer revealed the contents of her will, because she tells us the date in her diary. Then, almost immediately afterwards, you and your brother and your cousins start paying her a great deal of attention, visiting almost weekly, whereas previously you hardly saw her from one year to the next.

"A cynical person might draw conclusions from that change in behaviour. I'm a cynical person. And I'd expect the typical juror, hearing about that, to be the same.

"I said that you lied to us previously, and you repeated that lie this morning. If you have never been inside the garage, how do you explain that your fingerprints appear on the garage door knob?"

Mrs Wade flushed. "I vaguely remember trying the door one day, but found it locked."

"A good try, Mrs Wade – but nowhere near good enough. Your prints were also found on the door knob on the inside of the garage. You had been inside. Why lie about it?"

Mrs Wade turned to her solicitor. I refused to give my fingerprints yesterday – they're trying to bluff me."

"What do you say to that, Chief Inspector?" enquired Jones.

"A very simple answer, Mr Jones. Your client handled a paper, and drank from a beaker. We checked the prints on those with those taken from the door. A perfect match. In due course, when your client is charged, we'll take formal prints."

Jones looked out of his depth, but said nothing more. Mrs Wade scowled again.

"My memory must be faulty, she said. I don't remember going in there, but I was looking all around the property one day, and I must have looked inside."

"Yes, Mrs Wade. And no doubt you've forgotten obtaining the key needed for access – that door was always locked – as you yourself have just told us."

Mrs Wade was silent.

Now, let's talk about Doctor Acres again. You were present on every occasion when your aunt was taken ill. But who actually called Acres in each time?"

"I think I did once or twice; perhaps

a servant on another occasion. I really don't remember."

"No, Mrs Wade. No servant ever telephoned him. You made the calls. How did you get his number?"

"What? I used the directory, I suppose."

"I don't think so, Mrs Wade. There was no directory anywhere near the telephone, and on none of the occasions when you called the doctor was it removed from its normal home in a different room.

"You told us that you had met the doctor when he called to treat your aunt. So you did, of course. But you knew him a great deal better than just seeing him in your aunt's house. You knew him well enough, for example to walk arm-in-arm with him in a public park. You are, in truth, lovers. You already had his telephone number committed to memory – no directory was needed."

"You summoned him on each occasion to carry out his pre-arranged function – to provide a series of false diagnoses."

Mrs Wade looked shocked, and then her head slumped onto her chest. Mr Jones started to say something, and then stopped again.

"A few minutes ago, you suggested that Acres himself could be the murderer. Not a very sensible proposal, given that there is irrefutable evidence that on every occasion he only arrived after the poison had already been administered.

"But without hesitation you are keen to point your finger in his direction to save yourself.

"So maybe it won't come as a surprise to you that your lover has also been somewhat ungallant. He has given us a signed statement, admitting that his task, previously agreed with you, was to create the 'gastritis' nonsense each time you gave Mrs Latimer a non-fatal dose."

"No, he wouldn't do that..." squealed Wade, before Jones stopped her.

"Then," continued Bryce, remorselessly, "after you'd killed your aunt, his job was to provide a plausible death certificate.

"Dr Acres is trying to save his own neck at the expense of yours. Whether he is successful in the first part of that remains to be seen – but his testimony, together with your lying and prevarication, will certainly be sufficient for any jury to decide on your guilt."

"Oh, by the way – you might care to think about an explanation for removing the jar of patum peperium after breakfast on Saturday. You couldn't stand the stuff yourself."

Wade didn't reply; but her hands, resting on the table, suddenly clenched into bunched fists.

"We'll leave you for ten minutes, Mr Jones," said Bryce. "Your client might care to make a statement. But in any case, I'll be charging her with murder. Acres will shortly be charged as an accessory – I can't say whether any other charge will be preferred later. He and your client will shortly be transferred to East Dulwich, and will appear, probably together, before a magistrate tomorrow. I don't know whether you'll represent her then, or at committal proceedings in a few weeks' time. But you'll certainly need to find counsel well before the next Assizes.

"Sergeant, ask the Custody Officer to put the constable on the door again. If you want to come out, Mr Jones, just knock."

Ten minutes later Bryce and Haig were talking by the front desk when Jones emerged from the interview room.

"My client is in a bad way, gentlemen. I really can't allow her to make a statement at present – partly because she seems to be breaking down, and partly because I don't want to pre-empt how a criminal law solicitor might choose to handle proceedings at the committal stage. Or counsel at trial, of course.

"But all you have is circumstantial evidence, Chief Inspector. I don't see that you have enough to charge my client."

"With respect, Mr Jones, every poisoning case that I can think of relies on circumstantial evidence. It would be a rare case indeed where an eye witness can say, in effect, 'I saw Mrs X buy rat poison, and I saw her put some of it in Mr X's food just before he died in agony'.

"Here we have a pile of evidence, some of which is circumstantial, as you say. The motive of the expected inheritance, for example. Or the change in visiting patterns soon after hearing about that bequest. But reinforced by your client's lies – about the garage, and about not knowing the doctor – I reckon there's ample to convince a jury.

"However, the testimony of Dr Acres isn't circumstantial – it's direct evidence. And, as far as your client is concerned, lethal."

"Oh, God," said Jones. Well, you'd better charge her then. You say you're taking her to Dulwich – I'm going to ask a more experienced colleague to take over her representation, so he can arrange to see her there."

The three men returned to the interview room, where Mrs Wade had collapsed over the table, weeping.

"Gwendolyn Wade, I charge you with maliciously administering a toxic substance, namely arsenic trioxide, to Eloise Latimer, on various occasions between June and September this year, with intent to injure her, contrary to the 1861 Offences Against The Person Act.

"I also charge you with the wilful murder of Eloise Latimer, at Court Lane, Dulwich, on Saturday last, contrary to Common Law."

Mrs Wade seemed to nod in acknowledgement, but made no reply. Leaving Jones in the room, the two officers went back upstairs.

"As you say, sir, there must be plenty to

convict her. Do you reckon her mouthpiece will try to argue insanity?"

"I don't see how anyone could argue that. Scottish law allows a plea of 'diminished responsibility' in homicide cases, but as yet there's no such thing in England and Wales. I don't see how that could possibly apply to Wade anyway. The equivalent here are the M'Naghten Rules which you know about – and just like our recent case in Great Castle Street, I can't see any barrister even attempting to show that Mrs Wade didn't know that what she was doing was wrong.

"I think her only hope is if she has such a mental breakdown that she becomes unfit to plead."

"Anyway; not our problem. Arrange to get her and Acres transferred, in separate vehicles, to East Dulwich. Talk to the station first. Make sure they aren't allowed to even see each other, let alone communicate. Before Wade goes, have someone take her fingerprints formally – I'd hate it if our use of 'accidental' prints was ruled inadmissible at trial.

"Thank you for your help, Sergeant – and please thank Yapp and Barker too.

"I'll just brief the Chief Super, and then I'd better inform the Coroner – I'm not sure whether he'll go ahead with an inquest with witnesses, or wait. I'll also inform the domestic staff, and the son. I don't feel like contacting the other relatives. Although as far as we know they didn't connive in the murder, they were just as cupboard-loving as Wade."

"Since I've worked with you, sir, this is the eighth murder case we've been involved with. Do you ever fancy something else – a nice little fraud, say?"

The DCI laughed.

"Something like that would certainly make a change, Sergeant. But it's so long since I've been involved in a non-capital case, I've probably forgotten how to conduct one!"

****

THE NORFOLK RAILWAY MURDERS

CHAPTER 1

Tuesday, 1st November, 1949.

The day that Dora Bloy would never forget started much like any other. The breakfast dishes were neatly stacked on the draining board as she wiped her hands on a small towel. Pushing a wisp of hair back into the folds of her cotton headscarf, she looked through the kitchen window to assess the Norfolk sky. Satisfied that there was no rain in the offing, she quickly sloughed her overall and exchanged her slippers for a pair of short, brown, boots. An extra cardigan, topped off with an old woollen coat, and she was ready to go foraging.

Taught from childhood by her late father, Dora was an expert in the art of gathering Nature's edible gifts. She saw the hedgerows, meadows and woods, as extensions to her pantry. These were the places where, depending on the time of year, she could find fruits, vegetables, herbs and mushrooms. It was simply a case of knowing where to go and what to look for – exactly as her father had shown her.

This skill had made a particularly valuable

contribution to the household's diet during the war, ensuring that her family enjoyed an abundance of nourishing and tasty supplements to their rations.

Beyond the benefit to her own family, Dora had been delighted to be consulted by the Women's Institute early on in the war. Invited to speak at meetings, she had freely shared her knowledge, giving seasonal advice on what to pick and where to find it.

In the autumn of 1942, her daughter had come home from a Girl Guides meeting and announced that all Norfolk Guides were to make every effort to contribute to the National Rose Hip Collection. Once again, Dora found herself instrumental in the local enterprise of picking the little fruits.

The hips, containing ten times the vitamin C of oranges (which, like all citrus and other imported fruits, had become almost unobtainable during the war), were duly taken to King's Lynn, mostly by cart. From there, they were sent onwards to be turned into rose hip syrup. Dora derived great satisfaction from knowing that the syrup had helped save the nation from vitamin C deficiency and disease.

Even now, four years after the war had ended, shortages and restrictions were still in place for many foods, and Dora's aptitude continued to eke out the family's rations.

Selecting a shallow wooden trug and a

deeper wicker basket as suitable receptacles for her intended harvests, Dora let herself out of the little Leziate cottage, and walked the half-mile or so towards the Gayton Road railway bridge. The wide and gently sloping banks which stretched down to the track boundary below were a favourite location, and offered the foods she sought that morning.

Rosehips and sloe berries would be in perfect condition after the recent frosts – their tough skins softened and their robust flavours made milder. She might also find sorrel for soup, and chicory. The latter was a favourite vegetable accompaniment to the rabbits which her husband reared for the table in their back garden. As many mushrooms as presented themselves would also be picked.

Arriving at a spot near the end of the bridge, Dora braced herself a little against the slope, and made her descent towards a group of wild rose bushes, flush with hips. Setting down her trug and basket, she started picking, her nimble fingers quickly stripping the fruits from their stems.

Having cleared one side of a bush, she assessed the level in her basket and decided to pick a few more. Shifting her position slightly, she stumbled against something and almost fell. Looking down at her foot in the long grass, she wondered what the unexpected obstruction might be, and was horrified to realise she had stumbled against a dungaree-clad human leg.

Shuddering uncontrollably, she sat down and was unable to move for what seemed like a very long time. It was the unexpected aspect of her discovery which had upset her so badly. Once the shock passed, she became calm and was able to think clearly. She moved around the bush until she was beside the rest of the body, and checked a wrist for a pulse.

Quite certain that the poor man was dead, Dora quickly thought what she should do. Gayton Road station was visible only fifty yards beyond the bridge, and she decided that was the best place to raise the alarm. Abandoning her trug and basket, she ran under the bridge, along the railway track, and up the sloping end of the platform.

The elderly station master was lifting a large teapot as Dora burst through the station doors. He needed no more than a glance at his unexpected visitor to realise something was very much amiss.

"Now then; now then. Whatever's put you in such a hurry?"

Two sentences from Dora told him everything he needed to know. Pushing a large enamel mug of scalding strong tea towards her, he made the necessary telephone call to the police station in King's Lynn, and gave his opinion that an unfortunate man had fallen to his death off the Gayton Road bridge.

After drinking some of her tea, Dora was sufficiently recovered to return to her baskets, avoiding even a glance at the dead body. She didn't feel like further foraging, and walked home.

An hour later, a uniformed officer arrived at the spot, and after a cursory inspection of the body, decided that the report was likely correct – the man must have toppled from the bridge above, possibly whilst intoxicated. It would be a matter for the coroner to decide how this had happened. He made no attempt to speak to the Station Master, nor to Mrs Bloy – although in fairness neither could have provided any further information.

This officer, confident that he was following all necessary procedures, made arrangements for the body to be taken to the King's Lynn hospital mortuary, for a *post mortem* examination.

The police surgeon was contacted and agreed he would perform this late the following afternoon, it having been suggested that there was no urgency in the matter of this death.

***

Tuesday, 1st November, 1949

As a railway platelayer, more often than not Jacob Goodall worked in a small gang of men. Today, however, he was working alone, employed on his favourite task of track inspection.

His three-day schedule required him to walk the eighteen miles of the little-used West Norfolk branch line between Heacham and Wells. Yesterday, he had walked the first six or so miles to Docking, catching a train back home to Heacham at the end of the day.

Today, a chilly but fine morning, he had taken the train as far as Docking, and was now walking the mid-section of track from there to Burnham Market. He would report any significant problem to his foreman, who would in turn inform the Permanent Way Inspector. Instances of the commonest problem – re-tightening the wooden keys holding the rails in position – he could remedy himself, using the long-handled hammer he carried over his shoulder with his knapsack. Hanging from his belt was a heavy spanner, ready to deal with any loose fishplate nuts.

In joining the Great Eastern Railway on his fourteenth birthday in December 1914, Goodall had started on the path to becoming a life-long railwayman. Like so many from his social class at that time, he had been an underdeveloped youth, a degree of malnutrition having limited his early growth. Despite this disadvantage, he had been a willing and hard worker, grateful to be given a job as an engine cleaner at King's Lynn.

As the war years progressed, he had

gained height and filled out. The combination of physical exertion, together with the better food which his mother could provide with his weekly pay packet, improved his health significantly, and the question of enlisting was one he frequently considered.

There had been many discussions at work about conscription and Goodall knew that he was exempt, his work being 'starred' as essential. During these debates, some colleagues had shared his mother's strongly held view: working men, on poor wages and without property to their names, shouldn't be called to fight for a country in which they had no vote.

Differences of opinion notwithstanding, some railwaymen volunteered to join up. Goodall also resolved to enlist, but he promised his mother he would not do so before he was officially eligible on his eighteenth birthday. Mrs Goodall was much relieved that this significant date had not been reached before the Armistice was signed in November 1918.

Initially wishing to become an engine driver, Goodall had soon decided that the progression from cleaner via fireman to driver was a lengthy and uncertain one. He had also noticed that drivers and firemen were sometimes even dirtier than he was at the end of a day's work. In 1916, when the opportunity arose to be a ganger's lad in a team of platelayers, he had jumped at the chance of an outdoor and comparatively clean job.

Thirty-three years later, it was a choice he had never once regretted; not during intense summer heat, or freezing winter cold. Not even in storms, when the wind-whipped rain slapped thousands of wet needles into him before he could reach shelter in a platelayers' hut.

He strode along, his well-toned leg muscles making easy work of the walk, his strong arms thwacking wayward keys back into place as he went.

Although he was officially working alone, Jacob had the company of Sheba, a lively red setter. The dog belonged to an elderly spinster for whom his wife 'did'. When that lady had been taken into hospital the previous year, Goodall had offered to exercise young Sheba while her mistress was away. The surgery had not gone well, and his wife told him that her employer would never again walk far. Having bonded with the beautiful animal, Jacob willingly extended his temporary offer indefinitely. He carried on taking the setter out, very much appreciating his surrogate status as master, but without the responsibilities and costs of ownership.

Happy in the knowledge that there was no chance of a supervisor seeing him, and a barely greater chance of some busybody on one of the few passing trains reporting him for taking the dog to work, Goodall continued on his way without fear of discovery.

For a railway line in the mostly flatlands of Norfolk, this branch actually had a slope, rising two hundred and fifty feet (a massive height for the county!) between Heacham and Docking, and then falling away again on the way to Burnham Market. Technically, yesterday's walk had been uphill, meaning that today's was all downhill. Goodall knew this because the gradient posts along the way displayed the information; but he would be the first to say that even the steepest climb yesterday – 1 in 99 – was hardly noticeable.

Man and dog made good time from Docking, and were soon nearing Stanhoe. It was here that Sheba, running ahead, suddenly started to bark, much excited by something. Goodall called her to heel, but the dog stood her ground and continued to bark.

Arriving beside the setter, he saw a body lying inside the boundary wire. In pre-war days, when more labourers were employed, there would have been no undergrowth inside the boundary. Now, there were established swathes of thistles, bracken, mallow, and other shrubs. Although these were dying back as autumn gave way to winter, the density of remaining cover meant the body was practically hidden.

Goodall took the dog's collar and pulled her away, gently urging: "Hush you up, my lovely; hush you up."

He cautiously bent forwards. Crouching down, he took a closer look. It was a man. Face pressed into the undergrowth, his full head of greying hair was disarranged and spiked with burrs. Parting some foliage, Goodall could see he wore a good-quality dark blue suit, and smart black leather shoes. One trouser leg was torn, revealing a navy-blue sock held in place by a black suspender.

Gingerly, the platelayer touched the hand nearest him and found it was very cold. Standing up, he moved aside with Sheba. Having stopped barking as bidden, the dog was now emitting rhythmic, warning growls, and clearly unhappy.

Goodall tried to work out what he should do for the best. Pulling out his watch, he saw it would be almost an hour before a train would pass in either direction, and there was no guarantee that one would stop if he tried to flag it down.

Alternatively, he could continue on to Stanhoe Station, only ten minutes' walk away, and raise the alarm. Gabriel Fisher was the solitary employee there, acting as stationmaster, porter, booking clerk, ticket collector, crossing keeper, and doing any other job that might be necessary. Gabriel would be the closest help to hand.

Goodall thought some more. He knew that the signal box at Stanhoe had been removed many years ago, and he wasn't sure if there was any telephone or telegraphic communication at the station. An absence of firm knowledge on this point decided him – he would return up the 'hill' to Docking. Somewhere in that larger village was a policeman whom the stationmaster could telephone. He started off, expecting the journey to take twenty minutes.

At Docking station, Goodall took Sheba's bowl out of his knapsack and reported his find to Wilfred Hoskins as he poured water for the dog. The stationmaster made a fuss of the friendly setter and listened to the platelayer's extraordinary tale of the well-dressed man.

"Oi'll say Oi hen't never heard o' such as that!" was his response, his wonderfully broad Norfolk accent not in any way obscuring his dismay at what he had been told.

Hoskins immediately set about contacting the local bobby, but in this he was unsuccessful. The constable's wife answered the telephone and said her husband was out on his rounds, and could be anywhere within several square miles of his little police house. He would return for his dinner at one o'clock, she said.

Hoskins contacted his railway superior in King's Lynn, instead. The British Railways official in the town was inclined to be less accepting of Goodall's tale than the Docking stationmaster had been. He told Hoskins to give the telephone receiver to the platelayer, and quizzed him sternly before he began to accept that this wasn't a prank. Still not completely convinced, he raised further questions, each of which brought more denials from Goodall:

"No, sir, that definitely warn't no discarded scarecrow.

"No, sir, I hen't mistaken a Guy Fawkes dummy, hidden up ahead o' bonfire night."

Patiently, the platelayer emphasised that no one would dress an effigy – scarecrow or Guy – in such good clothing and shoes. Moreover, he had touched the dead man's hand.

Finally persuaded, the British Railways manager undertook to inform the police without delay.

With the telephone replaced, and reassured that the police in King's Lynn were to be notified, Goodall talked over the consequences of Sheba's discovery with his Docking colleague. He suggested that he had enough time to walk back to Stanhoe and ask the driver of the next 'up' train to stop and convey the body to Heacham. This idea had superficial merit, but without permission from a higher authority that the body could be moved, the two men wisely decided against it.

Further discussion found the stationmaster and platelayer agreeing that there was no point in Goodall waiting with the body until the police arrived. The man was in the middle of nowhere, and nobody else was going to stumble across him in the next little while. The early November weather was cold, but clear; so there was no likelihood of harm from the elements. Added to which, Goodall had heard that the local hunt was bemoaning the lack of foxes, so the risk of the deceased being attacked was also minimal.

Shouldering his knapsack and hammer, the platelayer thanked the stationmaster and gave him a friendly "Cheerio then, Wilf!" as he set off again with Sheba.

Goodall intended to walk fast over the section he had already covered, and recommence his inspection after he passed the body. As he trekked along, he put his mind to the circumstances of how the poor man came to be lying by the tracks.

Other than a railway worker, why would anybody walk along the line in such an out-of-the way place? If someone had planned to walk from Docking to Stanhoe – or vice versa – they would surely have found the road and used that, its surface being far easier underfoot. To the platelayer's way of thinking, this last point was especially true for someone setting out wearing the 'town' shoes the dead man wore, rather than more robust footwear.

It was the anomalies of dress which taxed Jacob Goodall the most. The dead man wore an expensive, fine-weave suit – without an overcoat. True, the weather wasn't bitterly cold yet. But why would someone, who could obviously afford quality clothing, go walking at this time of year underdressed like that? From home to the local pub and back without an overcoat; yes, that was a different matter altogether. He could see someone doing that all right, and had in fact done it many times himself. A jacket, with muffler and cap, was good enough for Goodall in even the coldest weather for a short brisk stroll to his village pub.

But distance walking? In a lightweight suit and shoes? No, that didn't sit straight at all. And yet, to all appearances that was what the prosperous-looking stranger had done.

It wasn't long before Goodall concluded that the man must have fallen from a passing train. In which direction the deceased had been travelling was another question altogether, and he didn't attempt to answer it. The line was single-track along this section – as it was for its entire length apart from passing loops at some of the stations. So it wasn't obvious whether the man had been travelling towards Wells or towards Heacham.

He walked on.

Despite his energetic pace and the uplifting benefits of an emerging blue sky and cool morning sunshine, he remained uneasy. There was a certain aspect of his conclusion which, no matter how he viewed it, he couldn't reconcile and make to fit neatly in his mind. This was chafing away at him, and he slowed his pace for a while as he teased the snag out.

In the highly unlikely event of a faulty

catch – such that a compartment door swung open and the man fell from the train – Goodall believed that the open door would be noticed as soon as the train arrived at the next little station. He reckoned that would be true irrespective of which side of his compartment the man had fallen from – the platform side or the opposite side. So, what alternative explanation was there? Had the well-dressed man somehow *jumped* to his death, rather than *fallen*?

The thought that the man might have deliberately leapt from a moving train came to Goodall just as he was approaching the body again. Whistling for Sheba, he clipped her lead onto her collar and held her close by him, giving the deceased the widest possible berth. If the man had chosen this tranquil spot as the starting point for his eternal rest, the platelayer didn't want to disturb his peace a second time.

Arriving at the tiny Stanhoe Station, he offered Sheba more water, and told his jack-of-all-trades colleague about the incident, before continuing towards Burnham Market.

Still mentally turning matters over and over as he walked and periodically hammered at a protruding key, it wasn't long before Goodall rejected the idea that the man had '*jumped*' from a train on the same grounds as his earlier '*fell out of a carriage*' theory. In either case, the door could not be shut again afterwards by the man. Added to which, why would someone intent on harming themselves choose a slow-moving train at a point where it passed a relatively soft landing place?

Goodall came to a sudden standstill. Comprehension spread across his weathered face. The dead man hadn't fallen or jumped out of a carriage at all. He had been *pushed out*. This alone seemed to fit what he knew, and was the only version of sense that he could make of it all.

At that moment, he saw the next 'up' train chugging towards him in the distance, hauled by an aged Holden 2-4-0 locomotive. Stepping to one side of the track, Goodall made a spur-of-the-moment decision to try to flag down the oncoming locomotive, still a half mile away, and probably only travelling at twenty miles per hour on the slight upward incline from Burnham Market.

Slipping off his red neckerchief he quickly knotted it beneath the head of his hammer. Gripping the handle tightly in both hands he held the hammer aloft, and waved it in sweeping arcs. He knew his efforts had been recognised when he heard the whistle and saw the train slowing.

The engine halted level with him, the driver and fireman both leaning over the side of the cab.

"Wha's up wi' yew then, young Jaaycob?" called down the concerned driver.

Arthur Smith had known Goodall since his

arrival at King's Lynn in 1914. The flimsy new recruit had turned up with far too little to eat to sustain him through the working day, and Smith – a mere nine years older – had insisted the boy take a share of his own food. Although little more than a year from his fiftieth birthday now, 'young Jaaycob' remained forever youthful to the benign driver.

Goodall explained about the body a little way past the next station, but said nothing of his newly formed thoughts. "You'll hear when you gets to Stanhoe, I shouldn't wonder," he said, his Norfolk accent nowhere near as marked as the engine driver's. "But I thought you ought to be told in case Gabriel dun't say, and you happen to spot the man as you go by.

"And when you reach Heacham, Arthur, will you tell them I'll be back there later? Whosomever wants to talk to me can meet me there."

"Yew do depend Oi shall do that directly Oi gets to Heacham, young Jaaycob," came the reassuring promise.

Some trains on the line had two or three goods trucks coupled to the back of the passenger carriages, and in those cases a guard's van was also attached. This train had no trucks, and the train guard travelled in the last of the two elderly carriages. The man jumped down and joined the platelayer. It was an unexpected stop, and despite the negligible volume of traffic on the line the guard wondered how long the delay would be, and if he should be taking steps to protect his train in the rear, as 'Rule 55' demanded. However, having heard the news, and been told by Arthur that they were about to restart, he climbed back into the train.

Goodall carried on, his mind very much easier. He was glad to turn his thoughts away from the dead man, and reflect instead on the changes he had seen on the railways over the previous thirty or so years. The most recent of these had been the nationalisation of the independent railway companies by the Government in 1947.

As he walked, he amused himself with a favourite pastime - calculating what proportion of British Railways' extensive and varied estate he personally 'owned'. Today, he didn't dwell on his share of the many hotels, ships, and other assets – including tennis courts, wine cellars, and even a few farms. Instead, by the time he finished his shift he had generously endowed himself with a satisfying fraction of a locomotive, part of a station, and a section of track.

It somehow felt very good to think that the railways, and all their appurtenances, now belonged to millions of citizens – Jacob Goodall amongst them.

***

Elsewhere, matters relating to Goodall's discovery of the body were progressing very slowly. The British Railways official at King's Lynn, after his interrogation of the platelayer, was true to his word and quickly contacted Sergeant Knight at King's Lynn police station. Following that swift action, however, there was a considerable delay before the Sergeant managed to contact PC Hammond, the local Docking bobby.

Sergeant Knight had received sparse detail, and it didn't include mention of the dead man's clothing, because although Goodall had laboured the point the British Railways official hadn't thought to pass it on.

Ignorant of this crucial fact, Knight made the regrettable assumption that the body belonged to a tramp, unfortunately struck by a train while walking along the track. He therefore instructed Hammond to cycle the two miles from Docking to Stanhoe, and arrange to have the next 'up' train stop, collect the deceased, and transport the body to Heacham. The Sergeant told Hammond he would make arrangements with the Coroner, and ensure a vehicle was waiting at Heacham, ready for the transfer to King's Lynn hospital mortuary and the inevitable *post mortem*.

Goodall, his day's work done, boarded a train at Burnham Market and headed for home.

As the engine pulled into the tiny station at Stanhoe he spotted PC Hammond on the platform and correctly guessed why he was there. He left Sheba, happily stretched on the compartment floor, and joined Hammond, fully explaining his suspicions that the well-dressed man's death could not be accidental.

The platelayer's theory put the Constable in a quandary. Hammond knew there would be no further trains that evening and felt sure that, having already lain in the open during the day – and who knew how long before that – the deceased shouldn't be left in situ any longer. From Stanhoe there was no way to make a quick call to Sergeant Knight for further advice, and the train could only be delayed for a few more minutes.

Given that the platelayer's notion was not only unproven but also, Hammond believed, highly unlikely, he decided to go ahead with the collection of the body. He boarded the train as he had been instructed.

The engine steamed along the short distance to where Goodall, now riding in the cab while Sheba sat with the guard, indicated it should stop. The handful of passengers watched curiously as the body was carefully lifted and placed in the luggage compartment.

PC Hammond went through the dead man's pockets. Apart from a train ticket, he found nothing. This puzzled him. The deceased's anonymity was unexpected and extraordinary. The Constable privately acknowledged that Goodall's idea about the man's fate might indeed be more relevant than he had initially credited. However, he had done as instructed, and there was no going back. Asking the guard for a tarpaulin, Hammond respectfully covered the body.

The train, now running quite late, puffed towards the two remaining stations and eventually reached Heacham.

A waiting ambulance took the dead man away.

No one in authority wanted to speak to Goodall. He returned Sheba to her mistress, and went home to tell his wife about his day.

CHAPTER 2

Early on Wednesday morning, Goodall again caught the first branch line train at Heacham. Today, he would get out at Burnham Market and walk the last seven or so miles into Wells. Anticipating that the police would surely want to interview him somewhere along his route, he didn't take Sheba for company.

Although he made a point of speaking to the Station Master at Heacham, and leaned out of the train to talk to the men at Docking and Stanhoe, none had been contacted by the constabulary and there was no sign of a policeman at any of the stations. Goodall left the train at Burnham Market and set out towards Holkham. Either the police were disinterested in his involvement, or they had already solved matters to their satisfaction. He thought no more about it.

As Goodall worked, he came to a section of the Burnham track running behind a wood belonging to a house called *Little Goslings*. In one of life's countless but never-to-be-known coincidences, the lady of the house was at that moment making a telephone call to a firm of

King's Lynn solicitors. Her husband, Timothy Mayhew, was a partner in the firm, and had not returned home the previous evening.

He had travelled by train to London on the Monday, ready for a Tuesday meeting, and had been expected to return home that evening. He would ordinarily have arrived about nine o'clock, but there had been no sign of him, and he had sent no message.

On Wednesday morning, just as Goodall was passing by only a few yards away, she was calling her husband's office to see if, by some chance, anyone knew where he was.

Nobody did.

A few minutes later she telephoned the police to report a missing person.

***

Following Sergeant Knight's notification to the coroner, the mechanism for arranging a *post mortem* examination on the Stanhoe body had also creaked into motion. Just after lunchtime on Wednesday, Dr Bartlett, the local police surgeon, took a telephone call and agreed to do the PM at four o'clock that day, or a little earlier if he finished the PM for the Gayton Road man sooner.

When his morning surgery had finished, Bartlett went home for a quick lunch and then on to the hospital mortuary. He donned his gown and gloves and then, for no particular reason, changed his mind and asked his assistant to bring the more recent body out first.

He had been given very little background, the coroner's officer implying that some unfortunate and nameless tramp had been knocked down.

As Bartlett viewed the dead man on the ceramic table, however, he realised immediately that the vagrant suggestion was completely wrong. He took little notice of the man's suit and shoes – both of which were irrelevant to him because he knew the man wearing them. It was Timothy Mayhew lying on his slab. The doctor and solicitor were closely acquainted as fellow-members of both the medico-legal group and the bridge club.

"Oh dear Lord!" he exclaimed, and passed this identification to his assistant.

The two undressed the body, and while doing so Bartlett had his second shock. The condition of Mayhew's neck suggested he had been strangled.

"No accident this, Jim," was his terse comment to the mortuary attendant, who was also staring closely at the marks. "Someone should have gone through his pockets already, but do it again, will you. Put anything you find safely to one side for the police."

Autopsies weren't regular events in Bartlett's police surgeon workload. So far, police work had been only a tiny adjunct to his general practice, and had never been much more demanding than making clinical assessments of drunkenness. Had anyone asked him the previous day what the likelihood might be of his carrying out an autopsy on a murder victim he actually knew, the doctor would have judged the odds to be nil.

As he methodically went through his procedures, he noted five points of significance:

First, a contusion with severe bruising just above the solicitor's left ear. This, Bartlett determined, had certainly been inflicted before death, and with some sort of hard implement – perhaps a piece of piping, or even a purpose-made cosh.

Second, the actual cause of death was asphyxiation due to strangulation with a narrow ligature – possibly a piece of clothes line.

Third, Mayhew had died almost twenty-four hours earlier – somewhere between seven and ten o'clock the previous evening.

Fourth, the dead man had a broken hip and a series of minor abrasions – these had all been received *post mortem*.

Fifth, Mayhew's liver looked to be in a parlous state.

Alarmed by the external evidence of murder, Bartlett also took stomach samples for analysis, just in case the matter was even more complex than it already appeared. However, without the benefit of instant confirmation that toxins might also be involved, Bartlett was satisfied that Mayhew had been killed *on,* rather than *by,* a train.

Leaving his assistant to finish off, the police surgeon removed his gloves and gown, and hastily penned a preliminary report. Taking these notes with him, he went to find a telephone.

With the instrument in front of him, Bartlett had second thoughts. Returning to where his assistant was still restoring order in the mortuary he said "Get the other man out, please Jim. I feel I ought to do his autopsy as well, before I ring the police."

Jim Williams finished hosing down the slab, and deftly manhandled the second body onto it as Bartlett gowned and gloved himself again.

"At least I don't know this one," he muttered. "The police have identified him as Ralph Besant, one of Joseph Boam's employees. A widower, apparently walking home after work." The doctor dabbed at some tiny particles on the surgical table. "Pretty obvious from the fine sand in his overalls that he worked in the pits – I'd recognise that glass-making sand anywhere. Let's get his clothes off."

That done, the two men looked at the now-naked body, and then looked at each other.

"Don't hardly believe it, Doc – a second strangling!"

Bartlett was unusually silent as he carried

out his efficient examination. Eventually, he stripped off his gloves and gown for the second time.

"Strangled, yes, Jim – and with the same sort of ligature as poor Mayhew. But he didn't die of asphyxiation. He died from a blow to the head – which could, as the police thought, have been caused by falling from the bridge. The strangulation was done after he was already dead, although the killer may not have realised that.

"Also, this man has been dead for about four days.

"Clean up again, please Jim. I need to tell the CID a few things."

After rapidly making some more notes, Bartlett retraced his steps to the telephone.

***

Since 1837, the Borough of King's Lynn had employed its own police force, headed by a Chief Constable. That force had recently been subsumed into the Norfolk Constabulary, and King's Lynn police station had not yet settled down under the new regime. Inevitably, procedures and communications were somewhat disjointed.

Two murders in quick succession – with inescapable similarities – would have been a most exceptional occurrence anywhere in the country in 1949.

And then a third body was found. That discovery was to catapult Norfolk into an unenviable 'serial killer on the loose' location, whilst at the same time calling into question the operational effectiveness of the county's police force.

The third body was found by one of the King's gamekeepers. On patrol in the Wolferton Woods and less than a mile from Sandringham House, the gamekeeper, like Dora Bloy, had literally stumbled upon the man while crossing the track. Running as quickly as he could, he covered the few hundred yards to Wolferton station and alerted King's Lynn police.

Sergeant Walters, manning the front desk, took the gamekeeper's call. Walters was unaware of the almost identical call taken by his colleague the previous morning when Timothy Mayhew's body was found at Stanhoe. He also knew nothing about Ralph Besant's death, and no one at the police station had linked the earlier call about a missing person with those bodies.

Walters therefore unknowingly followed recent precedent, and assumed a train had struck an itinerant trespasser. He arranged for an ambulance to go to Wolferton to collect the body.

***

Dr Bartlett made his telephone call from the hospital. Bypassing Sergeant Walters, he asked for, and was put through to, the Criminal

Investigation Department. He reported his provisional findings on the two bodies, including his identification of Mayhew.

Detective Sergeant Gray shared the Doctor's shock. Tim Mayhew was someone he knew from occasional court cases. He had liked the solicitor, finding him to be competent and friendly. As for Bartlett's report on the similar circumstances between the two dead men, this was highly alarming to Gray. Wedging the telephone receiver between his shoulder and ear he first repeated, and then scribbled down, Bartlett's main autopsy points.

After the woeful lack of communication to date, a lucky chance occurred. Detective Constable Malan had been standing by the front desk when Sergeant Walters took the Wolferton game keeper's report earlier in the day. Now listening to Sergeant Gray's side of the conversation with the police surgeon, he urgently interrupted the senior man to relay what he knew about the Wolferton incident.

Gray asked Dr Bartlett to hang on while he grasped the import of what Malan was telling him. "Go downstairs and collect everything we've got about Stanhoe yesterday, and today's Wolferton body, too," he told his subordinate.

"Not sure if you heard all that, Doc, but it seems we have yet another body beside a railway track. Arrangements have already been made to bring in the deceased, but until you tell me otherwise, I think we should assume it's another murder. If I get him to the hospital morgue in the next hour or so, could you do the PM tonight?"

"I'll go home to eat," replied Bartlett, "and then return to the hospital. And I hope to high heaven that when I see this chap on the slab I don't find it's another from my social circle!"

Sergeant Gray replaced the telephone receiver and reviewed what he knew. Whether under the old or new line of command, the police at King's Lynn had very little experience of murder. Furthermore, the local CID inspector was currently on holiday, visiting his wife's family in Scotland.

Malan returned quickly and was able to pass on the few recorded facts about the discovery of Timothy Mayhew at Stanhoe. In rootling through the records he had also rounded up Mrs Mayhew's report, and realised its significance.

Sergeant Gray quickly moved everything up the chain of command. Dashing out of the CID office and taking the stairs two at a time, he sprinted up to the next floor at a speed which belied his fifty-two years of age, and caught his chief preparing to go home.

Superintendent Reeves was not best pleased to be detained. He was a bilious man, with an easily irritated disposition at the best of times. He listened to his subordinate. When the solicitor's name was mentioned he exploded.

"Tim Mayhew? Good God above! And two, possibly three, murders, you say? This is unheard of, man! Unheard of!"

Sergeant Gray withstood the blast.

"Have you rescinded Walter's instruction to recover the third body?" Reeves was correctly considering that premature removal might destroy critical evidence.

"No, sir," said Gray, and braced himself for another strong reaction to this admission. Already sure of his poor standing in the Super's eyes – he could never do right for doing wrong – he felt he had nothing to lose, and explained his decision. "In view of what Dr Bartlett said about Mr Mayhew, I thought it best to let it stand and get the body to the mortuary as soon as possible. I've informed the Coroner and arranged with Dr Bartlett to do the *post mortem* later tonight."

The Superintendent growled something unintelligible. Evaluating what his subordinate told him, he begrudgingly accepted it as the best arrangement, but didn't have the decency to say this to the junior man. He picked up a fountain pen and began to fiddle with its nib. The murder of an acquaintance was very disturbing, and his mind always worked more efficiently if his hands were engaged on a task as well. He thought for a bit and said, "You don't have the seniority to tackle this, Gray. In fact, we don't have the manpower or the expertise. I'll get on to the Chief Constable. He may send CID officers from

Norwich, but I hope he'll call in Scotland Yard."

When the small blockage of paper fibres was dislodged and the nib of his pen was functioning properly, the Superintendent unleashed his annoyance yet again.

"From what you're telling me, this hasn't gone well from the very start, Sergeant. It's now Wednesday evening, and Bartlett says Mayhew has been dead since Tuesday. You tell me his wife reported him missing this morning – but nobody connected her report with the body that was discovered quite near his home. In fact, if the Doc hadn't recognised him, we'd still be none the wiser!" he thundered.

Gray nodded unhappily, he could see exactly where the Super was going with all this, and he knew there would be nothing he could reasonably offer in rebuttal. It would be pointless to say that none of the errors were made by him, or indeed by the CID.

"We can't do anything useful now to catch Mayhew's killer until tomorrow morning. That's Thursday." Reeves now spoke slowly, as though teaching the days of the week to a particularly deficient scholar. "Today has been completely wasted, man. Wasted!"

Again, Gray said nothing. Whilst he didn't feel personally responsible – he hadn't dragged his heels in any way – he knew what Reeves said was correct: an avoidable delay on the part of the police had not been avoided. He also saw no point in mentioning something that had struck him and DC Malan as they looked through the paperwork downstairs. Something which would doubtless be picked up by whoever took on the investigation: Mayhew's wife had delayed reporting him missing to the King's Lynn police for a good twelve hours.

Reeves wasn't finished. "At first light tomorrow morning, I want men out searching around Stanhoe where Mayhew's body was found. Same goes for Wolferton. Thorough searches of both. D'you hear me?"

The Super now fiddled with a paperclip chain he had made earlier in the day. Working in reverse, he unlinked the clips and set them out in neat rows. He felt increasingly certain that when he sent the matter 'upstairs', the Chief Constable would call in Scotland Yard. Whilst that would be his preferred outcome, it nevertheless gave him a fresh anxiety: he felt he and his officers must inevitably look like parochial amateurs – a bunch of utter incompetents – to any London detectives.

Hoping for something positive to pass on to his Chief, the Superintendent plaintively appealed to his DS. "Can I at least assume that one part of this mess has been competently handled, Gray, and that detailed statements have been taken from whoever made the discoveries and anyone else involved?"

The Sergeant shook his unhappy head.

"Not that I'm aware of, sir."

"Well, clear off and find out who they are and get that organised!"

Gray's ears were throbbing with this last bellow as he escaped back downstairs.

The Superintendent made his telephone call.

The Chief Constable, like most of his ilk, hadn't come up through the police ranks. However, having been in post for over twenty years, he was unusually experienced. He listened to the facts, asked a few pertinent questions – none of which the Super could answer adequately – and gave his decision.

"Even if your DI was available, Reeves, this really is beyond us. I'll ask the Yard for help. Good that the third PM is going ahead; make sure you prioritise finding out who this third man was. Act on anything else that occurs to you or your DS, but be sure to do nothing which might hinder the London experts."

He gave a sorrowful sigh. "I know Mayhew's wife slightly, but I'm not doing this sort of thing myself over the telephone. If you haven't already made arrangements, get your officers to see her and break the news tonight. Tell her to expect someone from the Yard tomorrow. And, using a bit of discretion in the circumstances, get a statement from her if you can."

***

Dr Bartlett and the third body arrived at the morgue together. Anticipating the possibility of another unpleasant strangulation case, the doctor eyed the swathed figure without enthusiasm as it was manoeuvred onto the table. He pulled off the covering sheet himself, and instantly let out an involuntary and deeply felt "No!"

When he had recovered a little, he was able to explain his shocked reaction to his attendant. "I just don't believe this, Jim; I know this man too. Patrick Johns – another solicitor."

It didn't take the Police Surgeon many minutes to establish that Johns had been killed in an identical manner to Mayhew. Coshed, and then strangled. Similar injuries after death, too; but with a shoulder broken in the fall, rather than a hip.

However, somewhat to his surprise, his examination showed that Johns' death had occurred about two days earlier – a day prior to Mayhew's.

Bartlett cleaned himself up. Having noted his findings, he once again made his way to a telephone.

CHAPTER 3

Shortly after nine o'clock on Thursday morning, a black unmarked Wolseley pulled up outside King's Lynn police station. A slim, distinguished-looking man in his mid-thirties got out of the driver's seat. His front-seat passenger was only a little older, and built in a rather more squat form.

Moments later, a second Wolseley, a newer and slightly smaller model, pulled up alongside. The sole occupant of this was a man in his mid-twenties, with tow-coloured hair, an alert manner, and a particularly engaging smile. All three men wore grey suits of various shades.

"I was sure I'd beat you here, sir," laughed the younger man. "But I had to stop and ask directions in the town, whereas you had the Sergeant to navigate for you!"

His boss smiled. "True, but in fact I've been to the town before, and didn't need directions. Let's go inside."

At the front desk, the leader announced himself and his colleagues, "Detective Chief Inspector Bryce, from Scotland Yard, and these gentlemen are Detective Sergeant Haig and Detective Constable Kittow. We are expected?"

The Desk Sergeant had sprung to attention as soon as Bryce spoke. "Oh yes, sir, the Superintendent said to bring you up as soon as you arrived. Come through please, and follow me."

He lifted the hinged portion of his counter and led the London men up a staircase and along a corridor. Tapping on a door, he opened it and stepped aside.

"Ah, gentlemen! Come in, come in," said the uniformed Superintendent Reeves. His ulcer was not so painful today and he was consequently feeling less bad-tempered than he had with Sergeant Gray the day before. "Sit yourselves down. Organise some refreshment for all of us, if you please," he told the Desk Sergeant.

Mutual introductions followed, after which Reeves spent several minutes outlining what he knew.

"I'll say straight away that things didn't go as well as they should have. I'll make no excuses beyond saying that some of the staff here are ex-Borough men, and others are County men, and the operating procedures come from both forces, too. We haven't got everything properly integrated and running smoothly yet.

"Be that as it may, we should have realised earlier that the body found yesterday morning wasn't that of a line-side trespasser hit by a train, but was likely to be that of a solicitor who'd already been reported missing by his wife.

"Since we called for your help, the PM has been carried out on our third body. Same cause of death as the second victim – and this one was also a solicitor, from the same firm.

"The first of the three victims – and I think we have to assume there's a common assailant – died just before the weekend, but wasn't found until Tuesday. He was also beside the railway, but by the line out of South Lynn.

"So we now have two solicitors, both from the same firm, both apparently killed in the same way, about twenty-four hours apart, and one quarryman killed five days ago.

"Dan Bartlett, our Police Surgeon, is upset. He was called in to do autopsies on all three men, and it was he who identified the solicitors, both being very well known to him. Quite a shock, as you can imagine."

A constable arrived with a tray. When the beverages had been distributed Reeves continued.

"Anyway, to address the basics first; I understand you've met our Chief Constable, Bryce? He was very pleased to hear you're heading up this enquiry. Anything you want, we are to provide. For a start, we're lending you Detective Constable Malan, one of our brightest and best juniors. No experience of murder, unfortunately, but then nobody this side of the county has much of that."

Some rather noisy slurps, followed by a satisfied “Ahhh...” punctuated the Super’s narrative. His thirst slaked, he carried on. “Our local DI is away in Scotland, but frankly, even if he’d been available I think the Chief would still have called you in. The senior DS is holding the fort on various matters, and can’t be spared – but within these walls I’d say Peter Malan is far more intelligent anyway.”

More slurps and Reeves’ mug was drained and replaced on the tray. “Second, you have rooms booked at the Glebe Hotel in Hunstanton. It was the Chief’s personal choice for you. He thought you’d prefer to be nearer to where the bodies were found. And it’s only a short walk from the Glebe to the station, should you be investigating railway carriages and so on. He would have used the Sandringham – that’s the railway hotel actually in the station – but it’s closed at present. You have an extra room with a telephone, to use as your incident room, and there’s a small police station in James Street if you need a cell. We can always make space for you here, if you want to carry out interviews at this end of the line, for example.”

Reeves stood up. “Now, gentlemen, I’ll take you to CID and introduce you to DC Malan, and then you can get started. I wish you all the very best on this one, it all seems utterly inexplicable – and bizarre.”

The Yard detectives followed the local

chief downstairs. Introductions performed, Superintendent Reeves departed. Bryce made his preliminary assessment of Malan. About the same age as Kittow, the local detective constable was perhaps half a head taller than his Yard counterpart, with straight dark hair clipped very short, and sharp blue eyes. There was no mistaking his enthusiasm, something which Bryce had also recognised early on in DC Adam Kittow, and which had marked him out as worthy of development opportunities.

"Can you get a car, Malan?" asked the DCI.

"Already have, sir. I've got the one the DI normally uses, and he's not back for another week."

"Good. I anticipate we shall all be out and about quite a bit – and in different directions – so that'll give us three cars between the four of us. Collect everything you have on these deaths," the DCI told the local detective, "including the *post mortem* reports, if they're available. Bring the whole lot to the hotel at Hunstanton.

"So that the four of us are properly equipped with the same song sheets, so to speak, bring us each a railway timetable with you as well. We all need to understand how the various stations involved are linked. Once you've arrived with all the relevant paperwork, Malan, and briefed us, we'll think about what to do next."

Another question occurred to the DCI as he stood up to leave. "Where do you live, by the way?"

"In Snettisham, sir."

Malan started to explain where that was, but the DCI forestalled him. "I'm familiar with the stations on these lines. Basically, you're four down from Lynn and two up from Hunstanton."

Malan was impressed. He hadn't yet discovered that his temporary boss was a railway enthusiast.

***

Barely thirty minutes later, the two London police cars arrived outside the Glebe Hotel, followed not long after by Malan's car. Taking a quick break to book into their rooms and unpack, the Yard officers soon joined their new colleague in the extra room provided.

"Couldn't be better," said Bryce looking around and thoroughly satisfied. "The sea view – or I should say the view of The Wash – is wonderful from my bedroom, but would probably be a distraction down here in our incident room!" Pulling out a chair from under the main table, he sat down and organised his pen and a foolscap pad on the table, making it clear that he was ready to start.

"Right. You first, Malan; what do we know about these three, and what was found on them?"

"Well, sir, taking the victims in the order of their deaths.

"The first one is Ralph Besant; 58 years old. A widower; lived alone. He was apparently walking home from his job in the local sand quarry. He was found almost under a road bridge going over the South Lynn to Fakenham line, close to Gayton Road station.

"The police surgeon says he died somewhere around five o'clock on Friday evening. It's practically certain that he was pushed off the bridge, and sustained a very serious head wound in falling. That was the cause of death. Someone – possibly not realising he was already dead – then tightened a ligature, maybe a clothes line, around his neck.

"The body wasn't found until Tuesday morning. The uniformed officer who attended assumed it was accident or suicide, and Besant was taken to the mortuary without anyone noticing the strangulation marks. Dr Bartlett saw them at the PM, of course.

"I took a look at the bridge earlier this morning, sir, to see the lie of the land. The railway passes under the road. The line remains near enough horizontal, and the road is built up in a long gradual slope each side, to pass over it. That's a common arrangement in Norfolk, where most of the roads were probably only tracks when the railways first came along. There's a small station, Gayton Road, only a few yards from the bridge. Besant was found at the far side of the bridge, away from the station.

"It's a quiet road, and I can't think many passengers ever use the station. It actually won a 'Best Kept Station' award a few years before the war; thanks to station staff with time on their hands, probably. Anyway, if I'm right about the sequence of events, no one at the station could have observed anything that happened on the road, because the parapet of the bridge would be in the way.

"Getting down to the track is very easy – I did it myself, and apparently the woman who found the body had gone down there to forage. Once down there, you can't be seen from the road. In theory, someone on the station platform could have seen Besant and his attacker. But the chances of anyone being on the platform – even if a train were due – would be slim. Also, anyone who might have been around would be a good fifty yards away, and looking through the dark shadow under the bridge. And it would have been getting dark anyway." The local detective constable shook his head and pulled down the corners of his mouth. "I doubt we'll find a witness, sir.

"Besant didn't turn up for work on Monday, of course. When he didn't arrive on Tuesday either, his foreman apparently thought about sending someone round to the man's house. However, he hadn't got around to doing that."

Malan flicked through his pocketbook and

read from a fresh page.

"The next death was Patrick Johns, aged forty-four. Partner in Mayhew & Johns; a firm of Lynn solicitors. Bachelor. Lived here in Cliff Parade, just along the road from where we are now. He was killed between five o'clock and eight o'clock on Monday evening.

"Nobody has reported him missing. The only reason we know his name is because Dr Bartlett, doing the autopsy last night, recognised him. As yet, we haven't had time to do anything else about him.

"It seems he was travelling between Hunstanton and Lynn – the only thing found in his pockets was a rail ticket from Heacham to Lynn, so it's assumed that was his direction of travel.

"No keys, wallet, or ID on him. No small change; not even a nose rag, sir." Malan, as the 'new boy', was keen to share his thinking about the absence of ID and personal effects, but a little unsure as to how much he could say to these experts from Scotland Yard. He looked up from his notes and tentatively offered: "Seems odd for a well-dressed man not to have any of those things about him."

Bryce, recognising the local constable's restraint and correctly suspecting the reason for it, smiled faintly, but kept his head down and carried on drawing on his pad.

Sergeant Haig, observing his boss, and

knowing his habit of fully involving all his subordinates and encouraging opinions, took the unspoken cue and gave the local detective the confirmation, and confidence, he needed.

"Aye, you might well call it odd," he agreed pleasantly. "Or, as we would call it at the Yard, *very highly suspicious indeed*." He smiled at the young DC and added, "Not to worry though, Malan, we'll have you speaking your mind – and our lingo – in no time!"

Grinning his thanks at Haig, Malan continued. "Johns' body was found about half way between Dersingham and Wolferton, but wasn't spotted by the crews of various trains passing the site over the next couple of days. Eli Beavis, a gamekeeper on the Sandringham Estate, saw it while he was out patrolling in the Wolferton Woods yesterday, when he happened to cross the line just at that very point."

Malan paused, expecting questions, but when none were forthcoming, he continued again. "The doc says Johns was coshed, sir, perhaps with a piece of piping or maybe even a purpose-made cosh, and then strangled to death – with a ligature apparently identical to that used on Besant. Johns was then thrown from the train, and there are *post mortem* signs of injury consistent with a fall of that sort.

"The third victim is Timothy Mayhew. His body was actually found before Johns, but he was killed twenty-four hours after. Aged sixty-two, senior partner in the same firm. Lives in Burnham Market. Married. According to his wife's statement, it seems he went to London by train on Monday, stayed overnight, and was due to return on Tuesday evening." Malan pushed the statement across the table to the DCI.

"It was his wife who reported him missing yesterday morning. Problem was, as an adult, Mayhew being absent from home didn't merit priority treatment, and no one made the connection between her call and the report of a body. His wife hadn't rushed to report him missing, either.

"He was found beside the track on the Wells branch, this side of Stanhoe station, by Jacob Goodall, a platelayer. The PM shows an identical cause of death to that of Johns – coshed, strangled, thrown out of a train. The doc says that Mayhew also had advanced liver disease. He was killed between seven o'clock and ten o'clock on Tuesday evening.

"We've managed to contact the railwayman, Goodall, and he'll be at Heacham station at three-thirty this afternoon ready to give a statement, sir. I was detailed to go myself, but obviously you'll decide now. The gamekeeper has already made a statement, but it doesn't tell us anything apart from the place, date and time of his discovery." Malan pushed this across to the DCI.

"Again, there was no ID or anything at all

on Mayhew's body, except a ticket from Wells to Heacham. And again, it was Doctor Bartlett who identified Mayhew.

"Uniformed have been out searching at both locations since early this morning, sir. No word from them before I left Lynn."

One of Sergeant Haig's routine tasks was photographing victims and crime scenes. Appreciating that the way the three bodies had been moved after discovery meant this wouldn't have been done, he nevertheless had a question. "What about photographs of the deceased? Did someone do that at the morgue; or get some from the men's homes?"

Malan, much embarrassed, shook his head. It was only just dawning on him that photographs would be necessary when making enquiries, and now there would be yet another delay in getting some.

"What about contact with the solicitors' office? Anybody done that yet?" queried Kittow.

Malan brightened, "Yes, sir. The Super spoke to a solicitor at the office when they opened this morning, and got John's address at the same time, Mayhew's already being known from his wife's report. Near panic, apparently, when he told them that both partners were dead. He didn't mention that they were murdered, though. The Super said someone would be visiting today, not mentioning it would be Scotland Yard detectives."

Malan shuffled his papers together. "That's it from me, sir," he said.

Haig and Kittow had each made notes of the limited information. The DCI, who had produced paper and pencil and a ruler from his briefcase at the start of Malan's briefing, and seemed to have been doodling, looked up from what he had been drawing.

"I've just sketched the relevant lines and stations in this corner of Norfolk," he said, passing his plan to Sergeant Haig. "Might help you and Kittow to get your bearings when you're using the timetables."

Bryce began to outline the priorities for the investigation. "We need to find the actual train that each man travelled on, and who else travelled with them. From that, we'll hopefully be able to pinpoint the exact compartment for each murder. Although, even if we manage to do that, we may not turn up any evidence – strangulation obviously won't leave the same clues that a gun or knife attack would. In that respect, I'll go so far as to say I think our killer has either been a bit clever, or a bit lucky in his *modus operandi*.

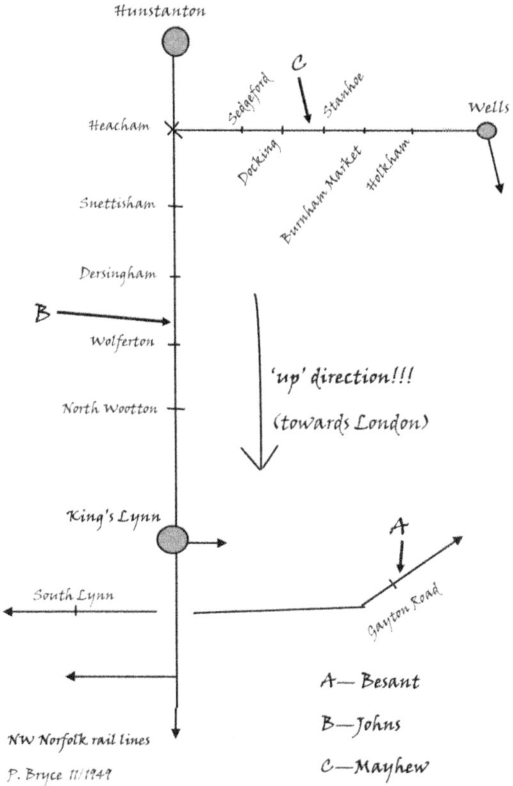

"As you correctly suspected, Malan, removal of all identifying items from both men – including handkerchiefs, which might well have been monogrammed – sends us a clear signal: someone wanted to delay identification for as long as possible after discovery. Why do you think that was?"

"To give himself the maximum time to escape?"

Bryce nodded. "Yes, that has to be a strong possibility. In which case, we might already be too late. The killer may have left the county, or even the country, by now. The thought that a particularly brutal and prolific murderer may get away, has me even more determined than usual to ensure that we catch up with them, though. We'll just have to work extra rapidly to make up for lost time.

"Another clear signal – and this one gives me hope, gentlemen, that the killer isn't particularly clever – is the fact that Johns, who worked in Lynn and lived here in Hunstanton, had a ticket from Heacham. Why? The time of death suggests he would have been travelling in the opposite direction, going home in fact."

Shakes of the head met his question.

"Likewise Mayhew. The man lived in Burnham Market. He reportedly travelled by train to London on Monday. So why, when he was supposed to be going home, was the only ticket he was carrying valid for the opposite direction?"

The DCI turned to the local constable. "Have you got the tickets here, Malan?"

The constable produced an envelope and shook the tickets out. Bryce's features darkened as he viewed the small pieces of cardboard.

"As I thought – neither has been punched. These were bought beforehand, and certainly weren't the tickets the men actually used for their last train journey. Someone is rather crudely attempting to muddy the waters about the victims' movements by planting decoy tickets."

Both Haig and Kittow were keen on railways, although not so knowledgeable as their DCI.

"Do you think that Johns, for example, wasn't going through Wolferton on an 'up' train from Heacham, at all then, sir?" asked Haig, using his forefinger to trace the relevant section on the plan for Kittow to see as well.

Bryce, resting an elbow on the table and his chin on his hand, shook his head slowly. "I don't say that he definitely wasn't on a train going in that direction, but it seems extremely unlikely. Even if for some reason he was, it's even more improbable that he'd take a ticket from another station when he lives close to this one – unless he chose to walk a couple of miles for exercise first. It seems pretty certain that he was actually on a 'down' train – going home to Hunstanton, in fact. If so, this was a deliberate red herring.

"Same for Mayhew. Why would he go back to Wells to buy a ticket? No – my guess is that he, too, was on his way home.

"Initially, at least, I propose we work on the assumption that both men were on their way home, Johns on Monday night and Mayhew on

Tuesday night. And that both were travelling in the opposite direction to that suggested by their tickets."

With the cardboard slips now resting on a clean sheet of foolscap, Bryce said, "There isn't much of a surface on these tickets, Sergeant, and both will have been handled by a number of people already, but you could try and see if you can lift anything useful off them later."

The DCI looked down at his notes, and the tasks for each detective he had planned. "The lack of photographs is unfortunate. But I'm sure we can get hold of some ourselves today when we're out and about. I certainly don't intend to delay starting our enquiries until we have some."

Turning to Kittow, he gave directions to his junior Yard subordinate first. "You're going to start at Heacham station. Find out how many tickets were bought for the Wells branch on Monday afternoon and evening. And, if possible, get details of anyone taking one of the few Wells trains – regardless of whether they transferred from a Hunstanton-bound train or started from scratch at Heacham. I doubt if there are ever very many passengers and you know the sort of questions to ask: was Mayhew known by staff at the station; did anyone see him; were there any strangers that day."

The DCI looked up at the ceiling, visualising the relevant train lines again. "Whilst you're there, Kittow, ask about people getting off a 'down' train on Monday evening, too. If the killer did push Johns out at Wolferton, he had a choice of four stations where he could get out himself, Heacham being one of them.

"Then, move up the line to Snettisham, Dersingham, and finally King's Lynn stations, and ask the same questions at each. You can skip North Wootton and Dersingham – I'm satisfied they can't be involved. Remember when you're at Lynn you have to account for trains that Mayhew may have taken on Tuesday, as well as likely trains for Johns on Monday."

The young Yard detective looked up from his pocketbook jottings. "That it, sir?"

Bryce nodded and turned to the local DC, outlining what he was to accomplish. "We know Johns was a bachelor. First task for you, Malan, is to find out if he lives here alone or has resident staff. Get access to his house somehow. Look through whatever paperwork you can lay hands on. See if you can discover any next-of-kin. In the absence of live-in staff, he probably has a daily cleaner or something. Find her, and ask what she knows about his movements.

"If possible, collect a couple of photographs of the man. Passport, or anything would do. I prefer not to rely on mortuary photographs for showing to members of the public, if possible.

"If you find someone connected to Johns, check whether he normally used the train to go to his office. And when you've done what you can in his house, you should ask questions about his movements at Hunstanton station. You're only concerned with Monday, of course, and whether he got on the train here in the morning; but like Kittow, you also need to ask about people getting off at Hunstanton in the evening, because this is the fourth station where the killer could possibly have ended his journey."

Bryce checked his watch and saw it was quarter to eleven. "As it turns out, I haven't organised this very well. We've only just come from King's Lynn and Sergeant Haig and I need to go back there now and interview the staff at the office. When we've done that, we'll get to Heacham at three-thirty to speak to Goodall, and Mrs Mayhew after that. Time permitting, I also want to talk to the station staff at Stanhoe.

"Let's all aim to meet back here at five, but that's not a deadline – take more time if you need it."

CHAPTER 4

"Ordinarily, I'd be very tempted to save petrol and trundle around on these picturesque little rural lines," said Bryce from behind the wheel of the Wolseley as he and Haig headed back to King's Lynn. "Trouble is, particularly on lines like the Wells branch, the few trains that operate tend to carry goods as well as passengers, and spend ages in remote places loading chickens, or sheep, or whatever. I bet there are more milk churns than human passengers carried between Heacham and Wells!"

"According to the timetables," said Haig, "there are five trains a day to Wells – six on Fridays and Saturdays, but none on Sundays. The Stanhoe station sees a grand total of ten trains in a sixteen-hour day – over an hour and a half between passenger trains, on average. Not exactly like London Bridge or Liverpool Street. It's a long working day, but it must leave a lot of time for gardening!"

"Certainly does," laughed Bryce. "It'll be interesting to see how well-tended the station is."

"Any ideas on motive yet, sir?"

"None at all, I fear. On the face of it, we have a particularly vicious killer who is seriously aggrieved with one or more solicitors. Your guess is as good as mine as to why that might have been. Perhaps the murderer lost out in some inheritance dispute. Or was convicted of an offence and blamed the solicitor for not getting an acquittal. Or for not mitigating well enough to avoid a custodial sentence.

"Alternatively, if there are junior partners and staff solicitors, someone might feel that promotion prospects would increase if the upper ranks were thinned out. Although I'd be the first to say that anyone motivated in that way would have to be seriously deranged.

"But then we have the quarryman, Ralph Besant. Although it seems he wasn't on a train like the other two, there are still strong connections – railway line and ligature – which leads one to assume, as the Super did, that the assailant is the same in all three cases.

"Given what I'm convinced has been deliberate messing about with the evidence, I'm keeping a very open mind. In fact, two of the victims being solicitors from the same firm may not even be significant."

Sergeant Haig stared at his boss, his dark eyebrows rose as far up his forehead as they could go. "Aye, well sir, that would be stretching coincidence a wee bit far for me!"

"I agree it's unlikely. But strange things

happen, and even Superintendent Reeves described the situation as bizarre. I've found that the longer I do this job, the harder it is to surprise me," said Bryce as he turned the car into Tuesday Market Place.

"A lovely square, this," he commented, pointing towards a fine building as he spoke. "A mid-nineteenth century Victorian oddity – the Corn Exchange – in front of us here; and directly across from that, a beautiful late-seventeenth century coaching inn. Almost every other building on all four sides has some architectural merit as well."

The Yard detectives walked towards an ivy-clad building. Stencilled on two of the windows they saw:

Mayhew & Johns
Solicitors
Commissioners for Oaths

Haig pulled the front door open and held it for the DCI to go through first.

They found a young woman at a desk in the bright reception area. A cloaked mound sat in front of her – a typewriter with its dust cover still in place. Two other women stood beside her, all three wearing black armbands and looking miserable. The Yard detectives had clearly interrupted an intense conversation. With the slightly unfocused gaze of someone prised away from a more important matter, the seated woman nevertheless politely enquired if she could help.

Bryce introduced Haig and himself by name and said that they were detectives. For the moment, he didn't intend to mention their ranks or their Scotland Yard status. Having been told earlier that morning that the police would visit, the women had expected to see uniformed officers. All three now looked at the besuited detectives with much more interest, realising they were not the potential clients for the firm they had assumed them to be.

"You all obviously know what has happened, and I'm very sorry for your loss. We shall, of course, need to inspect the rooms of both Mr Mayhew and Mr Johns, and at some point take statements from people who work here."

Bryce's voice conveyed exactly the right degree of sympathy for the women, combined with unmistakeable professional purpose. Addressing the seated receptionist he enquired, "Who is the senior person in the firm now?"

"Well, Mr Bullen is the only solicitor now, sir, so I suppose he's the senior in the office today, although he just popped out a few minutes before you arrived."

Hesitant glances were exchanged with her colleagues before the girl continued. "The thing is, none of us knows for sure who's in charge. We do know that Mrs Mayhew is also a solicitor, but she doesn't ever work here. All the same, we were wondering, just between ourselves, whether she might be a silent partner in the business, and that maybe she'll step in to take control of the firm now."

The receptionist's tone, together with the expression on her face – mirrored on her companions' faces – told the Yard men that this solution was the one all three were hoping for. Both detectives also silently registered that taking the helm of a successful company could perhaps provide a lead to unlocking the murders.

"Anyone else in the office today, apart from Mr Bullen, who might be considered in charge right now?" asked Bryce.

"There's Mr Boyd – Douglas Boyd – he's the office manager, I suppose he comes next. After him there's Carter Stanley, our articled clerk."

She sniffed twice in quick succession before explaining with a catch in her voice, "We're ever so worried about what's going to happen to us and our jobs."

Her colleagues nodded their agreement almost violently.

"That's very understandable," acknowledged Bryce. "For the record, tell us who you are, please."

The two slightly older women were Janice Henderson, secretary to the late Mr Mayhew, and Patricia Kendall, secretary to the late Mr Johns. Anne Percival, the youngest, was general clerk and receptionist. There were apparently two more female clerical employees in the building.

Addressing the receptionist first, Bryce made a request, "When Mr Bullen returns, send him straight to me, please." Turning to the two secretaries, he said: "Mrs Henderson, "I'd like you to show me Mr Mayhew's office; Mrs Kendall, kindly take the Sergeant to Mr Johns' office."

As Haig prepared to follow his guide, Bryce told him "Gather up all the keys you can find, Sergeant, and lock up everything in Mr Johns' room – cabinets, drawers, and his office door if possible – then come and find me. We'll look through all his paperwork later."

Haig had only just re-joined his boss when an angry-looking young man threw open the door of Mayhew's room without knocking. Large and heavy-set, his build was of the type often described as 'beefy'. He strode towards the late partner's desk, where Bryce now sat opening drawers. Not content to address the DCI across the desk in the conventional manner, the newcomer walked around it and loomed over Bryce, his deeply flushed face glaring down at the Chief Inspector.

"Look here, you!" he stormed. "What's the meaning of all this? You can't barge in here and take over our office! And I'm told you've locked Patrick's room when we shall obviously need to get papers out of there. How dare you!"

Bryce, suspecting that he was being

harangued by the solicitor whom he'd summoned, gestured to Haig that he should shut the door. Frowning slightly, he turned in his seat to look up at his loud and indignant visitor. "Suppose we start by introducing ourselves," he suggested pleasantly. "I'm Detective Chief Inspector Bryce, and this is Detective Sergeant Haig. Who are you?"

"I shall complain to Superintendent Reeves about your high-handed conduct!" shouted the man, ignoring the question and clearly disinclined to co-operate. "You can't just come in here as if you owned the place. I'm a solicitor, and the pair of you would do well to grasp that I bally-well know the law!"

"Let's see about that, shall we?" replied Bryce, not at all pleased by this response to his reasonable overture. Leaning further back in his seat, he crossed his legs and folded his arms. Maintaining his pleasant tone, he proceeded to dismantle his hector's objections.

"Allow me to make a few points. First, this no longer has anything to do with Superintendent Reeves because the Chief Constable has handed the case to Scotland Yard. That's us, as far as you are concerned.

"Second, this is a murder enquiry. We are empowered to do all it takes to solve it. Should you have a need to access Mr John's room or this one, between now and the time that this matter is concluded, you only have to ask us. Politely.

"Third, I was called to the bar while you were still in short trousers, so please don't lecture me on the law!

"And finally, any further obstruction to my investigation and I shall arrest you.

"So, for the second and last time, who are you?"

The solicitor stared down at Bryce, speechless. Retreating backwards to where a chair stood against the wall, he literally fell into it, his bombast completely spent. Rubbing both hands hard over his face, he gave a mumbled apology from behind his fingers, and then emerged to supply the required information in an unsteady and somewhat breathless voice.

"I'm Fergal Bullen. This is...this is all such a shock! When Reeves rang me this morning, all he said was that Tim and Patrick were dead and police would see us in due course. But murdered? Both of them?"

Having arrived roaring and in high dudgeon, the solicitor now finished on a near whisper, almost unable to speak the word 'murdered', and with his face once more behind his hands.

Bryce allowed Bullen some time to recover. Soon the solicitor's breathing and colouring became more normal, as did his disposition and manners. "Look, can we get you some coffee or something?" he offered. "I know I could do with some."

"That would be very welcome, thank you. But please don't mention anything to the staff, at this stage," Bryce warned him. Bullen nodded, and left the room.

"Potentially useful that Mr Reeves didn't tell them it's murder, do you think, sir?" asked Haig as soon as the door closed again.

"Perhaps. And we'll certainly watch the rest of them closely when we tell them. The news may not be a surprise to someone."

Fergal Bullen returned and sat down again. Very calm now, he appeared to have splashed his face with water, judging by the wet patches on his shirt collar. "Apologies again for my outburst," he said. "Am I allowed to know what happened? We just assumed that there must have been a road accident, although we couldn't understand why Tim and Patrick would be travelling together."

"I shall certainly answer your question," said Bryce, "but before I do, just help us by answering a few of mine. As far as you know, when was Mr Johns last in the office?"

Bullen fidgeted with his pinkie signet ring as he spoke, "Well, this is only hearsay, as I didn't see him myself, but I understand that Patrick was in the office all day on Monday as usual. His secretary says he wasn't expected on Tuesday – but he didn't turn up yesterday when he was expected. When he'd missed a couple of appointments, she tried unsuccessfully to call him at home."

"I see. What about Mayhew?"

"I last saw Tim very briefly on Monday morning. Later in the day, he went to London – he had a meeting on Tuesday. At least, as far as I know he went. Janice can probably tell you more about his travel arrangements.

"Apparently, he should have been in here again yesterday, but as he didn't have any clients to see, Janice just shrugged off his absence – thought perhaps he'd decided to take a day off after his foray into the Great Wen.

"When Mrs Mayhew called to ask if we knew where he was. Janice told her he hadn't been seen and suggested contacting the police. Mrs Mayhew said she would do that. The two promised to let each other know if they heard anything. Yesterday morning was the first time we knew for sure that something serious was up; but it was Reeves, not Clarissa Mayhew, who contacted us this morning."

"Good. Just a bit more background for both partners, please. We know Mayhew was married, he lived in Burnham Market, yes?"

"That's right. He was the senior partner. His wife is also a solicitor by profession, but she has her own practice."

"Do you know if he generally came to work by train?" asked Haig, neatly recording key points.

"Normally, no. He could drive from

Burnham to the office in a third of the time a train would take. But he went up to London at least a couple of times every month by train. I understand that on those days sometimes he drove as far as Lynn and caught the Liverpool Street train, but at other times he did the whole trip by train, starting with the branch service from Burnham Market."

Anne Percival tapped on the door and came into the room. Aware that she was interrupting, she quickly poured and handed out cups of coffee and set down a plate of biscuits. When she had gone, Bryce continued:

"What about Johns?"

"He was a bachelor. Lived alone in Hunstanton, in one of those huge Victorian houses on the seafront. He occasionally had a small gathering there – afternoon tea parties, really. I've been three or four times. I think he engaged caterers when he entertained.

"A nice fellow, but quite private. I know he had two passions in life: photography and his cars. But there may have been a third."

Bryce was immediately intrigued. "Please explain."

"Well, the cars are straightforward. He has three – all Alvises. You'd need more than a bob or two to keep even one of them, never mind three. There's a practically brand-new TA14; a 1938 4.3 litre drop-head coupe, and a 1939 Speed 25 Charlesworth Sports Saloon. All, especially the pre-war cars, are magnificent. I drool every time I see one of them.

"I'm envious of Patrick's cameras too, speaking as someone who can only afford a box Brownie. I know he had several cameras, because I've seen them. They were always lying around in his house, and on his desk here sometimes, too.

"A couple of first-rate 35 mm cameras for a start – Leica IIIs, he told me. Then a couple of larger-format ones – a Rolleiflex Automat, and an expensive-looking Yashica as well.

"What he used them for might be a bit more sensitive. Every wall that I've seen in his quite extensive house is plastered with framed photographs – all, I think, taken by him. I'm no expert critic, but all of them look to be of a professional standard.

"Some are of churches – exteriors and interiors. I once heard him say that he'd photographed every church in the county, and a good few in Cambridgeshire and Suffolk, too. There are lots of other subjects: waves breaking on the shore; fishing boats at Lynn; Hunstanton pier, and so on. Some pictures of his cars, too.

"But interspersed with all those are photographs of ladies not wearing very much, in what might be called 'artistic' poses. There must be at least thirty such pictures on the walls of the hallway and the reception rooms in which he entertained us. I've never been in any of the bedrooms.

"I can tell you that he didn't invite the ladies from this office whenever I visited. Actually, I don't recall many female guests at any of his gatherings. But he definitely had female help around the house – cleaning and so on. No idea what they thought about that side of his photography, though.

"He took me up to his darkroom once. Fantastically well-equipped. The attics in those houses are vast, and his has a photographic studio as well, complete with different props, screens and backgrounds. It's supposition on my part, but I guess that's where he took his models – although there are some outdoor shots of them as well.

"Obviously, he wasn't ashamed of that side of his hobby, but he never spoke about it with me in the same way that he discussed the pros and cons of capturing a sunset over water, or the texture of tree bark, for example."

Bullen fell silent and Bryce thanked the solicitor. "That's all very useful to us for building up a picture of the victim. I don't have high hopes that you can help us with this, but we're interested in these gentlemen's wills, and also in their partnership agreement for this firm."

A shake of the head was the solicitor's response. "I see that you need those documents, of course. I can tell you that Patrick appointed me as his executor, I suppose a couple of years ago. But I had nothing to do with drafting his will, and I've never seen what it contains. I know nothing about Tim's will.

"It may be that Tim and Patrick kept a copy of their wills at home, but I'd be surprised if the originals aren't kept here in the strongroom. I can get you into the strongroom easily enough, if you'd like, but I'm pretty sure that both men would have their private papers in one of our locked steel boxes, rather than in our more usual cardboard box files. I've no idea if you'll be able to access them without keys."

Bryce said nothing to this, but Haig could read his boss' mind on the matter: necessary force would be used on the boxes if no keys could be found.

"As far as the partnership agreement is concerned, if it's in the building I'd expect it to be in the same boxes," continued Bullen. "Although I suppose Clarissa Mayhew may be able to tell you what it says in the event of a partner dying, without your having to find the actual document. That's a matter of considerable interest to all of us here, I might say. If the agreement is silent on the point, the partnership ceases to exist. You'll be aware of the normal rule about deaths – in the absence of other clear information, the elder is presumed to have died first. So Patrick briefly became the senior and, as far as we know, sole partner.

"I had hopes of becoming a partner in the next three or four years; Tim was talking of winding down about then." He sighed. "I'm not the only one who's worried about what will happen next. Everyone's anxious."

"All right, Mr Bullen. After your first intemperate outburst you've been very patient," said Bryce. "I'll answer your question now, and tell you what happened. Both the partners died in identical ways. Each was coshed, strangled, and thrown from a moving train." The DCI deliberately spoke quite slowly, watching closely as each brutal detail of the murders made its impression on the solicitor.

Bullen stared back, apparently even more shocked than before. He leaned forward and thrust the palms of his hands towards Bryce, the entreaty in his voice completing the image of a thoroughly distressed supplicant. "Are you really sure?" he asked. "There isn't some ghastly mistake? Some sort of mix-up with bodies and paperwork at the morgue?"

"I'm afraid not. But although the order of their deaths may well prove important, for the future of this firm if not in solving the crimes, you're wrong in your assumption that they died together. The medical evidence is that Mr Johns was killed a full day before Mr Mayhew."

Bullen was still goggling at the policemen when something occurred to him. "On different days – so on different trains then? This is incredible! Who would go out of his way to kill one of them – let alone both?"

"Very good question, Mr Bullen. We don't have an answer yet, and I don't want to go into more detail at this stage. However, it seems the two partners aren't the only victims – a third man was killed on Friday, and his situation is also connected with the railways. His name is Ralph Besant – does that ring a bell?"

Bullen was now reeling from this additional news. He shook his head and said weakly, "You'd have to check with the other staff, but I've never heard the name before."

Bryce, conscious of how much needed to be accomplished before the three-thirty rendezvous with Jacob Goodall at Heacham, made a request. "Well, let's just see the strong room first, please, if you would lead the way."

A short walk through reception to collect a key, and then down into the building's cellar, brought them to a reinforced door which the solicitor unlocked. Feeling for the light switch, Bullen stepped back again and let the Yard men pass him.

The room was not especially large, and had the characteristically musty smell of paper shut away in a little-used and windowless cell. That aside, it was very clean and very efficiently organised, with sturdy 'library' steps by the door to assist with access to the higher shelves.

Ignoring the many box files lining two of the walls, Bryce and Haig searched amongst the black metal boxes on the shelves of the third wall. Clearly stencilled labels displaying the owners' names in alphabetical order, made this an easy task. The detectives quickly identified the two partners' boxes and removed them, the solicitor stepping back into the room to turn off the light and then lock the strong room door behind them.

"We'll take these to our car straight away, Mr Bullen," said Bryce. "While we do that, perhaps you would get all of the staff together in Mr Mayhew's office. Reassure them that we won't detain them very long. And again, please say nothing about the nature of the deaths."

With the two strong boxes safely stowed in the boot of the Wolseley, Bryce and Haig returned to find the receptionist posting a notice on the front door advising that *Mayhew & Johns* was closed until after lunch.

Everyone else was already assembled and standing disconsolately in Mayhew's office when the Yard detectives arrived with Miss Percival. A large table at one end of the room had sufficient chairs around it for a sizeable meeting, and Bryce invited the staff to sit down.

"Ladies and gentlemen, for those who haven't met us already, I'm Detective Chief Inspector Bryce, and this is Detective Sergeant Haig. You all know that Mr Mayhew and Mr Johns are dead, and I'll talk some more about that sad matter in a moment.

"First, though, let's go round the table, and

each of you can tell us who you are, where you live, and what you do in the firm."

Ten minutes later, all the relevant information was in Haig's pocketbook and Bryce made his announcement.

"I regret to inform you that Mr Mayhew and Mr Johns were both murdered. That is why we have been called in from Scotland Yard to investigate."

The staff looked uniformly stunned; even Bullen, who had already received the shock, seemed affected again.

Carter Stanley, the articled clerk, broke the unhappy silence. In his late twenties, his voice conveyed bewildered disbelief:

"But how? Where? Why?"

"Well, the 'how' is quite an easy question to answer, although I realise the details will be distressing to all of you who knew both men well. No doubt everything will be in the newspapers very soon, but I apologise in advance to the ladies in particular, for having to describe this to you all now."

Sergeant Haig needed no further priming that he was to watch the employees very closely. The absence of an appropriate emotion on anyone's part would definitely merit closer questioning.

Bryce delivered his information. "Each man was struck on the head and then strangled. Both were then thrown from a train."

Patricia Kendall, already pale on hearing that the partners had been murdered, now looked even ghostlier. Making a heaving noise, she clamped her hands tightly over her mouth, jerked up to her feet and kicked back her chair. Haig, noting her horror and pallor, rushed to open the door as she ran from the room.

Bryce looked at Janice Henderson and judged that she could also do with some additional time. As personal secretaries, the two women would have worked most closely with the partners, and the DCI reproached himself for not anticipating how strongly they might react. "Go and see how your friend is," he told her. "Come back again when you're both ready."

Silence had fallen over the remainder of the staff. Bryce made no attempt to break it. Boyd, the office manager, Stanley, the articled clerk, and Bullen, the solicitor, all seemed to be studiously avoiding each other's eyes. The two junior women and Ann Percival, while not as visibly distressed as the secretaries, sat gazing miserably at the table.

Bryce resumed when the two secretaries returned. He felt the group was now ready to take in more information and some necessary instructions. He addressed the articled clerk:

"You didn't ask 'when', Mr Stanley, but the answer is sometime on Monday evening for Mr Johns, and on Tuesday evening in the case of Mr Mayhew.

"The 'where' is also known, at least approximately. Mr Johns was found in Wolferton Woods, and Mr Mayhew between Docking and Stanhoe.

"As to 'why', well that is what the Chief Constable has asked the Yard to determine – plus the 'who', of course."

No one made any response to this and there was a further silence.

"Just a few more questions. We have approximate times of death, but we still don't know exactly which train each man was on. Can anyone help us?"

Heads were shaken, but Mrs Kendall volunteered some information about Mr Johns:

"I don't know for certain, sir, but unless he left the office early, there is only one suitable train, really – the 5:43. There isn't another until after half past seven. But at least two days each week, Mr Johns would come in by car, because he sometimes had to visit clients out in the Fens or somewhere."

"Thank you; that's helpful, and Monday was clearly a day when he didn't come by car. Can anyone say what train Mr Mayhew would take after arriving back from London?"

More shaking of heads.

"If, as you say, he was going home on the local train, I think there would only be one or two connections from London in an evening," said Fergal Bullen.

"I don't know his reasons for coming into Lynn by train instead of car on Monday," said Mrs Henderson, "but he did do that occasionally. I can give you the telephone number and address of the company he was visiting in the City. They could probably tell you what time he left them on Tuesday, which might help you work out his likely onwards train from Lynn."

"That will certainly be useful, Mrs Henderson, thank you; perhaps you can find that for us before we leave. Did he, to your knowledge, ever come back into the office after one of his trips to London?"

"No. As far as I know, he always brought in all the papers the following day. If the papers for the St Mary Axe meeting were still in his briefcase when he was found, then he didn't come back into the office on this Tuesday either."

"Ah, yes. Briefcases. Mrs Kendall, was Mr Johns in the habit of taking a briefcase home, too?"

"Without fail, sir," she replied.

"I see. Unfortunately, no briefcase has been found for either man. Nor were they carrying wallets, money, or identification."

Once again there was general disbelief. It clearly struck the staff as inconceivable that both men would set out on any sort of journey with nothing on them apart from what they were wearing.

Mr Stanley diffidently raised his hand

again, "I realise it's not at the front of your mind, sir, but have you any idea what will happen to the firm? I believe I speak for everyone when I say that this has been well-paid employment for all of us."

"The short answer is no, I don't; but I can assure you the status of the firm is very important to us as well. In any case of murder, the motive is paramount. It's possible that the partnership agreement – and perhaps the wills of the deceased men – could provide a clue. We hope to find all the relevant documents in the strong boxes we've removed.

"I'm not sure how far your own legal studies have progressed, Mr Stanley, but if the partnership agreement doesn't specifically cover this situation, then the 1890 Partnership Act does. As I said, we'll have to see what we find in the boxes, and of course we'll also speak to Mrs Mayhew.

"You might bear in mind, as you prepare your notes, that the severity of the blows to the head suggests it is unlikely that the attacker was female. The strength needed to apply and tighten the ligatures, and to throw the victims out of a train and close the door again, takes that a step further, and makes it even less likely to have been a woman. I appreciate that hardly helps you gentlemen, and I'm drawing no inferences. Anyway, I'm not actually ruling anyone out – male or female – at present.

"There has also been a third murder – a Ralph Besant. Will you all check please and let me know if he is, or has ever been, a client of this firm."

More shock registered on the faces around the table, only Bullen having already heard of this additional murder.

"I think it's possible that some of you, without realising it, may have some enlightening information. I'd like each of you to write down what, to your knowledge, happened in this office in the last week, say, right up to this morning.

"I don't want this in official statement form, and I don't want any collaborations, either. You must each work entirely alone to make your notes, giving names, dates and times. Include any appointments or diary entries you are aware of.

"Also – and this is potentially crucial – there may be one or more clients of this firm who have felt particularly aggrieved or badly treated, for whatever reason. So please be sure to include any behaviour by a client or a visitor, anything at all which seemed strange at the time, or with hindsight seems odd now. Even if such incidents fall outside the period I've just asked you to cover, make sure you include them."

The next few minutes were taken up with questions about the content required. Bryce answered these, dealing with the final one by saying "I want your notes finished in the next hour. Sergeant Haig and I will be using that time to go through the partners' offices more thoroughly before we leave for our next appointment."

Bryce prepared to conclude the meeting. "Once again, I'm sorry to have given you all such distressing news. If anyone thinks of something after we leave, we'll be at the Glebe Hotel in Hunstanton, and you can contact us there."

Bullen, Stanley, and Boyd all looked even unhappier than the women as they left the room.

With the door of Mayhew's office shut again, the telephone rang before Bryce could speak to Haig. After Bryce lifted the receiver, it was quickly clear that he was hearing something positive. "Excellent," he said. "Get everything over to us here quickly as you can."

Replacing the receiver he confirmed what his Sergeant had already surmised. "Reeves' search parties have found two briefcases. By the time we've got everyone's notes and that London address, the briefcases should have arrived here. Then we'll get back on the road and find somewhere to eat on our way to Heacham. We'll look in the cases later – I think we can assume that if they did contain anything incriminating, the killer will have removed it before throwing them out."

CHAPTER 5

With Haig at the wheel this time, the police car left King's Lynn and arrived in Dersingham via Castle Rising and the Wolferton Woods, the crisp November weather making this a pleasant journey. At a signal from Bryce, Haig pulled into the yard of the *Dun Cow* public house. Haig thought *The Black Horse* in Castle Rising had looked far more appealing, but his leader had given a shake of his head as they had approached it. Here, however, the chief had said, "This looks okay. Should be able to give us something to eat."

Haig knew that his boss didn't approve of drinking much alcohol at lunchtime, and wondered what the DCI would order to drink. In the past, a half pint of bitter had been agreed, Today, it seemed that a pint of bitter shandy was acceptable, and Haig followed suit. The choice of food was very limited – a ploughman's lunch or a bacon sandwich. Both men opted for the former.

While waiting for their meals to arrive, Bryce pulled out the little bundle of notes prepared by the staff. They didn't take much time to peruse. He handed each one to Haig as he finished it.

When both men had finished reading, Bryce said, "Well, a couple of possible angry clients. And as each secretary mentioned both names, each of the clients seems to have been upset with both partners – assuming the secretaries didn't collude. We'll have to find out more."

The food arrived, and the officers were pleased to find that the helpings were generous. Each man's plate held plenty of crusty bread, a decent piece of Cheddar, a hard-boiled egg, and an apple. A dish of butter and jars of pickled onions and chutney were provided for sharing.

In accordance with Bryce's unwritten rules, during the meal there was no further discussion about the current case. Instead, the officers reverted to one of their favourite topics – railways.

"I've never been on any of the railways around here," said Bryce. "The Hunstanton line is remote enough, but at least there are occasional visiting engines from the Midlands and, as we heard, there are a few through carriages to and from London. And Royal trains, of course, bringing the King and his guests to Sandringham House via Wolferton station.

"But while we're here I'm really hoping to find a reason to view the trains on the Wells branch. I believe the line is about the last in the country still operating with gas-lit clerestory carriages. As for the locomotives, well, there may still be one or two of Holden's Great Eastern E4s from the 1890s." The DCI's grey eyes lit up in anticipation of seeing one of these veterans.

"Going back to Malan's timetables, guv; I worked out that the fastest train on the branch barely averaged twenty miles per hour. Not exactly express speed!" said Haig as he spread chutney over his cheese.

"No indeed, Alex. And as some of the intermediate stations were built so far outside the tiny villages they purport to serve, I can't think that there are many passengers anyway. The whole system is neither swift nor even convenient in some cases. I doubt if the line ever came near to showing a profit."

The men enjoyed their simple meal. Bryce settled the bill and the two detectives continued their journey.

"It's easy to appreciate why Mayhew often drove to his office, rather than take the train," said the DCI surveying the Norfolk countryside. "But on Monday he made the fatal decision to go all the way by train. If he'd taken his car to Lynn station in the morning, he couldn't have been killed in the way he was. Somebody else also knew very well what Johns was doing that day."

"Someone in the office then – or possibly with a connection to someone in the office?" said Haig.

"Yes. And that's exactly why we can't rule out any of the women yet. Information about

Johns' travel plans – Mayhew's as well – may have been deliberately, or quite unthinkingly, passed to our killer by one of them."

Arriving at Heacham, Bryce turned into Station Road and pulled up in front of the little carrstone building. It was still some twenty minutes before their appointment with Goodall, but they wandered inside to take a look around. Nobody seemed to be about.

There was a platform on each side of the two running lines, the one on the eastern side also acting as a bay platform, presumably for the Wells branch trains to pull into. Bryce and Haig each noted the very odd fact that there were two signal boxes, both at the same end of the station. Neither could have much to control, and a single box sufficed at stations far larger and more complex than this out-of-the-way location.

All was quiet. No passengers were waiting on any of the three platforms, and there was no sign of any train. Bryce spent a few minutes examining a timetable posted on a wall, and then joined Haig, who had taken a seat on a bench – its ironwork bearing the marking "L&HR".

The two men sat in companionable silence for a few minutes, before Haig remarked that he thought he saw a figure in the distance. Sure enough, a man soon came fully into view, walking along the line from Snettisham. Spotting the two policemen, he raised a hand in greeting, and came off the track and up the platform slope to join them.

"'Afternoon, sirs," he said as he reached them. "I'm thinking you'll be the police. I'm Jacob Goodall."

The DCI made the introductions and the three shook hands.

"Let's sit down and have a chat, Mr Goodall. We won't keep you long."

"Be easier, p'raps, if we go in the waiting room," suggested the platelayer. "You can face me proper there."

He led the way down the platform and into the smallest waiting room the detectives had ever seen. Supplementing a bench along one wall were three chairs tucked under a small table. The Yard men sat down, Goodall carefully propping his long-handled hammer against the mantelpiece of the little cast iron fireplace, and removing his heavy spanner from his belt, before taking the seat opposite them.

"Well, Mr Goodall," began Bryce, "presumably you've heard that the man you found was murdered?"

"I've heard nothing, sir. Nobody has spoken to me until this morning when I was told to meet you here. Murdered, was he? Well, I thought when I saw him he can't have been hit by a passing train."

"What made you think that?" asked Haig.

"He's lying by the track, miles from anywhere, and there was no sign of blood on the bit of him I could see. If he'd been a tramp he wouldn't have been there – he'd've used the roads."

This was a firmly given assertion, and both detectives wondered what caused the platelayer to be so sure about how a tramp might get from place to place.

"Following the track would be more direct and quicker for tramps, surely?" said Haig.

"That's so," agreed Goodall, "but they dun't want to put themselves more into the wrong than they already do on occasion, and trespassing on the tracks is never a good idea anyway."

Seeing that both officers were looking less than convinced, the platelayer shared some additional thoughts. "There's a reason why they're called 'gentlemen of the road'. We has one knocks at our back door quite regular, every six months or so; he's known hereabouts as 'Sunshine'. The wife has been giving him a cup o' tea and a sixpence for nigh on four years now. Finds a bit o' grub for him, and some of my old clothin' if there's any spare. Sunshine's told her he sticks to the roads, doing a tour of villages and towns hereabouts. He calls at the houses where he knows he can get a bit o' help, and where he won't be cussed or driven off.

"That being Sunshine's ways, I wouldn't expect to see a tramp on the track, much less find one knocked down by a train – and I never have in all the years I done this job. But the thing about the man on Tuesday was his clothes. A sharp suit and good shoes. He warn't trampin'.

"First, I reckoned he fell out of a train. Faulty door catch, maybe, or perhaps he was drunk at the time, and opened the door by accident thinkin' he was on a corridor train. But if so, someone surely should've seen an open door at the next station – Stanhoe or Docking – dependin' which way he was going."

"Then I think on it a bit more, and begins to wonder if he jumped deliberately, to do away with himself. But that dun't fit the bill neither, because a slow-moving train and a softish landin' place very likely wouldn't work. And in any case, unless he jumped out o' the window – which dun't strike me as likely neither – the door'd still be open at the next station; same way as if 'e'd fell out.

"Took me a bit o' time to get around to thinkin' he'd been pushed out, and someone closed the door behind him."

"Very good thinking, Mr Goodall," said Bryce, impressed. "You're quite right about this not being an accident. He was travelling on a train, was attacked, strangled, and then thrown out."

Goodall nodded slowly. "Strangled, was he? I didn't look close enough to see that, or I could've saved myself quite a bit o' thought. Well, I hope you dun't think the murderer is me?"

"Frankly, we have no idea who it is. But the matter is complicated by the fact that a second man has been found murdered in similar circumstances, this time in Wolferton Woods. Turns out he died a day before the man you found."

Goodall stared at the detectives. "Two murders? Here in West Norfolk? I never heard of such a thing before, sirs." Something else occurred to him. "Were the two men related, or is there a crazed maniac around?"

"They were related in a sense, in that they were both lawyers in the same firm. But whether there is some understandable reason for the murders, or whether we are indeed looking for someone carrying out random killings, it's too early to say.

"However, it's three murders, not two – there was another by Gayton Road station on Friday."

This was almost too much for the platelayer to take in. "Three? Inside of a week? That must be more'n we get in ten years!"

He shook his head sadly at what the world – or at least what his county – was coming to.

The DCI asked Goodall to recap Wednesday's events, and the platelayer delivered a precise report of his doings. He even mentioned Sheba, anticipating that, as the staff at Heacham, Docking, and Stanhoe were likely to be interviewed, and all were aware of – and might mention – Sheba's presence, he'd better declare her himself.

Bryce hadn't really expected new information, and wasn't disappointed when none was forthcoming. The interview effectively over, the three men chatted for a few minutes about life as a platelayer, the Yard men unsurprised to find that Goodall had extensive knowledge of the local lines.

Sergeant Haig asked the question which had been puzzling both detectives earlier. "Do you know why there are there two signal boxes at the same end of this station, Mr Goodall?"

"Ah, not for sure, I dun't, but I'll tell you what I think," replied the platelayer. "This station was built in 1862 by the old Lynn and Hunstanton Railway – and at first it was single track and a single platform. Later they put in a second platform and a passin' loop.

"But the Wells line, that was built by a different company, the West Norfolk Junction Railway, four or five years later. They must've got an agreement with the L&H to put in the bay platform. And I think they put in the turntable themselves, for it's not much use to the main line users. But my guess is that sharin' a signalman was perhaps a step too far for the L&H, so the WNJ had to build their own little box to control the signals and the points for the branch. The two companies joined together in about 1874, and in 1890 were taken over by the Great

Eastern. Matter of fact, the GER really ran the lines for years even before it properly took them over. But the separate signal boxes have stayed unchanged – a proper curiosity."

"Thanks for that, Mr Goodall," said Bryce – I was wondering exactly the same thing as Sergeant Haig. We're both interested in railways, and it's always a pleasure to meet someone who is so knowledgeable on the subject."

As the detectives stood up to leave, the Stationmaster appeared in the doorway. He greeted Goodall with a slap on the back and a hearty "How do, Jacob!"

Turning to Bryce and Haig he said "And you gents must be the Scotland Yard policemen. I had an officer come round with questions earlier; he said you'd be coming to meet Jacob."

Bryce performed the introductions, and learned that the man's name was Turner, and that he was eager to repeat what he had already told Kittow that morning. With a little time in hand, the DCI was happy to listen.

"There were only two Wells trains that would fit in with the times your Constable gave me, and I saw both of those off myself," said the Stationmaster. "As I told your man, that day there weren't above half a dozen passengers on each. And all those had through tickets from further up the line. No ticket was sold here that day for any station up to Wells.

"While your Constable was asking me, and

all the while since, I've tried to remember who I saw. On the 6:27 there were two pairs of regulars – husbands and wives. Maybe a couple of other men – but not as I recall wearing suits, like the man Jacob here told me he found.

"But on the last Wells train I'm pretty sure there were two men in suits. And three or four others, who were workmen. They all crossed the line together and came to wait on the bay platform. I've seen one of the suited gents several times before."

"The two suited men – were they waiting together, talking to each other or anything?" asked Haig.

The stationmaster thought for a moment. "That I can't truly say," he replied. "They stood quite near each other, as I recall. But that's not surprising, because there's usually only two carriages on a Wells train, so waiting passengers are never far from each other anyway."

"I assume the two carriages were non-corridor," said Bryce. "Could you see whether they got into the same compartment?"

"No corridor," Turner confirmed. "After the engine ran around, they were both near the end of the last coach. But I couldn't say for sure if they got in together. No reason why they should; plenty of empty compartments on that service at that time of day for everyone to have one to himself."

He suddenly realised the significance of

what he'd been asked: "Oh – you mean one might have been the killer travelling with his victim!"

Bryce nodded. "Now, let's go back to Monday evening. The officer who came earlier will have told you that there was a murder that day too, beside the line near Wolferton."

Turner moved his head from side to side, clearly still astonished at the situation. "Yes, he did," he said, "and I'm still struggling with it."

The Chief Inspector probed some more, "Any chance you saw someone – perhaps wearing a suit, perhaps not – getting off a train from Lynn that evening?"

"Can't say as I did, no. That would either be the 6:14, or the 9:44. Maybe ten or a dozen passengers got off both trains, but I don't think there was anybody that I hadn't seen before. I'm sure I'd have remembered if there was a stranger – we get very few of those outside of the holiday season."

Bryce thanked the two railwaymen for their help, and promised Goodall his statement would be taken later.

CHAPTER 6

The DCI sat behind the steering wheel of the Wolseley, and thought about what they had learned.

"As these trains probably slow down almost to a stop in some places, have you considered the murderer might have dropped off between stations?" asked Haig.

Bryce nodded. "Yes, but we have to hope that isn't the way he did it, otherwise I'll not rate our chances of ever finding him."

"What if the killer isn't a stranger to Turner at all? Not likely, perhaps, but he could just be someone that Turner didn't really notice because he was used to seeing him at the station."

"Very good point, Sergeant. The sooner we get some photographs the better." Turning the key in the ignition and pressing the starter button, Bryce added, "I think we'll have to concentrate on motive for the present. Dig out Mrs Mayhew's address and let's get over to Burnham Market."

Reaching into the back Haig pulled forward Bryce's briefcase and found Mrs

Mayhew's statement with her address on it. "Little Goslings, Herrings Lane," he told his boss.

"Good," said Bryce, pulling out of the station yard. "Won't take us twenty minutes to get to the village, and we can ask for directions when we get there. We'll go via Stanhoe, and take a quick look there first."

***

Stanhoe Station, over a mile from the hamlet it notionally served, wasn't even in the same league as some of the other lowly stations in the county. The track was single, with no passing loop. Most rural stations could at least boast a siding for goods wagons, but even that basic facility was absent here. Indeed, this station was not significantly larger than some of the unstaffed 'halts' which, as both officers were aware, were dotted all around the country, typically serving isolated golf courses and the like.

There was no sign of life in the booking office, so the policemen walked through to the platform. Across the track was a sizeable patch of garden, mostly given over to growing vegetables. A man was busy with a hoe. Seeing the officers, he laid his implement across a wheelbarrow, stepped over the track, and climbed up to join them on the platform.

"You'll be police, most likely, about the body?"

Bryce confirmed their identities, and learned that the man's name was Gabriel Fisher.

"You don't get many people buying tickets here, I dare say?"

"That'd be correct, sir. Bookings clerk isn't a big part of my job, and most weeks I don't sell so much as a single ticket. Few people ever go anywhere at all, never mind by train; and as you see, we're well out of the village anyway."

"So, if a man got off a train from Heacham on Tuesday evening, say the one getting here around nine, you'd probably notice?"

Turner's response was unequivocal. "I certainly would! Nobody got off here from that particular train. Nor the one before it. Nor the same one yesterday, come to that."

"You didn't notice anything unusual on Tuesday night – no door swinging open before the train got into the station, for instance? I appreciate that an open door might not be on the platform side where you would be standing, but would you even have noticed an open door on the side opposite to where you were standing, I wonder?"

Another emphatic response came from the railwayman. "Yes, I would, sir. But no, there was nothing untoward. First I knew anything was wrong was Tuesday, when Jacob Goodall come through and told me there was a dead body a bit towards Docking. Do you know who it was?"

"Yes," replied Haig. "Mr Mayhew, a King's

Lynn solicitor who lives in Burnham Market."

"Oh, I've heard the name. His wife is big in the Burnhams. Another lawyer."

An exchange of glances between Bryce and Haig confirmed that neither had any more questions for Fisher. However, this time it was the DCI who raised a railway question.

"Stanhoe obviously isn't a block post, Mr Fisher, but didn't it once have a signal box?"

"That's right, sir. Most of this branch is single track. There's a passing loop at Docking, and there's a loop just outside Burnham station which can be used as a passing place if required. But trains usually cross at Docking. Even with the odd goods service, the traffic doesn't warrant more sections. And yes, years ago, there was a signal box here. Don't know why. It was just signals for the level crossing, really. No points for sidings, or anything. Maybe they thought that the line would be doubled one day – little chance of that. Anyways, the box here was taken away twenty years ago and we just have the ground frame now."

"Thank you very much, Mr Fisher. If anything else occurs to you, please get a message to us at the Glebe Hotel in Hunstanton."

"'Huns'ton', sir, corrected the local. "We like to shorten names hereabouts. You likely passed through 'Ingulsthorpe' earlier – well that's spelt I-n-g-o-l-d-i-s-t-h-o-r-p-e. And on the east coast is H-a-p-p-i-s-b-u-r-g-h, pronounced

'Hazebrugh'. And no local says King's Lynn – it's just Lynn.

"In fact, in days gone by it used to be *Bishop's* Lynn, until that king with too many wives decided he wanted all the Roman Catholic churches and monastery money for himself, and booted the Bishop of Norwich out."

Bryce and Haig smiled at this potted history of the English Reformation, and set off for Burnham Market.

CHAPTER 7

The light was just beginning to fade, but 'Herrings Lane' was easy enough to find and 'Little Goslings' was soon spotted only a short distance along the unmade road. Bryce turned into a gravelled drive and pulled up in front of a large detached house. They were evidently observed, because a ground-floor sash window was flung up, and a woman leaned out and called to them as they got out of the car.

"Good afternoon. Are you the London policemen? I'm Clarissa Mayhew. I'll let you in myself."

The front door opened and the detectives were taken inside. Sergeant Haig introduced them both as they stood in the hallway.

"Come into the drawing room," said Mrs Mayhew, leading the way. "I'm sure you'd like some tea," she added, pressing a button in the wall without waiting for a reply. Seating herself on a chintz covered easy chair in front of the fireplace, she gave a welcoming "Please, gentlemen," as she motioned that Bryce and Haig should sit on the sofa opposite.

She was in her early fifties, and probably

her husband's junior by fifteen years, thought Bryce; noting at the same time her unrealistic hair colour and the heavy application of makeup their hostess was wearing.

The men were barely seated when a maid arrived. "Tea for three, please, Maudie, and something to eat," instructed her mistress.

"I'm very sorry for your loss, Mrs Mayhew," began Bryce. "And I apologise for bothering you again – I know you've already made a statement to the local police."

"No apology is necessary, Chief Inspector. Tim is dead, and nothing can be done to bring him back."

Clarissa Mayhew lowered her head before continuing, such that neither detective could now observe her face as she spoke, and found themselves looking instead at the line of grey on either side of her parted red hair.

"I loved my husband, and despite our age difference, we got along very well. Naturally, I want you to find his killer."

Her words were all the right words. But there was something about Mrs Mayhew's manner which, in Bryce's experience, was atypical in a close relation who had very recent knowledge of a loved one's murder. Simultaneously, he and Haig called to mind Janice Henderson's response earlier in the day. True, Mrs Mayhew had been informed twelve hours or so ahead of the office staff; but both men were struck by the contrast between the effect of Mayhew's death on his secretary, and the effect on his wife.

Bryce decided to question the apparently impassive, newly widowed woman, on a material point. "Regarding your statement, Mrs Mayhew, you said that you expected your husband home on Tuesday evening, but you didn't report him missing until Wednesday morning. Why was that?"

"Because I wanted to check other possibilities first. I used to live in London, and that's where Tim and I were first introduced to one another. Mutual friends knew we were both keen theatregoers, and it was that shared love which ignited our romance." Clarissa Mayhew managed a small smile at the memory. "I had a rather nice little flat in Holborn at the time. After we married we decided to keep it as a *pied a terre* for our London theatre trips. It was also handy for those occasions when Tim's work in the capital spilled over. Timothy wasn't a well man, and it wasn't actually unusual for him to stay an extra night in London to recover after a stressful meeting.

"So on Tuesday, after the last train arrived at Burnham without him, I thought he must have gone back to the flat. What was more unusual was that he fact that he hadn't telephoned, either from the firm he was visiting or from a public call box. The flat has never been connected.

"I still thought he would be at the flat, but about ten o'clock that night I contacted Barts and other hospitals around the City, and also the hospital in King's Lynn. There was no news of him anywhere, and so I had to assume that for some reason he'd been unable to get through to me.

"On Wednesday morning, he would have called from Liverpool Street before getting on the train. When he didn't call, I contacted his office first, and then the police."

"You're both wondering two things. Why I telephoned hospitals, and why I'm not prostrated with grief now."

In fact, both detectives were now anticipating what was to come, since Malan had mentioned Mayhew's liver damage earlier. Clarissa Mayhew continued:

"Tim was dying – cancer of the liver. Mentally, I've prepared myself to be told of Tim's death countless times since he told me how ill he was. I have lain on my bed and sobbed and punched my pillow until I didn't have another tear to shed, nor the energy to make another fist. That is how you find me today; rather worn out, I'm afraid.

"I was getting ready to travel to London myself yesterday, fully prepared to find Tim dead in the flat, when I was told he'd been found quite near here."

It was a moving little speech. Her detached indifference now had a convincing alternative explanation, which tied in with Dr Bartlett's post mortem report.

"I understand; thank you for clarifying that." Bryce spoke gently, intuitively knowing that their hostess would continue without prompting, when she felt ready.

"As far as this business is concerned, I'll repeat what I told the officer yesterday evening when he brought the news. Tim was going to London, as he does at least twice a month. Sometimes he drives to Lynn or Hunstanton, and takes a train from there. Sometimes, as on Monday, he goes all the way by train. This branch line is very under-used, gentlemen, and although it is quite a rigmarole to go from here, we both felt obliged to support it whenever we could. This could not have happened if he had driven to Lynn this time. But I suppose, if he was targeted, the killer would have found another way. In any case, Tim's life was not shortened by very much.

"Let me say something else about this dreadful matter. Only a few minutes ago, when I called Tim's secretary, I heard that his partner, Patrick, was killed in very similar circumstances. You must agree that one such murder of an inoffensive solicitor is unusual, but two must be unprecedented. No doubt that is why the Yard has been called in. Presumably someone has an exceptional perceived grievance against Mayhew & Johns."

"That does seem a very strong possibility," agreed Bryce. "However, you may not have heard that, last Friday, there was a similar murder – of a man with no apparent connection to the firm. So we haven't completely discounted a deranged maniac on the loose."

Mrs Mayhew looked astounded at the news of a third murder, but said nothing. Bryce continued.

"Are you aware that Mr Johns died about a day before your husband?"

"No, I wasn't," she replied in surprise. "That might alter things."

"Do you mean in regard to their business?" asked the DCI.

"Yes. I haven't had time to assimilate this information. I assumed that they were killed together – although if I'd thought clearly I'd have realised that Patrick would never be on a Wells train. But if they had died together, then Tim as the elder would, in law, have been deemed to die first. But from what you say, that isn't the case. I need to think this through to see the possible implications."

The maid returned with the tea before Bryce or Haig could say anything further.

Mrs Mayhew spoke next while straining the brew into cups and inviting the detectives to help themselves to cake, which was declined by both men. "I've heard about you, Chief Inspector. The Chief Constable is one of Tim's golf-playing associates, and I know him too. He rang this morning to commiserate. I gather that he knows you slightly. He tells me that you are a barrister, and that you are held in extremely high regard throughout Scotland Yard."

Haig grinned to himself, he was beginning to lose count of the number of times he had heard a similar statement. He hoped that one day he might be working with a subordinate detective sergeant and hear such compliments, his own reputation having preceded him.

"You embarrass me, Mrs Mayhew," replied Bryce, partly from habitual modesty, and partly also because it was true. He had always found hearing praise, however sincerely given, an uncomfortable experience. He made a light-hearted quip as a means of stemming any further conversation about himself, "I'll admit to being a barrister, but I absolutely deny the rest!"

"Very well, I shall say no more," said their hostess with a small smile.

Bryce, keen to move on, broached the topic for discussion. "We actually came to see you to talk about the partnership agreement. We haven't seen a copy as yet. In fact, we don't even know if there are any other partners – perhaps yourself, for example? We have deed boxes belonging to Mr Mayhew and Mr Johns, but we haven't yet located a key for either.

"We may have to force the locks, but we're hoping that you might know the terms of the agreement, as it is of course a possibility that it may help to find a motive. Wills may be crucial too."

"Yes, of course. I can tell you straight away that Tim and Patrick were the only partners, but I'll come back to that. You say there were no keys found – what about wallets, papers, and so on?"

"Nothing whatsoever for either man, I'm afraid. Only a railway ticket for each, which looks like a crude attempt to distract us. I don't think for a minute that robbery was the motive here."

"No, clearly not," agreed Clarissa Mayhew. "Well, first of all, I can give you a key for Tim's box before you go. I have a similar box myself at my firm, and Tim and I each kept one another's keys. Second, I can certainly tell you about the agreement, because I actually drafted it myself.

"The terms are very clear. On the death of either partner, a new person automatically and immediately enters the partnership. I am the agreed person. That avoids the clause in the Partnership Act which – in the absence of alternative directions – would otherwise close the partnership down when only a single partner remains. When I heard yesterday evening that Tim was dead, I was already contemplating what that would mean. However, although I wasn't aware of it until a few minutes ago, I actually became a partner in the firm at the moment of

Patrick Johns' death."

She paused. "That alone gives rise to further thought.

"Allow me to divert very slightly. I know that Tim and Patrick were contemplating amendments to the agreement, with a view to offering a partnership to Fergal Bullen. As he isn't in a position to put any capital into the firm, there would have to be adjustments to profit-sharing. Although I know they'd talked to him about it, nothing was finalised. As soon as Tim got his diagnosis it became rather more pressing, of course. But as far as I know Fergal hadn't actually been told about Tim's illness – it wasn't in the firm's interest for that information to get out until other arrangements were in place.

"That was another reason why I didn't mention his illness when I reported Tim missing. With hindsight, that was overly cautious of me, but I'm not really myself at present. Patrick was the only other person who knew.

"Which brings us to something else which I think will interest you, Chief Inspector. On the death of a second partner – Tim, as we now know – the agreement provides for another immediate appointment: Patrick's brother Jeremy. He's also a solicitor, in Nottingham. With that provision in place, the firm could continue seamlessly after the second death.

"To be frank, when drawing up the

agreement, I didn't really envisage a time where two partners died before other amendments could be considered. I just thought that the situation should be covered, so Tim nominated me, and Patrick nominated Jeremy. They agreed that I should 'go first', as it were, as I was nearer the office in Lynn, and apparently Jeremy wasn't really interested in being nominated anyway; he did it as a favour to his brother – the tying of a loose end for Patrick's peace of mind, really.

Anyway, the position now is that Jeremy and I are the partners in the firm of Mayhew & Johns. It's ironic, really. It seems that the partners were Mayhew and Mayhew for a few hours, but now the original name once again reflects the two current partners."

"Another very strange thing is that I've become the business partner of a man I've never actually met. I assume someone will be informing Jeremy of his brother's death; his details are all in the partnership agreement, if needed."

Mrs Mayhew took up a poker and stirred the coals in the grate, sending a cloud of bright flaming dust up the chimney.

"Now, the wills. I have no idea what might be in Patrick's. As far as I know he has never married, and apart from his brother I don't know about relatives. He was very comfortably off, certainly.

"Tim's is very straightforward. Aside from

a gift to the Church, and bequests to our domestic staff, I am the sole beneficiary. We have no children."

Mrs Mayhew paused again to replenish teacups. "Are you sure you won't have some lardy cake, gentlemen? It's fresh this morning."

Both officers again politely declined a piece of the bun cake, Haig explaining that their lunch at the Dun Cow had been enjoyed "not long ago" – but each man was actually thinking that he wouldn't be able to enjoy his evening meal if he accepted a slice of the solid cake.

Bryce looked at their hostess. "Thank you for that information, Mrs Mayhew. I have to say, this is the first we've heard of Jeremy Johns. One of my men has been looking through Patrick Johns' house and I expect he will have found the details, but the partnership agreement is a good fall-back if not, and we obviously need to speak to him.

"Not being in any way flippant, and as you don't know him I don't think you'll be offended, but Jeremy Johns is the first person we've come across so far who has anything approaching a motive!"

Clarissa Mayhew's smile almost reached her eyes. "From what Patrick said, Jeremy is doing very well indeed on his own account, so I doubt if a partnership here would attract him. Anyway, if he turns out to be the beneficiary under his brother's will, he'll inherit what I imagine will be a sizeable sum when Patrick's assets are all realised, and so had no need to kill Tim as well – let alone this other poor man."

Bryce said nothing in response to this, but swift thought was taking place behind his intelligent grey eyes. It had to be a possibility that Johns' murder was motivated by greed, with Mayhew's murder purely an act of removal – a means of ensuring that some form of incriminating knowledge about the killer was never revealed by Mayhew.

Their hostess stood up. "While you're still drinking, gentlemen, I'll go and fetch the key for the deed box."

"Might you also find us a couple of fairly recent photographs of your husband at the same time, ma'am?" asked Haig. "That would help us find a witness who can confirm which train he was on."

The two officers rose as she left the room. Resuming their seats, they discussed what they had been told.

Haig spoke quietly: "The brother needs a bit of looking at, sir. Bullen, though, would surely have waited until he was made a partner, before bumping off Mayhew and Johns?"

"Yes, I agree. We also need to explore the other two male employees, as well as those two aggrieved clients. When we get back to the solicitors' office, I'm hoping people can expand on what's in the notes."

"What about Johns' activities with the ladies he took up to his studio, though, sir? What if they were married or promised elsewhere, and a husband or fiancé took umbrage?"

"We'll explore that angle too. But the trouble is, if Johns was killed because of his photography, there wouldn't seem to be any reason to go after Mayhew as well – let alone Besant."

They rose again as Mrs Mayhew returned, a small key dangling from a piece of red ribbon in her hand.

"This will be the one you want," she said, offering it to Haig, together with two photographs of her late husband in what looked like solid silver frames.

Haig smiled his thanks at her and set about carefully releasing the photographs from their expensive surroundings. Issuing receipts and taking responsibility for valuable personal possessions were things to be avoided wherever possible.

"Thank you very much, Mrs Mayhew," said Bryce. We won't sit down again – we've encroached long enough on your time. But before we leave, were you aware of any, er, hobbies that interested Mr Johns? And did your husband ever mention any incident where the firm didn't perform to the satisfaction of a client?"

Mrs Mayhew's expression showed her

swift grasp of the thrust of the DCI's questions.

"You're alluding to Patrick's penchant for taking pictures of semi-clad or even naked females, I imagine. Yes, I was aware of that; it wasn't a secret. I only went in his house a few times, but you could hardly miss them – hanging somewhat incongruously among the church exteriors and the beach hut scenes. It has to be said that he was a skilled photographer, and in my view the pictures were artistic rather than in any way offensive, much less obscene – although I suppose there will always be some who would disagree. However, I've never heard of any complaint about his actions, and none of the photographs are explicit to anywhere near the same degree as a Rubens or some other classic paintings of the female form, for example.

"As for aggrieved clients, I know of nothing unusual – but we didn't really discuss each other's work, unless on a rare occasion one of us wanted a legal opinion from the another. I do know that, like most solicitors, Tim and Patrick tried to keep their civil litigation clients away from court where possible. Occasionally, no doubt, a case would get to court and the client wouldn't get the judgement he or she wanted. Tim would have explained the risks, of course, and might even have warned that the case wasn't winnable; but as you know, there are clients who want their day in court, regardless.

"The firm also handles criminal matters,

which almost always end up in court – magistrates' court, quarter sessions, or even the Assizes. And once charged, the probability of conviction is very high.

"But whether civil or criminal, Tim has never mentioned any particular case where a client has been especially aggrieved.

"I should probably tell you of something else, but I don't see that it is particularly helpful. Last week – Wednesday, I think it was, Tim seemed a bit upset when he came home. He wouldn't say what the trouble was. Of course, with his illness one could hardly blame him for feeling down, but that was really the only time I saw any sign that he might be depressed."

Bryce thanked Mrs Mayhew for her assistance and hospitality and the two men took their leave.

The DCI debated calling at the station in Burnham Market to enquire about any passenger who had alighted from a Heacham train on Tuesday evening. He quickly decided against this, reasoning that he would need to do the same at the remaining stations – Holkham and Wells – and there wasn't time to do all three now. It would be better to return the next day, hopefully with photographs, and visit all three stations in succession – or perhaps get Kittow or Malan to do it.

"You drive this time, Sergeant. I want to think. Get us back to Hunstanton. Don't return via Stanhoe – take the coast road via Brancaster.

CHAPTER 8

Each carrying a metal deed box and one of the briefcases, the two officers found that Kittow and Malan had already returned to the incident room, and were exchanging anecdotes, the pair obviously getting along very well.

"Right, gentlemen, let's see what has emerged from our various doings. You start, Malan."

"There was nobody in at Johns' house, sir, but I found a neighbour who shares a cleaner with him, and got a name and address from her.

"I found the cleaner – Mrs Brumby – at home. She was very upset when I told her how Johns died. Said he was a good employer and landlord – apparently he owned her house and others. She gave me her key to his property, so we've got access whenever we like now. She also gave me the details of another lady – a Mrs Goode – who cooked and so on for him, but I couldn't get hold of her. Both the women are dailies; no live-ins at the house.

"I couldn't find a will, sir, nor anything else of obvious help apart from his passport and an address book, and another photograph – a better version of the passport one." Malan set these out on the table.

"What I can tell you, though, is that Johns wasn't short of a bob or too. The place is very well done up, and the cleaner said he keeps three swish motors at a lock-up nearby, because there's no garage at the property. What with his house – and the others the cleaner mentioned – someone's in line for a tidy haul of spondulicks."

"Good," said Bryce. "We heard about his cars. Did you see any keys lying about?"

"Yes, sir, plenty; all on a row of hooks in his study. Car keys, and others, but I didn't bring them – just the front door key."

"We may be lucky then, Malan, as we're looking for the key to these strong boxes we've taken from the office, one of which is his," said the DCI. "Tell us about his wall decorations."

Malan looked surprised for a moment, before realising what the DCI was getting at.

"Ahhhh...you mean his photographs, sir?"

Bryce nodded.

"Over every wall in the house. Feels like a gallery as soon as you step through the front door. Not a single painting that I saw. But if you've heard about this, sir, you'll know that a number of the pictures are, you know, a bit revealing."

"Yes, we had heard. Did the cleaner mention them?"

"No, sir – well, only to say that they were

all by Johns himself.

"I asked about next of kin. She said Johns once mentioned a brother, but he's never visited whilst she was in the house." Malan flipped through the address book and slid it towards the DCI. "Under 'J' there's details for a Jeremy – with no other name beside it, which makes me think it's someone close to him. Could be Jeremy Johns, perhaps?"

"Good logic there, Malan. We learned from Mayhew's wife that there's a brother called Jeremy, in fact, so your book will be useful."

"I visited the station next, sir. No help there, although the staff were co-operative. There were at least thirty people who got off each of the last two trains on Friday evening. Some were regulars – although nobody knew any names – and a few were strangers. Maybe if we had a photograph of a suspect that might jog a memory, but as it stands at the moment, they can't help."

"Right, Kittow, what did you learn?"

"A lot less than Malan, I'm afraid, sir." Kittow repeated the facts that the Heacham stationmaster had volunteered to Bryce and Haig earlier.

"At both Snettisham and Dersingham, the railway staff were quite certain that on Monday no stranger got off from either of the last two trains from Lynn."

"Well, it's obvious that our killer would

be much safer getting off at Hunstanton, in the middle of a larger group. But, as Sergeant Haig pointed out to me earlier, it's quite possible that the killer wasn't a stranger at all, but was a regular on the line. What about King's Lynn?"

"Pretty hopeless, again, sir. There are typically twenty or so passengers on the Hunstanton trains in the evening. As we've heard, a few get out at intermediate stations, including those changing at Heacham for Wells. But probably a majority stay on until Hunstanton.

"When I explained what we were looking for, the stationmaster at Lynn reminded me that passengers' tickets are collected at each station. I think the railway sometimes uses them to check on takings, and line usage, and so on. He suggested we might go to each of the relevant stations, and see what might have been saved."

"Interesting," said Bryce, "although I don't immediately see how that would help us, unless we had a suspect and could get a fingerprint off a ticket to prove he was on the train. As I said earlier, the surface of an Edmondson ticket might hold a print. Probably a waste of time, but perhaps we should get hold of them anyway. We're not far from the station here, and you've already introduced yourself, Kittow, so you go back for the tickets later. However, I have a horrible feeling that, even if they are retained they won't have been kept in date order and will be just jumbled up in a sack.

"Anyway, Sergeant Haig will brief you two on what we've seen and heard."

Haig had been expecting his boss to delegate this task, and was prepared. He summarised what Goodall had told them, and then gave a clear report on the members of the firm, including their reactions and the main points of what they had said. He mentioned the two allegedly aggrieved clients. He then moved on to what little they had found at Stanhoe, and what of greater significance they had learned from Mrs Mayhew.

When he finished, there was a silence, each detective mulling over the new information they had been given.

Pushing back his shirt cuff, Bryce glanced at his watch, "It's almost six o'clock now, and I want those keys from Johns' house. We'll all go now and have a look. How far did you say it is, Malan?"

"Less than a couple of hundred yards from here, sir."

"Good, a nice little stretch of the legs by the seaside, even if it is rather dark now."

The four men left the hotel, Malan leading them down Cliff Parade. The houses here were substantial, five-storey double-fronted affairs, arranged in terraced blocks on either side of a public garden. The houses faced the road, on the other side of which were more public gardens up to the edge of the cliffs, and beyond those, The Wash. There was also a good view of the pier.

The entrance to Johns' house was on the upper ground floor. Malan, familiar already with the property, led the way up a flight of stone steps and unlocked the front door. Switching on the hall light first, he left his Yard colleagues and went from room to room throughout the house, illuminating them all, leaving the doors wide open as he went.

The hallway of the property had depth rather than width, and ended with a staircase leading up to the three higher floors and down to the lower ground floor. The front rooms on either side of the hall were a study and a sitting room, each leading to a smaller room facing the rear.

Bryce's first impression of the house was that it had not been cheaply erected in its day, which he guessed to be around the 1880s, but neither had any unnecessary expense been lavished on the fittings. The staircase was solid, but of the plainest construction, as were the covings, ceiling roses, and fireplaces. The nods to grandeur on the entrance floor came from the high ceilings and the vast bay windows facing The Wash. It was dark now, but headlamps from an occasional vehicle passing on the road caused Bryce to feel sure that any view on this level would be obtrusively interrupted by passing traffic and pedestrians.

For the three detectives who hadn't been inside before, Malan's description immediately struck as very accurate – well-kept, expensively and tastefully furnished, with the walls liberally covered in photographs.

"The kitchen and scullery are on one side of the lower ground floor, sir, and there are windows and doors front and back down there as well. There are two more rooms which were apparently once occupied by a live-in domestic and a handy-man husband, but the daily told me there hasn't been a couple living-in like that in her time.

"The principal day rooms are on this floor and on one side of the floor above, with a bedroom and a bathroom on the other side of the landing up there. Beyond that, on the fourth level – what I suppose you'd call the third floor – are three more bedrooms and another bathroom. The top floor – the attic really – is given over to darkroom and studio."

The four detectives went up to the next level. The ceiling height was only slightly lower on this floor, and the windows were the same huge floor-to-ceiling bays. Despite the lack of daylight, Bryce could see that the view, with the road now well below the eye-line, would be very much better. The quality of the furnishings was even better in these rooms, suggesting that Johns had felt the same.

Bryce was pulled away from his reflections

by Kittow, who had just whistled as he closely examined one of the photographs. Malan grinned – he had done exactly the same on his first visit.

"All very well for you young bachelors," muttered Haig. "Just remember the Chief and I are happily married men!"

Bryce smiled. Leaving his subordinates, he went back down to the study and collected some likely keys from the array on the wall, ignoring those which were clearly car ignition keys.

A quick check of the drawers showed him Malan was correct – there was nothing but domestic bills and receipts, together with similar car-related paperwork. He was still contemplating the situation when his colleagues came back downstairs.

"Let's get back to the hotel," he said.

"Huge house for just a single bloke," observed Kittow, as they went out into the hall.

Malan agreed. "All the grander houses like these terraces were designed for the well-monied. When Mr Le Strange built Hunstanton, effectively from scratch, he planned it as two separate areas, on either side of the green. Class distinction, really. Big houses to the north, with the best ones along Cliff Parade. Then rows of small terraced houses to the south – which is where I found Johns' maid."

"I know a bit about that chap," said Bryce. "He pushed for the railway to come here, although I think he died just before it opened. He gave land for the line, and persuaded other landowners along the route to do the same. But he was also a skilled artist, and designed decorations for the nave roof and the tower of Ely Cathedral – and painted much of them himself.

Sergeant Haig was used to his boss's erudition, and Kittow had heard the odd example too. But Malan, who had hardly recovered from the revelation that a Met DCI could pinpoint where he lived on the Lynn to Hunstanton line, was amazed. Seconds later he was even more flabbergasted when Bryce said:

"Wonderful name the man had. Henry L'Estrange Styleman Le Strange – with the two Le Strange bits written differently.

"Blimey, sir, you must have been to Hunstanton before,"

"No," replied Bryce. "I once spent an hour in King's Lynn, but that's the furthest incursion I've previously made into Norfolk. I've never even been to Norwich. I read a lot, you see."

Back in the hotel, Bryce excused himself to make a personal phone call and Malan took the opportunity to raise a question.

"How the hell does he know things like that, Sarge? I've lived here all my life, and I have a bit of an interest in local history – but I bet a lot of people in Huns'ton don't know half of that about Mr Le Strange."

"He's really interested in railway lines and so on. But it's not just what he's read, laddie – it's the fact that he can remember so much. I've worked with him for six months or so, and I've lost count of the number of snippets of information he's come up with. And it's always interesting stuff, too."

Bryce returned, and the four men sat down again. The DCI slid the key which Mrs Mayhew had provided across to Haig.

"See if that opens Mayhew's box," he said. Using a similar-looking key which he had taken from Johns' house, he successfully opened the second box. Haig's key also worked. Neither box was anywhere near full.

"Not much here at all," said Bryce, "but probably all we need. Will, dated just over a year ago – I'll come back to that. Deeds for the Cliff Parade house. Deeds for three other properties in Hunstanton – two in Seagate Road and one in Southend Road. And the partnership agreement."

"Those roads are in what I was calling the second-class area, sir – Mrs Brumby, the cleaner, lives in Seagate Road."

Bryce passed the deeds to Malan, who checked the numbers against his pocket book.

"Yes, sir, Mrs B lives in one of Johns' houses. The address I've got for the other help also belongs to Johns."

"I doubt if it's significant. I suppose it's

remotely possible that one or both of them engaged some 'heavy' to deal with Johns – but if so, we come back to the same question again, why Mayhew and Besant? However, check on the other woman tomorrow, and ask both of them to describe frankly what their employer was like. "What have you got in your box, Sergeant?"

"Ditto a partnership agreement and will – dated about five years ago. Title deeds for 'Little Goslings' – freehold held jointly by Mr and Mrs Mayhew. Deeds for the office premises in Lynn." He quickly scanned the latter document. "The freehold of that is also held jointly by Mr and Mrs Mayhew. So not in the name of the firm, and Johns isn't mentioned either. It would seem he had no direct interest in the commercial premises."

Haig dug a little further into the papers in Mayhew's box. "Ah, there's also a lease here, sir. Looks like the firm leases the property from the Mayhews. Bit of a tangle, I should have thought."

"Oh, I don't know," mused Bryce. "Lots of companies lease their premises. Anyway, let's see what the wills say." He opened that of Patrick Johns as he spoke. It wasn't lengthy, and it took less than a minute to absorb the principal contents. "It's mercifully free of the jargon usually employed by solicitors in will-writing," he announced. "Fergal Bullen is appointed Executor, as he told us . The principal beneficiary is his brother, Jeremy. However, there are various bequests – about twenty of them, varying in size from £100 to £500. All are to females. Mrs Brumby is one recipient, and Mrs Goode is another. One can hypothesise about the remainder – but I shouldn't be surprised if they turn out to be some of his models."

Haig passed Mayhew's will over to the DCI. In no time at all Bryce looked up and confirmed: "Exactly as Mrs M told us; including that she is her husband's executor.

"Now, the partnership agreement. I'll read Johns' copy. We'll check later to ensure both copies are identical.

"Quite a bit of jargon here, but the essence is again exactly as Mrs M told us. It's a 60/40 partnership, because Mayhew initially put in more capital. It doesn't cease 'by effluxion of time', but provides for automatic and immediate replacement of partners in the case of death or incapacity. As soon as Johns died, Mrs M became her husband's partner. A day later, Jeremy Johns succeeded Tim Mayhew as partner.

"Let's set this all to one side for the moment and look at these briefcases, Sergeant. It's a complete waste of time, given that several people have handled them, but just dust them for prints, please."

That done, the now-powdery cases were placed in front of Bryce. He found that both were unlocked. Pushing one case back to Haig, he told him to open it. Opening the other, he quickly scanned the few papers inside.

"This is Mayhew's case. Nothing apart from documents relating to the London meeting."

"Nothing here of interest either, sir," reported Haig. "Handwritten notes on a criminal case, and some stuff on a probate matter."

Bryce grunted.

"What we can't know is whether the killer removed anything incriminating. But if he did, he could well have handled these documents while doing so. If we find a suspect, we may have to check each individual document for prints. We'll put the papers back in the cases anyway. Let's sort out what needs to be done tomorrow.

"We badly need is a photograph of our murderer – and that we obviously don't have. However, we don't have many suspects at present, and we could try to get photographs of those few, and show those to the railway staff. A bit naughty, perhaps, but in their interests if they're innocent. Now, does any of you fancy yourself as a photographer, and think you could take some decent shots without being noticed?"

"I'd be happy to have a go, sir, if I could use Mr Johns' equipment," offered Malan. "He had a 135mm Hektor lens for his Leica. With that, I wouldn't need to get too close to the subject, and the quality would allow a good enlargement. I could park near the office and photograph them as they come out."

"Good. Pick up the camera and lens in the morning. If there are no spare film cassettes in Johns' house, buy some. But don't do any Julia Margaret Cameron stuff until I give the go ahead. I'll make a decision later.

"Anyway, we now have photographs of Mayhew and Johns to show to railway people.

"Kittow, you take them both and go to every station on the Wells branch including Heacham – see if that jogs a memory to confirm a specific train.

"Malan – when you've collected the camera, go and see the cleaners again – ask them to tell you anything they can about Johns. There's nothing in his telephone book to suggest any of the entries are for his 'models', so see if you can get any names and so on.

"Then contact this firm in London," he passed over the slip with the details Janice Henderson had given him, "and ask if they can say what time Mayhew left them on Tuesday. You can work out from that his most likely train back to Lynn.

"After that, take the pictures of Mayhew and Johns to the stations on the Hunstanton line – leave Heacham to Kittow."

"Yes, sir. Er – who is Julia Cameron?"

"One of the earliest and best portrait photographers. Middle of the last century, when cameras, lenses, and photographic paper were primitive, but the quality of her pictures was unequalled in her time.

"If Malan gets the other photographs, we'll have to go over the same ground again, and by the time we've finished the railway people will probably be fed up with us, but perhaps each visit will sharpen their minds a bit more.

"Sergeant Haig and I will go back to the office in the morning, and see if we can find out about these unhappy clients.

"In a few minutes, I'm going to try to contact Jeremy Johns. If he isn't at home, I'll make myself unpopular with Nottingham police and ask them to find him.

"Now, what does everyone think about this case so far? Malan?"

"Couldn't Beasant's murder be a sort of diversionary tactic, designed to take our attention away from the firm?"

"Indeed it could," replied the DCI.

"How about the first two murders both being 'dry runs', and that Mayhew alone was the real target?" asked Haig.

"Yes, that possibility has to remain on the table until we can safely remove it.

"I agree with Malan that Besant is likely a diversion, sir," offered Kittow, "but with respect to the Sergeant I favour the angry client theory – and that both partners were important to the killer."

"Provisionally," said the DCI, "I favour that theory too. The second two cases couldn't have happened without careful planning – in fact I believe that Mayhew and Johns were deliberately targeted. That also makes it unlikely, I think, that we're dealing with a casual killer. If the first case was a combination of dry run and diversion we're looking for someone with a very specific motive for killing both Mayhew and Johns."

Haig frowned. "I take your point about the planning for the murders of both solicitors, sir. And before I forget, there's no help with fingerprints on the tickets. But I still think it's likely that only one solicitor was the 'real' target. Surely an aggrieved client would only have a grudge against the solicitor who dealt with his case not the firm as a whole in the shape of both partners? Taken to the extreme, that might mean that other members of the firm are still at risk."

There was another silence, while everyone digested this thought.

"Yes, you're right, of course, Sergeant. And if there was only one 'real' target, then as you suggest it could have been either Mayhew or Johns. We must bear those possibilities in mind too, but I'm not totally convinced. If I were a killer, with a specific target, I wouldn't risk dry run. I'd get rid of my target, and either make a run for it or lie low thereafter. That's because I'd be doubling my chances of being caught by doing a practice. And don't forget that Johns and Mayhew were killed twenty-four hours apart – I might even be caught before I could get to my real target."

"You think it's probable that the killer had reason to kill both solicitors, then, sir?" asked Kittow.

"More likely than not, although as we've just discussed, there are other options which we can't yet eliminate.

"We need to have some means of staying in contact. I don't want to trouble the police at Lynn, so this is what we'll do. Every hour or so, call the desk here at the hotel and leave a message if you have anything for me. I'll call in as well, and leave a message for you. Got it?"

Everyone nodded.

"Now, that's enough for today. Let's lock these documents back in their boxes, and then lock the door of this room. Malan, are you able to join us for dinner?"

"That's very kind, sir, yes please."

"Good. We'll eat here tonight, and if the food or service is poor, we can always look for somewhere else tomorrow.

"When I've called Nottingham, I'd like a walk by myself to clear my head – perhaps along the pier. It hardly compares with Southend's in length, but I've always enjoyed walking over the sea. Let's meet in the dining room at seven o'clock. I don't suppose we need to book, but do it anyway please, Alex."

After the DCI left the room, Haig smiled at the look on Malan's face. "On duty, Mr Bryce is a stickler for discipline and so on. But off duty, he likes informality. It's Christian name terms. Or for him, 'guv', since few of us would feel comfortable using his first name. Not 'sir'. But remember, it's always very clear when we switch back to being formal, and then you must follow the rules very carefully!

"There are one or two things you should know. The guv is very bright. He's a barrister, with a first-class degree in law from Cambridge. He's the youngest DCI in the Met. He's also a very brave man – won a Military Cross in the war, and is still a major in the reserves. Incidentally, very few people at the Yard know most of those things – I only found out by accident. His fiancée was killed in the war, and he only got married a few months ago. In fact, that will have been his wife he rang earlier. Can't call mine, as she's staying with her sister for a couple of days, and there's no telephone. You should ring home yourself, Malan, if you can. Wouldn't want someone filing a missing person report about you!

"There's another point about the DCI that you need to know: never, ever, mention any of his personal stuff. He's a very private person and hates people talking about him to his face. Today, Mrs Mayhew said she'd heard he was the star of Scotland Yard – he immediately changed the subject.

"Anyway, I'm Alex, as you heard, and this is Adam."

"I'm Peter or Pete, and there's no telephone at my digs, so I think I'd better just nip back to Snettisham and tell my landlady that I won't be in. I'll be back by seven, sarge – Alex."

CHAPTER 9

Haig and Kittow were sitting in the hotel lounge when Malan arrived. The three officers were just chatting when the DCI joined them.

"Just one point before we leave business," said Bryce. "There was no answer from Jeremy Johns' number, so I've set the Notts boys on to him. Now, let's eat."

They sat down in the hotel dining room, and each looked without enthusiasm at a menu card. Nobody felt like a starter. Bryce, Haig and Malan had opted to share a bottle of red Burgundy, while Kittow had a pint of bitter.

While waiting for the food, Bryce opened the conversation with:

"Well, Peter, tell us about yourself."

Before replying, another look of astonishment passed over Malan's face. When he told Haig and Kittow his name, the DCI had already left the room, and as it appeared he had only just returned from his walk, Malan couldn't see that either of them could have told the 'guvnor' his name.

Bryce saw the look, and correctly interpreted its cause.

"No, I'm not omniscient," he smiled. Your Super told us your name earlier."

Malan smiled, and relaxed again.

"I'd have to say I'm surprised that he knew it, guv. Anyway, me, I'd just got called up into the army in the last year of the war, but by the time they'd taught me drill and how to shoot, the war was over. When they let me out, I joined the police. I was lucky enough to get transferred to the CID a few months ago. Didn't expect to get involved in a murder so soon, though!

"I do like history, so topics like Mr Le Strange interest me."

"What about railways?" enquired Haig.

"Sorry," replied the young man. "I wanted to be an engine driver once, of course, like most boys. And I'm familiar with the lines around this part of Norfolk; I don't know much else."

"Never mind," said Bryce. "What about cricket?"

"Well, I play for my village team, guv; I bowl slow left arm stuff, and usually bat at number 10. Unfortunately, Norfolk is only a Minor County, so we have no first-class matches to see around here. I look at the county averages, and listen to test matches when they're broadcast and when I'm off duty, but I don't think you'd call me knowledgeable."

Bryce and Haig both laughed.

"That's as good as we could have hoped for, Peter," said Haig.

"Yes, indeed, added Bryce. "Tell us please – and this isn't related to our work on this case – do you get involved at Sandringham House when the King is there?"

"The uniformed lads do – I did a few stints helping to patrol the grounds soon after I joined the force. It was rumoured that the Queen's corgis – and Princess Elizabeth's – would bite your ankles, given half a chance. In fact I never even saw one. But our CID doesn't get involved. The King has protection officers from the Met, of course."

The four men waited while two waitresses delivered their meals. Everyone quickly brightened up, as it seemed that the kitchen staff were more than capable of turning what had read like an uninspiring menu into appetising dishes.

When the waitresses had gone, the conversation restarted.

Kittow, who was almost exactly the same age as Malan, mentioned that his own experience was very similar, even to an early – and very fortunate – transfer to the CID.

Haig, concerned lest the talk might drift towards war service and embarrass his boss, changed the subject.

"Did you enjoy your walk on the pier, guv?"

"Yes and no, Alex. The tide was in, so that was good. I imagine that at low tide there's little or nothing of the pier over water. But the structure looks to be in poor shape. A sort of zoo, and some roller skating at the end of it. All very tatty. And the little steam railway looks to be on its last legs."

"It's very sad," agreed Malan. "It must have been wonderful towards the end of the last century. Originally, there was a proper pavilion at the end, but that burned down just before the last war. And there used to be steamers from the pier, making trips to Skegness."

"You said earlier how Le Strange built the town up from nothing," said Bryce. "That showed incredible foresight. But it was the railway that really turned it into a popular resort. For years after it opened, the Lynn and Hunstanton Railway was one of the most consistently profitable in the country, and even in Great Eastern and LNER days it did well – excursion trains from the Midlands and so on."

As the men came to the end of their first course, something occurred to Kittow. "There hasn't always been a Royal residence here, I think. Did the railway have anything to do with that coming?"

Malan, by now realising that the DCI would probably be able to answer, waited, but Bryce, seeing that, indicated that he should speak.

"Hard to say," said Malan. "Queen Victoria had apparently been looking for a country estate for the Prince of Wales for some time – allegedly to keep him out of London where he used to get into mischief. He was only about twenty, and involved with what Her Majesty thought was rather a raffish set. Many properties around the country were inspected, but after months of negotiation she bought Sandringham in 1862. The railway opened in the same month, but I doubt if that swayed the decision."

"That agrees with what I've read, Peter." Turning to Haig, Bryce continued the conversation, "Alex, you saw Stanhoe station earlier today. Almost embarrassingly primitive. Well, when the line was first opened, Wolferton probably had much the same population as Stanhoe. But a few years later, the Great Eastern, as it was by then, completely rebuilt Wolferton station into something suitable for a monarch to use. I believe it's a sight to be seen, and hope we can find time to visit before we leave."

Malan laughed. "Yes, it's very grand. Even used to have its own miniature gas works to supply gas for the station lamps!" And the waiting rooms and so on are so big that they are sometimes used for lunches during the royal shooting parties."

Haig smiled, "Just think what Stanhoe station might look like today, if Queen Victoria had bought a house near there, guv!"

Four steaming plates of apple crumble and custard were delivered, and the men tucked in happily again.

Malan, evidently well up in local history, volunteered a further point:

"It's said that one of the other estates the Royals considered was Houghton Hall, only a few miles away. Perhaps the Cholmondeley family wouldn't sell, but over eighty years later they still own the place. Anyway, if the Queen had bought that, the nearest station would be Massingham, on what was then the Midland and Great Northern railway – that's the line on which Besant was found. Massingham – also a good way from its village – is the M&GN's equivalent of Stanhoe, really."

"Good comparison, Peter. Now, as you'll be around here in the morning, sorting out cameras and so on, perhaps you'd like to join us for breakfast – seven fifteen sharp suit you?"

"Certainly does, sir – apart from the company, the breakfast here is bound to be better than my landlady dishes up for me!"

The DCI rose, "Right, I'm for my room and a quiet read before bed. Goodnight to you all."

CHAPTER 10

On Friday morning, after a breakfast which exceeded even Malan's expectations, the four set to work.

Bryce and Haig went back to visit Mayhew & Johns, to find out more about the two clients with alleged grievances against the firm. Anne Percival looked to be a different woman – she greeted them with a smile.

"From your expression, Miss Percival I'm guessing that you've had some better news?"

"Oh yes, a little, sir. Well, of course it doesn't overcome the sad business with the partners – but Mrs Mayhew called half an hour ago, and said to Mr Bullen that he should tell us all not to worry."

"Excellent," replied Bryce. "I'm glad she said that. We had a meeting with her yesterday, and she seems a pleasant lady.

"We're going to park ourselves in Mr Mayhew's office, and talk to some of you again. Ask Mrs Kendall to join us, please."

The two officers collected Mrs Henderson as they passed her desk on the way into Mayhew's room, and Mrs Kendall arrived a few seconds later.

"Take a seat please, ladies," said Bryce. "First, I understand you've been advised by Mrs Mayhew that you shouldn't worry. I'm glad about that, but it isn't what we want to talk about.

"In the notes you wrote for us, both of you mentioned clients who were somewhat disgruntled – Messrs Crowley and Seager. Can you expand on those, please?"

The two secretaries looked at each other, and Mrs Kendall indicated that Mrs Henderson should answer.

"We both know about those two – in fact everyone here in the firm knows. Incidentally, they are the only two that I can think of with any real grudge at all. Mrs Kendall nodded in agreement.

"One is a deeply unpleasant man named Crowley. He wanted to sue a company for breach of contract. They made an offer, but he said it was derisory. Mr Johns advised him to settle, but he refused, and asked for Mr Mayhew's opinion. Well, that was exactly the same. Mr Mayhew told Mr Crowley that it was actually a generous offer, and that if he went to court it was most unlikely that he'd be awarded any more – and it could well be less.

"Well, Mr Crowley wouldn't listen, and insisted on issuing proceedings in the High Court. So Mr Johns briefed Harry Preston, from chambers in Cambridge, to take the case. Mr

Preston also advised Mr Crowley to settle. He confirmed that advice in writing, and we have a copy of that letter on file. But again, there was no persuading the man, and eventually it got to court.

"Mr Crowley was awarded notional damages only, and the judge refused his application for costs, ruling that he brought them on himself. Worse, the judge awarded half of the respondent's costs against him as well.

"Apparently Crowley was within a whisker of being committed to prison for contempt, because he started abusing Mr Preston in open court while the judge was still present. The wretched man then complained to the Law Society, saying that the partners had 'briefed the wrong or an incompetent barrister'. That matter is pending.

"Given that Mr Preston has over thirty years' experience at the bar, and is a very successful specialist in just that sort of case, nobody here gives much for Crowley's chances with the Law Society!

"But we've also heard that he is trying to find another solicitor who will take on the job of suing this firm. Mr Mayhew said, only last week, that he wished Crowley could find some dodgy solicitor who would take the case. He looked forward to winning with ease, and the firm being awarded a substantial sum itself – Mr Crowley is a rich man.

"The second person is Andrew Seager, not rich like Crowley but equally unpleasant. He's a recidivist, with a record longer than your arm. Well, Mr Mayhew and Mr Johns almost took turns to defend him – or at least to mitigate for him when he pleaded guilty – in the police courts for some years. Eventually he found himself at the Assizes. He was convicted of an assault, and the judge, after looking at his record, gave him two years' preventive detention on top of the two-year sentence.

"Seager got out a couple of months ago, and came in here, creating such an awful fuss that the police had to be called. When he was taken outside, he was still shouting threats, and he was arrested and charged under section 5 of the 1936 Public Order Act. The magistrates sent him down for six weeks, and the Chairman made some very pointed remarks about Seager's appalling history, and actually said the bench wished that the lower courts had the power to impose preventive detention too. Unless Seager's been locked up for something else – quite likely, I should think – he would have been out of prison at the relevant times."

"Thank you very much for that," said Bryce. "We'll certainly look very carefully at those two charmers. Please dig out an address for each of them."

***

"It's just possible that the receptionist here could listen in to a conversation on this office telephone," remarked the DCI, "so let's pop into Lynn police station and call from there to see whether anyone has left us a message at the hotel."

The same Sergeant who had received them the previous morning was on duty again. He quickly directed the Met officers to an interview room with a telephone installed, and asked if they'd like some coffee, an offer which they gratefully accepted.

Bryce gave the hotel number to the GPO operator, and was soon connected to the reception desk at the hotel. After identifying himself, the girl immediately volunteered that there were some messages.

One was from Malan, who confirmed that he had acquired the camera. He also reported that the staff at Lynn station recognised the photograph of Mayhew.

Kittow reported that the stationmaster at Heacham had also recognised the picture of Mayhew.

Bryce thanked the girl for passing the messages, and asked her to tell both officers, when they next called, to meet at the hotel at half past one, or as soon afterwards as might be convenient.

Sitting back as best he could in the

uncomfortable chair, he sipped at the coffee which an officer had brought, and passed on the gist of the messages to Haig.

"Are we right in eliminating females from this enquiry, Sergeant?"

"I think so, sir, yes. We don't know how heavy the partners were, although the photographs don't suggest they were huge. But even if they were lightweights, the power needed to strangle someone, to open the door on a moving train, manoeuvre a body out, and then somehow get the door shut again – that last action in particular appears to be quite a physical task for anyone.

"We haven't seen the last site, but Malan said there was a quite a high parapet running along the road over the bridge, and the killer would have had to hoist Besant over that. No, I think it's a man – and probably a strong and maybe youngish one at that."

"Mmm – I can't fault your logic. And it has to be said that the three male Mayhew & Johns employees are all large, young, and strong-looking. Do you go along with me that the solution to this must have some connection with the firm?"

"I have to, sir. You suggested earlier that the first two were so carefully planned that it must mean that the solicitors were targeted. I cannae argue with that. But I still think it's likely that one solicitor was the real target. Depending on which, the other was either a dry run or a diversion."

"I'm not ruling out the dry run completely, but I am going to rule out killing two men from the same firm as a diversion tactic, because to my mind it makes me focus more on the firm and the partnership. Hopefully we'll find out. We should have heard back from Nottingham by the time we get back to the hotel. Then we'll have to see.

"I've done nothing about trying to identify the exact carriages and indeed compartments in which the later murders were committed. It just doesn't seem likely that there would be anything to identify them – no bloodstains. So although there can't be many carriages to choose from – especially the Wells ones – it would be very difficult to identify the right ones. I'm not convinced the time and effort spent in trying to pinpoint them would be worthwhile."

"Agreed, sir. Anyway, I can't see this murderer accidentally dropping his ID card on the carriage floor!"

"All right, Sergeant. Drive us back to Hunstanton; we'll take an early lunch. We passed the Golden Lion on the way in this morning – let's see what they can offer us."

In fact, the Golden Lion did the two men proud, to such an extent that both felt the need of some exercise afterwards.

"We aren't really dressed for a walk on the beach, but I'd like to look at the famous cliffs from the seaward side. The tide is well out. If we walk over the green and past the lighthouse, I think we can get down to the shore, and then come back to the promenade along the base of the cliffs."

"What are these cliffs famous for, sir?"

"Three different layers. Brown carrstone at the bottom – that's the sandstone used to build the Golden Lion and indeed Johns' house. Above that, a deep layer of red or rose chalk, also known as Hunstanton red rock – bet you've never seen any of that before. And at the top, another strata of white chalk. I've seen a black-and-white picture, but that can hardly do justice to the reality. Actually, there are two types of carrstone. The commonest is the brown or 'ginger', but there's also a rare silver variety, dug only I think in Castle Rising."

The two officers walked up the road to the now disused lighthouse. As Bryce had surmised, a couple of hundred yards past it the ground fell away almost to sea level, and there was an easy path to the beach. They walked back towards the town, partly on hard sand and partly over rocks. Both were impressed as they looked up at the unique cliffs. Re-joining the promenade, they returned to the hotel. There were no further messages, and the DCs had not yet come back.

The Yard officers had hardly sat down in the incident room when the telephone rang. Bryce picked up the instrument, and the receptionist asked if she should put through a caller on the outside line.

When this was done, Bryce identified himself, and then listened intently to the caller for two full minutes almost without speaking, occasionally scribbling a note. Then he said:

"I see, well, if he was anywhere in Nottingham at that time he's in the clear – at least for two of our murders. If you could just check that alibi, I'd be very much obliged. Yes, the witness may not be independent, but still. Anyway, we'll meet that train, Inspector, and thank you for your help. Hopefully, after you report on the alibi I won't have to trouble you again."

Putting the telephone down, the DCI turned to Haig.

"As you will have gathered from that, Jeremy Johns was in his office until at least five o'clock every day this week. His staff confirmed that. Last Friday he wasn't in the office, but was staying with a lady friend – which is also where he was when I called last night. Seems he's a divorcee, and is hoping to re-marry soon. Nottingham will check with the lady, but she's probably not much more reliable as an alibi-provider than a spouse would be. However, given that it would take three hours or so by train, and probably not much less by car, it looks as though he couldn't have killed any of our three.

"The Nottingham boys had to inform him

about his brother's murder, of course – they could hardly question his movements otherwise.

"Anyway, he's catching the train that arrives at South Lynn just after seven o'clock, and wants to come straight here. Apparently he said that, as we want to speak to him, perhaps we'll meet him at the station, so he can save on a taxi fare! Not sure if he has a sense of humour, or if he's a cheapskate.

"Ah, here come our colleagues."

The DCs arrived together. Neither looked to be bursting with urgent tidings.

"Before you sit down, Kittow, just ask for some tea and biscuits to be brought in, please. I assume you've both had something to eat?"

Both nodded, and Kittow went out for a minute. When he returned, Bryce asked Malan to report first.

"I saw Mrs Brumby again, and Mrs Goode who as well as helping with cleaning sometimes did 'plain cooking' for Johns in the evenings, although he often ate out. Each woman also works for at least one other household.

"Both women are aged somewhere about fifty, and both have husbands. Mr B is at the gasworks – I actually met him – and Mr G works on the railway. Not a scrap of hostility towards Johns from any of the three, just genuine sadness. We talked briefly about the artistic photographs. Neither woman seemed at all put out by them.

"The only concern they have is what will happen to their houses. They rent by the quarter and would like to stay put. Mr B said Johns was a good landlord – fair rent, and always quick to do any repairs.

"The firm that Mayhew visited in London said that he left their office at just after five o'clock. That means he almost certainly caught the 5:52 from Liverpool Street, which would have taken him to Heacham for the last Wells train.

"At King's Lynn, they recognised Mayhew from the picture, and one man remembered he took the London train on Monday afternoon. But everyone was vague as to whether they saw him on Tuesday evening."

"What about you, Kittow?"

"Turner at Heacham was pretty sure that one of the 'suits' on that train was almost certainly Mayhew, sir. He'd seen him before, too.

"Then, as you instructed, I went to the last few stations on the branch line to see if anyone remembered anything about Tuesday evening. At Burnham, the station staff think about four people got off each of the two relevant trains. All are regulars – no strangers at all. They knew Mayhew, of course.

"The stationmaster at Holkham is pretty certain that nobody got off either train. He says he would notice a stranger anyway.

"That leaves Wells. As you might expect,

more passengers got out there. I was told about ten on the earlier train, and maybe eight on the last one. The station staff did their best to be helpful, but were pretty useless. They all agreed that there were a few regulars, but nobody could actually state that he saw a stranger. Incidentally, the idea about the tickets being collected was also a non-starter It's exactly as you suspected, sir – they just go into a big bag at Wells. Nobody from head office has called for them for audit purposes for years, apparently, so there's no care taken. Nobody admitted it, but I got the impression that the bag was just emptied into a bin every few months."

Bryce grunted. "Can't be helped.

"Now, our report. Sergeant, please."

Haig gave the details relayed by the Nottingham police regarding Jeremy Johns. "He's coming here straight away, to be collected by one of us from King's Lynn later."

"You know the area, Malan," said Bryce. "Go to South Lynn station for ten past seven, collect Johns, and bring him here. I'm not expecting any trouble, and no question of an arrest; we're just inviting him to help with our enquiries.

"Having heard brother Jeremy is no longer a prime suspect, I want to concentrate on the partners' office. You've got the camera, Malan?"

"Yes sir, and I've familiarised myself with its workings."

"Good. Take it to the Tuesday Market Place this afternoon. I don't know how you can make yourself inconspicuous, but try. See if you can get an individual shot of all three men as they come out of the building. You haven't met them, and so it may be that you'll also get shots of some innocent clients. Doesn't matter, as the rest of us can identify the ones we want. I imagine, though, that the three of them will come out pretty soon after the office closes at five o'clock." Bryce paused, although the clocks hadn't yet gone back the level of light would be poor at that time. "What sort of film have you got, Malan?"

The local DC grinned; he had anticipated this question. "I've picked up some fast film, sir."

"Good. If you are questioned, be honest. If someone – and from what we've seen Bullen is the likeliest – gets difficult, you can threaten that you'll charge him with obstructing the police. I don't know if you can get the film developed tonight, but see what you can do. Do you have the expertise to develop and print yourself?

"Yes, but I don't have facilities at my landlady's, sir. If someone else picks up Mr Johns, I could use the Cliff Parade darkroom...?"

"Yes, okay – I'm pretty certain now that he isn't involved, so I'm sure he wouldn't object. But you'll need to be clear of the house by say eight o'clock, as he'll no doubt going there.

"Sergeant, I want you to take Kittow and try to see Seager and Crowley. Seager lives in

North Lynn, and Crowley in South Wootton. You know what you are looking for – alibis for the three crucial times.

"When we were in the office, I was leaning towards the view that this was an external killer, albeit one with a connection to the firm – hopefully either Crowley or Seager. So I didn't ask people what they were doing at the times of the murders. But I want you to drop into the office and inform those you see that I'll be coming in tomorrow to enquire about alibis. You only need to tell one person, probably – I imagine the office grapevine will do the rest.

"By the way, pretend you don't know Malan if you see him outside.

"Now, you and Kittow will have to collect Johns at seven. You'll need to find where the South Lynn station is, but depending how long it takes to find your two disgruntled gentlemen, you'll probably still have an hour or so to kill. If by some chance he isn't on the Nottingham train, you'd better hang around – there's another arriving about an hour and a half later.

"Malan, if they get Johns back here by say a quarter to eight, we should be finished with him in time to eat at eight-thirty. If you've managed to take some pictures, and do the darkroom stuff afterwards, come back here and join us again, if you will."

The local detective was happy to accept.

"That leaves me. I shall spend the rest

of the afternoon writing reports, and in the peace and quiet resulting from your absence, gentlemen, I'll try to exercise my brain cells."

CHAPTER 11

Bryce spent a little time looking more carefully at the notes produced by the eight staff members from Mayhew & Johns. However, apart from the mention of the two obnoxious clients, he could see nothing else which would merit a closer look. Mrs Kendall mentioned a special meeting that the partners had held on the previous Wednesday, but there seemed to be nothing in that.

It was a very pleasant late-October afternoon, and after completing the draft of his report to date, Bryce left the hotel and went for another walk – this time turning south along the promenade towards Heacham. There were surprisingly few people about, and those he saw were mostly unaccompanied ladies. Widows from one or other of the wars, or perhaps with husbands at work, he surmised, as he raised his hat for the sixth time.

Eventually, near the end of the promenade, the trickle of pedestrians stopped altogether. There was a convenient bench, and Bryce sat down and gazed out across The Wash. He had forgotten that Hunstanton was the only resort on the eastern side of England which actually faced west – and so the sun was setting over the water. He sat still for over half an hour, watching the sun sink lower and lower, and the colours of the sky turn more and more beautiful. He found, as he had hoped, that the seascape was particularly stimulating for his little grey cells. He didn't have a 'Eureka moment', but he did decide that this unusual meeting of the partners might indeed be important. He thought of another question that should be asked.

Eventually, he got to his feet, a little stiff after being still in the chilly air for so long, and turned back towards the town. There was a single message at reception, to the effect that the Nottingham 'lady friend' was eminently respectable, and unlikely to perjure herself. No messages from his own men, but then he hadn't expected any. He went to his room to lie down for three quarters of an hour. Then, after freshening up, he went downstairs again. He paused to ask the receptionist to arrange for a pot of tea to be brought, and also to reserve a table for four for dinner at eight thirty. He had contemplated, but immediately rejected, the idea of inviting Jeremy Johns to join them.

Back in the incident room, he was idly making a few trivial alterations to his draft report, when his tea arrived. It was now just after seven fifteen, and he hoped that his colleagues would be picking Johns up about now. He guessed that his colleagues should arrive back by seven forty-five. For the next half hour, he sat in deep thought, mostly reviewing the process he'd gone through earlier on the promenade.

What made sense? Very little. Could these three killings be the random work of a deranged person? But the pattern here didn't fit that theory. The odds against two solicitors being chosen at random would be enormous. Could the 'real' target have been Besant? Almost certainly not, for reasons already rehearsed. But what if a further murder – or more – was committed? He forced that thought out of his mind. There was nothing to suggest that this was even a possibility.

If one of the solicitors was the killer's 'real' target, why go to the lengths he did to kill the other? Surely an easier murder – like Besant's – would have sufficed.

No. He was convinced that the murderer had decided that both partners had to die. Although the idea of an aggrieved client couldn't be eliminated, he was now more inclined to suspect that one of the people in the office, probably one of the men, was responsible. But why?

At almost exactly seven forty-five, his reverie was disturbed by the arrival of Malan, who gave a vigorous nod to Bryce, and passed him a large brown envelope. He was followed into the room by Haig and Kittow. With them was a pleasant-looking, middle-aged, bald-headed man carrying a suitcase. He gave a brief smile as Bryce introduced himself and shook hands. They all sat down.

"Thank you for coming to help us, Mr Johns. I won't offer you refreshments, if you'll forgive me, as I don't think we'll need to take up many minutes of your time. I don't know how much you've been told about your brother's business affairs, and we'll come on to that in a minute, but I anticipate you'll be very busy over the next few days."

"Ghastly thing about my brother and his partner – and your Sergeant had just told me that there was a third murder. It's perhaps not decent to say this at a time like this, Chief Inspector, and it probably isn't relevant anyway, but you should know that there was little love lost between Patrick and me. That dates back many years. He took my fiancée away from me – but he never married her." Johns gave a fastidious look down his nose. "Naturally, I didn't want her back after that."

"I see. Well, it probably isn't relevant, as you say, although looking at various documents it would seem that he didn't bear you any grudge.

"Obviously, we've been looking into alibis. We do believe that there is only the one murderer, by the way."

Johns smiled again. "I think my alibis are unimpeachable. I was in my office every day this week, and staff can certainly bear witness to the fact that apart from today I was there until at least half past five. The local police spoke to several members of staff about that. My friend can tell you what time I got to her house – I should think about six-fifteen on both days. And on the Friday, we went out to dinner. It was at a restaurant where I am known, so not only can I provide a copy of the bill, but the staff there will be able to say that we were there. I think we left a little after ten o'clock, but again you can check for yourselves.

"Now, suppose you tell me why I, living miles away, and practically estranged from my brother, might be a suspect – not just in his murder but in two others as well?"

"Fair question," replied Bryce, also smiling, as he liked what he was seeing of the man.

"The Nottingham police were only aware of the murders, not any of this background. To summarise, you are your brother's principal beneficiary, although a solicitor in his office is the executor. I'll give you the will shortly. But you are also now a partner in the firm of Mayhew & Johns – your fellow-partner being Mr Mayhew's widow.

"Either of those facts would inevitably make you a suspect, but the will in particular – given what we've established so far about the size of your brother's estate – seemed particularly significant.

Johns looked steadily at the DCI for some seconds.

"Obviously, I didn't expect Patrick to die for many years, Chief Inspector. And I'd never given any thought to the possibility inheriting anything from him. I'm not a poor man anyway.

"I had completely forgotten about that partnership agreement. It must be about fifteen years ago that it was drawn up. Clarissa Mayhew drafted it – she was a newly-qualified solicitor then, and married Tim Mayhew soon after, I understand. Curiously, I never met either her or her husband – it was very soon after that that Patrick and I fell out. The partnership arrangements were agreed by telephone and letter, and documents exchanged by post. I may have a copy myself, somewhere, although I haven't set eyes on it since it was signed, and I don't remember the detail."

"Again, I'll give you your brother's copy of that agreement," said Bryce. "But I can tell you that at the instant of your brother's death, Mrs Mayhew became a partner. And when Mayhew himself died, you also became a partner.

"Mrs Mayhew is someone with whom I'm sure you can come to a suitable understanding. Incidentally, and I don't think she would mind my telling you this, her husband only had a few months to live anyway – so she had prepared herself for bereavement well before he was killed.

"Anyway, we have several items belonging to your brother which we don't need any more. You can take his deed box, which contains *inter alia* the will and partnership agreement. Also his briefcase, which held nothing of interest to us. Here is the deed box key. Malan, give Mr Johns the key of the Cliff Parade house, please.

"This key is the one used by Mrs Brumby, one of the cleaners. We haven't found your brother's own key – it seems the killer removed that along with the wallet and any other personal effects, which haven't been found. So you might consider having the locks changed.

"Also, Malan, let him have the names and addresses of the two dailies. When you obtain probate, Mr Johns, they'll be your tenants, as they both live in properties owned by your brother. And here is Mrs Mayhew's home telephone number." He passed over a slip of paper.

"One final thing, Mr Johns, and I apologise in advance for this. Your brother had a particularly well-equipped darkroom. This afternoon we had urgent need for some photography, plus some developing and printing. I somewhat high-handedly authorised the use of not only the darkroom, but also of your brother's Leica. Apologies."

"No problem whatsoever. No skin off my nose, and anything to help catch his killer gets my complete support."

"I left the camera and telephoto lens on a table in the studio, sir," Malan told Johns. "And cleaned up the darkroom before leaving."

"Thanks for that," replied Johns. "But as I have no interest in photography, I expect everything will just lie there until I can sort out a sale."

Observing Malan's wistful look, Bryce said:

"If you have no use for some of the photographic stuff, Mr Johns, I'm sure DC Malan here would be grateful for anything you can't sell."

"Understood. We'll have to see."

"Right, Malan, you and Kittow help Mr Johns with his case and the rest. Then drive him down the road and help him get it all into the house."

"That's appreciated, Chief Inspector – it's only a few yards, but I've only got one pair of hands. Shall I see you again?"

"Well, I imagine you'll be meeting Mrs Mayhew at some point soon. If that's in the firm's office tomorrow morning, then you'll certainly see me there. We've commandeered both partners' offices, by the way, but we can release one if you want a meeting."

After Johns and the others had gone, Bryce and Haig looked at each other.

"What about our two former clients?"

"Seager is out of the running, sir. He was certainly a free man at the time of Besant's murder, but on Saturday night he was arrested on a burglary charge. He was in Dereham magistrates' court on the Monday morning, and remanded in custody. He was safely in Norwich prison at the time both Johns and Mayhew were killed.

"We saw Crowley, sir. He was very abusive, to put it mildly, but you can't arrest a man for swearing at you in his own home!

"Anyway, it seemed he had just read about the deaths in the Lynn News. He was gloating in a quite sickening way, saying that it was someone's vengeance on a pair of crooked lawyers, and that it proves that he himself wasn't the only one who had been badly advised by them.

"When he'd calmed down a bit, we asked about his movements on the days in question. Well, that started him off again, but eventually we got some sense out of him. Again, I'm afraid he can't have been involved. He was, without doubt, at a dinner in Manchester on Monday evening. He'd travelled there on Sunday, and returned on Tuesday. He grudgingly gave us half a dozen names – people he'd known for years, he said, and who could confirm his attendance at the dinner. We made some calls from Lynn police station. Managed to get hold of two of the witnesses – one was the Manchester deputy chief constable, and the other an MP. Crowley is certainly well-connected. Both said they knew him well, and that they spoke to him at length during the evening. He couldn't have killed Johns, so that's that, I'm afraid, sir."

"Worth a try," the DCI shrugged. "Let's see what Malan's pictures are like." He proceeded to open Malan's envelope. He took out eighteen prints, but quickly realised that there were only six subjects, with three copies of each. The pictures were 'head-and-shoulder' shots. A professional photographer would have been ashamed of the composition – the subject either too high or too low in each frame – but they were perfectly adequate for the purpose required.

Three of the targets must have been clients, and Bryce pushed those aside, leaving the pictures of the male staff members.

"Not a bad job by young Malan, under the circumstances, sir," said Haig. "The men aren't looking at the camera, so perhaps they never even saw him taking their photograph."

"Yes, pretty good work. Tomorrow, he and Kittow can take these around the various stations, and we'll see whether any bells are rung."

Malan and Kittow returned, both laughing.

"Sorry sir, explained Kittow. "We helped Mr Johns carry the box and cases into the house. You should have seen his face when we turned into the study, and he saw the photos on the wall. After wandering round for a minute peering at them, he just said 'well, well, well'.

"Then as we were leaving, he looked into the studio. 'Well, well, well,' he said again."

"After we'd left, we visualised him going to all the other rooms, and wondered if he'd find any alternative to 'well, well, well' before he finished," said Malan – at which both men burst into giggles again.

"Very amusing, no doubt," said Bryce. "I don't begrudge you your simple pleasures, but before we eat let's look at where we are.

"I think we have to take Jeremy Johns off the list of suspects. I'm also ninety-nine percent satisfied that we aren't dealing with a random killer. We're told there are only two clients with anything like a grudge against the firm – and neither of those matters seems serious enough for anyone to kill as a result. Given that both men have cast iron alibis, I am more and more convinced that this was an 'inside job', as it were.

"Malan, you've provided photographs of the three main possibles, and you've done a very decent job under the circumstances. We'll probably never know who the other three men are in your pictures."

"It wasn't as hard as I'd expected, sir. I don't think any of them noticed that I was taking photographs at all. Only sad thing is, I see you've discarded the photograph of one of the men that I thought looked like a right villain!"

"Perhaps he was one of the firm's criminal

clients," smiled Haig.

"Or perhaps he was a peer of the realm, come in to make his will," replied Bryce, to general laughter.

"By the way, thanks for suggesting to Mr Johns that I wouldn't mind the odd bit of equipment, sir."

"Well, it'll probably come to nothing. Anyway," the DCI continued, "tomorrow I want you two DCs to take a set of pictures and show them around. Kittow, you do the Wells branch as before. Better start at Stanhoe, even though allegedly nobody got off there. Wells is the most likely, obviously. But if that produces nothing, try Holkham and Burnham.

"Malan, I don't mind which end you start. But you must cover Lynn, Dersingham, Snettisham, Heacham, and Hunstanton.

"Try to see every member of staff who was on duty at the relevant day or days. Push hard, without putting statements into their mouths, of course. If anyone is absent when you call get their address and take the photographs around to their homes.

"The Sergeant and I will be talking to some of the Mayhew & Johns office staff again.

"In the unlikely event that either of you comes up trumps, try to contact us at the solicitors' office. Don't use names; let's call these men 'A', 'B', and 'C'.

Turning the photographs over, he wrote

a letter on each photograph, double-checking afterwards to make sure that the three copies of each man's picture carried the same letter. He also made a note in his book.

"Let's all meet back here again at about noon tomorrow.

"Now, let's go and eat – and hope that tonight we don't get a call informing us about a fourth victim!"

***

Over another decent dinner, Bryce asked each man where he saw himself ten years ahead.

"You first, Alex."

"Well, guv, I can only hope. It would be nice to get to inspector – preferably in the CID but in the uniformed branch if necessary. By then I may have a second kiddie, so I'll need a bit more money. You'll have moved on long before that, so I wouldn't be leaving you in the lurch."

"I think that you may well be 'leaving me in the lurch', Alex. You see, I'll be surprised if you don't make inspector within two years at most. I'm not without some influence in high places, and the wheels are already in motion."

Haig stared at his boss and started to stammer words of appreciation, but Bryce cut him short.

"What about you, Adam?"

"If I could make DS within five years, guv, I'd be happy. Even happier if I reached DI eight or nine years after that."

"Well, this is the third case you worked on with me, and you must realise that I shouldn't have invited you on this one if I had doubts about you. I think your timescale is realistic. You're very young as yet, but I'll be amazed if you don't make sergeant within four or five years. If you do, you should bring your next target forward, and aim to become a DI after another five. You already have two good reports from me on your record, and I expect there'll be another after this case. So you're on target at the moment."

The DCI loaded his fork with more roast lamb, and before transferring it to his mouth enquired: "Peter, what about you?"

"Blimey, guv, I just don't know. I was incredibly lucky to get attached to the CID, and I spend a lot of my time just trying to learn – and making sure I don't make any silly mistakes. I get on okay with my DI, but not being disrespectful to him I don't think he has your standing or influence, guv. Anyway, we only have a small CID unit at Lynn, and promotion prospects don't look marvellous. The DS retires in about five years, and the DI a couple of years after that, but there is another DC ahead of me – and no doubt others in Norwich or even Yarmouth. I guess in ten years DS is about all I could aspire to."

"Would you be willing to move in the future, Peter?"

"Oh yes, guv. To get more experience, for a

start, even without a promotion. Lynn is a bit of a backwater, crimewise. I've no ties here, really, apart from my parents and a few friends."

"Good, very sensible. Well, I've been pleased with you so far, and you can certainly expect a positive mention in my report to the Chief Constable in due course. However, although you shouldn't count any chickens, I think I can say that your own superior, Superintendent Reeves, already thinks highly of you. He described you in flattering terms – and as I don't want your head to swell too much, I'm not going to tell you what he said! Just keep your nose clean – not brown, just clean."

The three officers all sat slightly stunned, but happy. The conversation moved onto other topics.

Malan would have liked to ask their boss about how he came to be a policeman, given that he was a barrister. But as he wasn't supposed to know anything about that, he was constrained.

"When does Fiona get home, Alex? asked Bryce.

"Tomorrow afternoon, guv. Her father has been on the waiting list for a telephone for over a year, but he's got no priority. I'll be able to phone her tomorrow evening."

"Perhaps we won't be here by then, and you'll be able to see her and Rosie in person," said Bryce.

All three officers looked at him.

"That'd be nice for you, Alex, and for the guv and Adam too, no doubt," said Malan. "But for myself, I'd like to see this case dragged out quite a bit longer. I'm not likely ever to get experience like this again. And, frankly, working with you three has been a real pleasure."

"Understandable, Peter," said Bryce, "but alas, we can't lengthen the time frame simply for your benefit!"

The others laughed. Their conversation became general and wide-ranging as food came and went. After the meal, Malan excused himself and went off to his lodgings.

"Come to breakfast again – eight o'clock this time, I think," invited Bryce as the local man left. The three Met officers had one drink in the hotel bar, and then retired to their rooms.

CHAPTER 12

The following morning the team split up as had been decided the previous evening. With Haig at the wheel, the two senior Yard detectives drove back to King's Lynn

Miss Percival, who was smiling even more broadly than the day before, gave the detectives a cheerful "good morning", as they made their way to Mayhew's room. In the outer office the secretary was sitting, apparently doing nothing.

"Good morning, Mrs Henderson," said Bryce. "We'd like to talk to you first, and then perhaps you can arrange a sequence of interviews for us, please. Mrs Kendall, then Mr Bullen, then Mr Stanley, and then Mr Boyd. After that, we'll see."

The secretary made a quick shorthand note on her pad. Haig unlocked Mayhew's door, and the three went in and sat down.

It seemed to Haig that Mrs Henderson looked less stressed than she had on the two previous occasions he'd seen her.

"You seem a bit happier today," he said.

"Well, yes, Sergeant. Mrs Mayhew has been on the telephone this morning. She's coming in later, together with the other new partner. But she's already assured Mr Bullen that the firm will continue."

"We're very glad to hear that, Mrs Henderson," said Bryce. "We spent time with both new partners yesterday, and they seem very competent people.

"I'm afraid that both your difficult clients have unbreakable alibis. Seager was in prison again, and Crowley was undeniably in Manchester with a string of the great and the good to bear witness.

"I'd like to focus on something else. In the notes that Mrs Kendall made for us, she mentioned that last week there was what we might call an extraordinary partners meeting. She presumably thought it was significant, but you didn't mention it. Before we speak to her, can you recall the incident?"

"Oh yes, Chief Inspector. It was unusual, but it wasn't something that came to mind when I was writing my own notes.

"Normally, the partners held a meeting, regular as clockwork, on the first Monday of the month. But last week, on Wednesday afternoon they had a meeting. It can't have just been an informal chat, because both partners cancelled meetings with clients.

"At the time, Pat and I did think it was a bit odd, because normally one of us would type an agenda for a partners' meeting, and then attend to take shorthand notes. We took turns at doing these tasks. It would have been Pat's turn to type up an agenda and take the minutes, had it been an ordinary meeting. But she wasn't asked, and neither was I."

"Was the meeting in this room?" asked Haig.

"Yes; and it lasted about an hour. Afterwards Mr Mayhew didn't say anything to me about it. In fact, looking back, he was a bit downcast for the rest of the day. It wasn't my place to ask him about it. Pat told me later that Mr Johns also seemed upset about something."

Did any other member of staff, or any outsider, come in here while the meeting was taking place?" asked Bryce.

"No, nobody. Is this meeting important, Chief Inspector?"

"Probably not, but in a murder case – especially a triple murder case – we have to examine everything.

"Anyway, please organise the list – and perhaps some coffee with a few spare cups for our interviewees?"

A few minutes later, both secretaries arrived, each carrying a tray. These were set down on the big table, and Mrs Henderson withdrew. Mrs Kendall offered to pour. Like her colleague, she now seemed very calm.

Before any questions could be asked, there was a tap on the door, and Mrs Henderson put her head back into the room:

"There's a call for you, Chief Inspector – shall I put it through here?"

"I'll come out," replied Bryce. Closing the door behind him, he picked up the secretary's phone.

"Malan here, sir. I went to Wells first, and we have success. 'C' on Tuesday night. They're pretty certain."

"Excellent. We may need to arrange an identity parade later, but for now I want you to come straight back to the Tuesday Market office."

Bryce returned to Mayhew's room, and apologised for the interruption.

Mrs Kendall also confirmed that the partners' meeting had been unprecedented, and that Mr Johns had said nothing about it – not that day, nor at any time since. She thought that her boss had been a bit distracted before he disappeared, but she hadn't associated his mood with the meeting.

After she left, Bryce briefed the Sergeant on Malan's report about the man in photograph 'C'.

Haig looked at his boss. "You'd already earmarked that one, hadn't you sir?"

"When you eliminated the two best outsiders, I decided this mysterious meeting was significant. He then seemed the most likely, yes. You made the point about it being pointless for Bullen to kill the partners before he was made a partner, and a similar point could be made about Stanley – he might never complete his articles if the firm closed.

And now we know Boyd seems to have been on the Tuesday night train, it's getting more certain. But we'll see the others anyway."

Mr Bullen followed, and was offered coffee. Bryce started off by talking about the new partners' forthcoming visit. Bullen seemed very positive about it.

"Early days," he said, "but I rather think the prospect of my getting a partnership may have improved. I gather that Mr Johns' brother isn't really keen to be involved. He wants to stay in Nottingham. I believe policemen always ask *cui bono?* Chief Inspector, so I appreciate that the fact that I look set to benefit must push me higher up your list of suspects.

Bryce smiled enigmatically, and questioned him about the unusual meeting the previous week.

"What meeting?" asked Bullen. Bryce explained. The solicitor looked surprised.

"I didn't even know there had been such a meeting. My room is well away from this end of the building, so I don't see much that goes on. Well, I'd like to think they were talking about inviting me into the firm, but as Tim and Patrick have gone I don't suppose we'll ever know. Probably one consulting the other about a case."

"Perhaps. Now, you'll all be expecting this

question, no doubt, and you've had plenty of time to think about the answer. Can you tell us exactly where you were between five o'clock and seven o'clock last Friday evening; between five o'clock and midnight on Monday evening; and between the same times on Tuesday evening?

"I can, Chief Inspector, but the only corroboration has to come from my wife. We're happily married, and I know with what cynicism the police treat such an alibi witness! Anyway, on all three evenings I was at home – certainly from about five forty onwards."

"Thank you, Mr Bullen, that's all. We may or may not need to talk to your wife."

The next interviewee, Mr Stanley, arrived. He also denied knowing about the partner's meeting, and made a similar comment to Bullen's about being his room being sited a long way from the centre of things.

Like the solicitor before him, he claimed to have been at home – or more accurately at his lodgings – at the relevant times. He offered his landlady as an alibi witness, as he had a half-board arrangement, and she had served his evening meal at six o'clock on each of the relevant evenings.

"We'll have to talk to her, Mr Stanley, but I'm sure she'll confirm what you say. That's all, thank you."

Stanley looked surprised at not being asked many more questions, and left happily.

A few minutes later, Boyd arrived. Bryce shook his hand, and sat him down, and fussed over getting him a cup of coffee.

"Now, Mr Boyd, we're asking everyone the same questions. Can you tell us, please where you were on these dates and times?" He listed them again.

"I was at home – or on my way home – on each of those dates."

"What about corroboration?"

"I live alone, Chief Inspector – I'm separated from my wife. I rent a little house in Gaywood. So no, I'm afraid I can't offer a witness. But my alibi is genuine, regardless."

"No convenient neighbours?" enquired Haig.

"Alas, I don't often see any of them. We keep ourselves to ourselves."

"Do you have a car, Mr Boyd?"

"Yes, I have a little Austin Seven Opal tourer. Quite elderly now, but it still gets me about as and when required. Petrol is a perennial problem, of course."

"Yes, it certainly is," said Bryce. "What's the registration number?"

"NG 8947, although I can't imagine why you want that."

Bryce ignored the implied question, and said:

"Let's change the subject. We've heard that the partners had a meeting last week – not the usual monthly one. What do you know about that?"

Boyd didn't hesitate. "Nothing," he replied.

The DCI stood up, walked over to one of the windows, and looked out at the square. There was a complete silence in the room. He turned round, and sat down again. Leaning forward towards Boyd, he said:

"That's not quite true, is it, Mr Boyd. I think you have reason to know – or at least to suspect – that the meeting concerned you."

"I know nothing of the kind."

There was another silence, both police officers looking at the manager. There was a tap on the door, and Mrs Henderson put her head inside again.

"Excuse me, sir, but there's another call for you. Will you come outside?"

Once more shutting Mayhew's door behind him, Bryce again picked up the instrument on Mrs Henderson's desk and heard his younger Yard colleague's voice.

"Kittow here, sir, I haven't been everywhere yet, but I thought you'd like to know this straight away. It's 'C' at Heacham on Tuesday, without any doubt."

"Excellent. You mean Turner's satisfied about him being the second 'suit'?"

"Yes, sir. He says he's happy to swear on a stack of bibles. I started at the Lynn end, so Hunstanton next."

"Good. I've already had a similar positive from Malan about Wells the same evening. Well, carry on, it'd be nice to get a third positive. When you've been to Hunstanton, just wait in the hotel."

Bryce returned to Mayhew's room, and sat down.

"Sorry about that, Mr Boyd. Now, where were we? Ah yes, you were just saying that you have no reason to think that the meeting had anything to do with you."

"That's right."

"You'll have to forgive my cynicism, Mr Boyd, but I don't believe you. You had good reason to fear the partners, didn't you?"

"I don't know what you mean," blustered Boyd.

"I think you do. Caution him now, Sergeant."

The caution administered, Bryce continued:

"We'll come back to the meeting in a minute. Why did you take a train from Lynn to Wells on Tuesday evening?"

Boyd replied spiritedly enough: "I didn't. You can't say that I did."

"Oh, it's not just me saying it, Mr Boyd. We have a witness who says you boarded a Wells train at Heacham."

"He must be mistaken. Anyway, how could he possibly think it was me?"

"Oh, it was very simple, Mr Boyd. We showed him a selection of photographs, and he picked you out. But, if he is mistaken, what about the people who say you got off the same train at Wells. Are they mistaken too?"

Boyd was silent.

"We'll arrange a proper identity parade, and ask the witnesses if they can pick you out in real life, rather than from a photograph. It may be that we'll soon have a witness to say that you were on a train to Hunstanton on Monday evening, as well."

Again, Boyd said nothing.

"I'll tell you what I think, Mr Boyd. I think you've been embezzling monies from the firm. I think one of the partners suspected something was going on, but didn't know who was involved. I think it's possible that another member of staff may be an accessory. The meeting was almost certainly to discuss the matter. You knew about the meeting, and perhaps there was some other alarm signal – a comment or question from one of the partners, maybe.

"Your only hope was to eliminate both partners, before they could call in an accountant, or go through the books themselves. You thought – although you were mistaken – that the firm would be dissolved on their deaths, and that in the confusion that would undoubtedly follow, your malfeasance wouldn't be spotted."

"That's for you prove, and you can't," said

Boyd after a further period of silence.

"We'll see. I anticipate that the fact that you were on board the train on which Mr Mayhew was killed – and then lied about being at home – will be sufficient to convict you of that particular murder.

"Then, I'm hopeful that witnesses will be found to say you were also on the train with Mr Johns on Monday night.

"Incidentally, you knew that, even if Mr Johns was found soon after he died, there was practically certain that Mr Mayhew wouldn't have heard about it before arriving back at Lynn on Tuesday evening. So whatever reason you'd given Mr Johns as to why you were travelling to Hunstanton, could safely be repeated with Mr Mayhew for the Wells trip on Tuesday. But in fact Johns wasn't found until much later anyway.

"You didn't have much time to plan this, but I think you spent much of Thursday or Friday setting up the scheme, buying tickets to confuse us, and so on. Then you probably had to get your car in the right place, in advance, so you could return home after the murders. We'll see what your colleagues know about your attendance recently."

Boyd remained silent, still looking down at his lap.

"Tell him what else we'll be doing, Sergeant."

"We'll be enquiring as to whether people

saw your car near the stations in Hunstanton and Wells, on the relevant days," said Haig. There aren't that many Austin Opals around now, and probably hardly any in Norfolk. And we'll ask whether anyone at the stations can remember you coming in to book tickets for various journeys. That must have involved some train travel, and no doubt we'll find some witnesses to it.

"Then, we'll enquire about sightings of your car near Gayton Road station last Friday. Poor Mr Besant. In your mind, someone else had to die to foul the pitch and mislead the police. Your own self-protection trumped everything else.

"We'll search your house, and car. Maybe you're so stupid as to have retained the cosh that you used so effectively. Or a piece of clothes line.

"Your neighbours – the ones you said wouldn't have seen you at home on the various dates – will be asked about your movements anyway. I expect one of them will have seen or heard you arrive home late on Monday or Tuesday.

"Of course, you may have worn gloves when you went through the two briefcases – but if you didn't, we'll find your prints on papers there – and I wouldn't have thought that the office manager would ever need to handle a solicitor's handwritten notes – probably not clients' documents either.

"Finally, a competent auditor will go through the firm's books. Of course, when they find what's been going on, you won't need to worry about a charge of embezzlement."

Still Boyd looked down without speaking.

"Your silences have been noted, Mr Boyd," said Bryce, and was then interrupted by yet another knock on the door.

"There's another police officer here, sir. Can I show him in?"

"Not yet, Mrs Henderson. I'll come and speak to him."

With Mayhew's door shut again, Bryce greeted Malan.

"You must have driven very fast to get back so soon! Anyway, by convention, the honour of making an arrest rests with a local officer. I want you to come in with me now, and when I give you the nod, arrest Douglas Boyd on suspicion of the murder of Timothy Mayhew. That's the one we have the best evidence for at present. He's been cautioned. Take him in your car to Lynn police station – Sergeant Haig can accompany you."

The secretary sat listening to this open-mouthed. The DCI gave her a tight smile. "You heard all of that, Mrs Henderson – please say absolutely nothing to anyone until we have left."

Malan looking pleased, followed the DCI into Mayhew's room.

"That was a good summary about what we're going to do, Sergeant. I'm sure that we'll find evidence for other matters later, but for the moment we'll start with the murder of Mayhew. Proceed, Constable, please."

DC Malan, who hadn't expected to have this opportunity, carried out the formal arrest, and then produced handcuffs to restrain Boyd.

Boyd opened his mouth at last. "Can I speak to Mr Bullen?" he asked.

"You can, and indeed you may," replied Bryce. "Sergeant, please ask Mrs Henderson if she can get Mr Bullen in here."

The solicitor arrived inside a minute, and looked amazed to see Boyd in handcuffs.

"Mr Boyd has been arrested on suspicion of the murder of Mr Mayhew," he informed the solicitor. "He's asked for you. He'll be formally charged at the station. That will only be a holding charge, of course – there will undoubtedly be other matters. You should be aware that there will be investigations into the finances of this firm, so before agreeing to represent him you might remember that there must be the possibility that you could be a witness.

"Anyway, he wants you to look after him initially, and if you are happy to do so, I suggest you come along to the station.

"Potentially, there's an interesting legal point about a future trial in these matters, Mr Bullen. With the precedent of the so-called 'brides in the bath' murders, the question of 'system' could arise here. Three cases of coshing, each followed by ligature strangulation would seem to be sufficiently similar and unusual to qualify – even without the railway connection.

Bullen nodded slowly, understanding Bryce's point but still struggling to come to terms with the whole situation.

"Malan, take Boyd to the station, and get him booked in. Sergeant, go with them. I'll follow you."

With his subordinates and the prisoner gone, the DCI stopped to speak to the secretary.

"Is Mrs Mayhew here, by any chance?" he asked.

"Yes, she's in a little interview room with the new Mr Johns," she replied.

"Good; just point the way, please."

Bryce knocked at the door indicated, and went in. The two new partners looked up.

"News," said Bryce.

"Do squeeze in and take a seat, Chief Inspector," said Mrs Mayhew.

"Apologies for this. Had I realised, I would have unlocked your brother's room, Mr Johns. In fact, you can have both rooms back now. But I won't keep you a moment. Douglas Boyd, the office manager here, has just been arrested on suspicion of the murder of your husband, Mrs Mayhew. We have witnesses to say that he was on the train when your husband was killed – and there is no earthly reason why he should have been. No doubt other charges will follow.

"No need for me to explain to either of you that he's entitled to representation, and he's asked for Mr Bullen, who has gone with him to the police station. As a potential witness, however, Mr Bullen may not be able to continue to represent him; and if the look on his face was anything to go by, I don't think he wants the job anyway.

"There's another matter. I strongly suspect there has been embezzlement, and that would provide the motive for the murders of both partners. Someone will need to go through the books with the proverbial fine-toothed comb.

"Bearing in mind that there could possibly be an accomplice among the staff, would you like to make a suggestion as to how we might proceed?"

The two new partners looked at each other, and then back at Bryce.

"I'd only met Douglas a couple of times," said Mrs Mayhew. But I'd never have marked him down as a killer. Anyway, if you agree to leave it to us, the firm will be very happy to look into this – unless you object, Jeremy?"

"Oh, I concur, Clarissa, it's obviously in our interest to get this sorted out quickly. I suggest we get an independent auditor in, and in the meantime seal the books – and indeed the whole of Boyd's office. We'll provide you with the details of whatever we may find, Chief Inspector, of course."

"On that basis, I'm agreeable to leaving it to you two," said Bryce. The police don't really have the resources for that sort of investigation – yet it may be an important part of getting a conviction for murder. If we get that, Boyd will never be tried for embezzlement, of course – probably he'll never even be charged with it.

"Here's the key to your brother's room, Mr Johns. And your husband's room is now open, Mrs Mayhew, so you can vacate these cramped quarters.

"Once again, my commiserations to you both. Hopefully, we'll get a conviction."

"You're a barrister, Chief Inspector," said Mrs Mayhew. (This was news to Johns, who looked surprised.) "Has the possibility of 'system' occurred to you?"

"It has indeed – I mentioned it to Mr Bullen a few minutes ago. But in the Smith case, Sir Edward Marshall Hall failed to persuade either the trial judge or the Court of Appeal that evidence of system shouldn't be allowed. Frankly, I can't see any modern counsel doing any better, should the question arise in this case."

"Probably not, Chief Inspector – even if there is one around with the oratorical powers of Hall in his heyday!"

Mrs Mayhew looked across at Johns, and added:

"We'd both like to thank you. You and

your team have solved this in a remarkably quick time. I'll certainly praise you to the Chief Constable when I next see him. No doubt he'll see to it that your star rises even further at Scotland Yard!" she added with a mischievous smile.

"I see in the papers this morning that there has been a murder in a tiny Suffolk hamlet," remarked Johns. "It seems remote spots in East Anglia are becoming somewhat lawless. Perhaps you'll be called in to solve that one too."

Bryce smiled, and shook his head. "Very unlikely. Scotland Yard is only asked to help in a small percentage of provincial murder cases – and anyway we have other peripatetic DIs and DCIs."

Neither he nor Sergeant Haig, as they said 'goodbye' to the two solicitors, dreamed that Johns' comment was actually prophetic. Within twenty-four hours, an incident in Liverpool Street would quickly prove to have links to the death in Suffolk – and both Yard officers would indeed be involved.

****

AFTERWORD

For readers interested in the demise of the railway system in NW Norfolk

In 2023 the only passenger line remaining in the whole of West Norfolk is that running south from King's Lynn, to London via Ely and Cambridge.

Were he around today, though, Tim Mayhew couldn't take a through train to Liverpool Street – he would go into King's Cross. (If he really wanted to finish in Liverpool Street, he could change at Cambridge and board a train which would probably stop at least seven times between there and London. It would probably be easier to take the underground or a bus or taxi from King's Cross to Liverpool Street!)

The fates of the other five lines marked on Bryce's 1949 diagram are outlined here. The plan on the following page reminds us of those lines, numbered for reference.

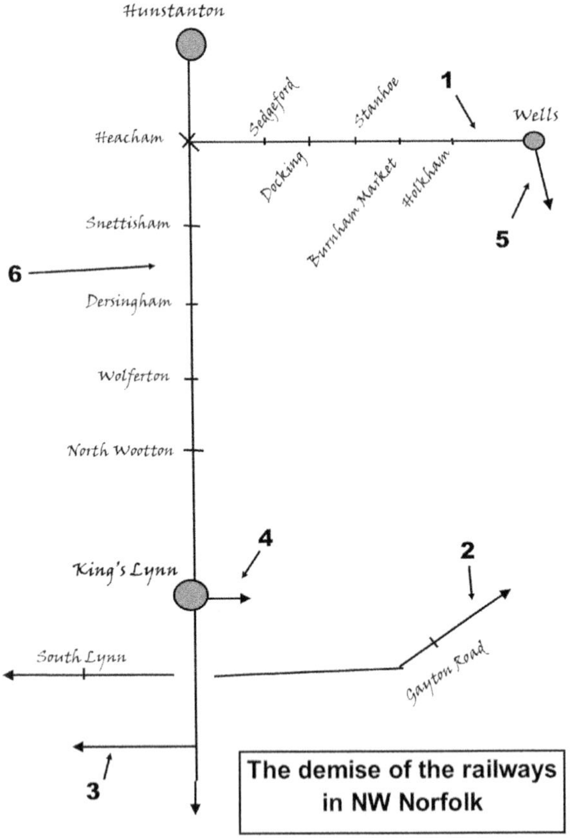

LINE 1. The branch from Heacham to Wells-next-the-Sea lost its passenger service in 1952. The next year, the disastrous 'East Coast Floods' washed away some of the line near Holkham, and it was never reinstated. Goods traffic

continued over part of the line for a short time, but soon the branch was completely abandoned.

Stanhoe station is now a private dwelling.

LINE 2. This line ran all the way from the Midlands via South Lynn station to Great Yarmouth, with branches off to Norwich and Cromer – a total of some 180 miles. The section through Gayton Road was closed in 1959, and over the next few years almost all of the remaining stretches disappeared. This closure predated the 'Beeching Plan'.

Gayton Road station building no longer exists, although there are remnants of the platforms in the middle of what is now woodland.

Off the map, a heritage railway operates over a few miles between Holt and Sheringham.

LINE 3, line branching off to the west just below King's Lynn used to go to Wisbech, and thence onwards to March and Peterborough. It closed in 1968. There are proposals to restore sections of this line.

LINE 4 ran eastwards from King's Lynn and meandered to Norwich via Swaffham and Dereham. Although not on Beeching's 'hit list', it also closed in 1968. The only remnant is a short section which runs for good trains only between King's Lynn and the sand quarries mentioned in the story.

LINE 5 ran from Wells to connect with Line 4 at Dereham, and went onwards from there. Passenger services were withdrawn in 1969 – goods services continued over part of the line until 1989.

A narrow-gauge heritage railway operates between Wells and Walsingham.

LINE 6. The King's Lynn to Hunstanton branch wasn't earmarked for closure under the 'Beeching Plan' either, but controversially it went anyway in 1969. Unusually, goods services were withdrawn even before passenger services.

The Monarch can no longer travel to the 'royal' station at Wolferton – it's necessary to leave the train at Lynn and go the rest of the way by car. The late Queen often did this, travelling on a public train.

Hunstanton station has been completely demolished, and the area once covered by that and the extensive station yard and sidings is now a combination of shops and car park. The other five stations on the line have all been converted to private houses.

Anyone who has struggled in the horrendous queues of road traffic trying to get into Hunstanton on any day in summer might think that closure of this railway was a serious error of judgement, and over fifty years later there are plans to re-open the line. The inherent difficulties are considerable; time will tell if they are insuperable.

BOOKS BY THIS AUTHOR

The Bedroom Window Murder

It is 1949. Sir Francis Sherwood – WW1 hero, landowner, magistrate – is shot dead while standing at an open bedroom window in his country house. A rifle is found in the grounds.

The county police seek help from Scotland Yard.

Detective Chief Inspector Bryce and Detective Sergeant Haig are assigned to the case. The first difficulty for the Yard men is that nobody with even a mild dislike of Sherwood can be found.

But before that problem can be resolved, others arise...

The Courthouse Murder

In July 1949, an unpopular and deeply unpleasant man is stabbed in the courthouse of an English city. As the murder has been committed in a room to which the general public doesn't have access, it seems probable that the culprit is someone involved with the business of the courts.

Suspects include a number of lawyers, police officers, and magistrates.

For various reasons, the local Chief Constable decides to ask Scotland Yard to investigate the murder.

Chief Inspector Philip Bryce and Sergeant Alex Haig are assigned to the case.

Theirs is a recent partnership, but the two men worked well together in another murder case a few weeks before. (See 'The Bedroom Window Murder'.)

The Felixstowe Murder

In August 1949, Detective Chief Inspector Bryce and his new bride are holidaying in the East Anglian seaside resort of Felixstowe.

During afternoon tea in the Palm Court of their hotel, a man dies at a nearby table.

Reluctant to get directly involved, Bryce

nevertheless agrees to help the inexperienced local police inspector get to grips with his first murder case, turning his own honeymoon into a 'busman's holiday'.

Multiples Of Murder

Three more cases for Philip Bryce. The first two are set in 1949, and follow on from The Bedroom Window Murder, The Courthouse Murder, and The Felixstowe Murder.
The third goes back to 1946, when Bryce – not long back in the police after his army service – was a mere Detective Inspector, based in Whitechapel rather than Scotland Yard.

1. In the office kitchen of a small advertising agency in London, a man falls to the floor, dead. Initially, it is believed that he had some sort of heart attack, but it soon becomes clear that he had received a fatal electric shock. A faulty kettle is then blamed. But evidence emerges showing that this was not an accident. Chief Inspector Bryce is assigned to the case.

2. Just before opening time, a body is found in the larger pool at the huge public baths in St Marylebone. The man has been shot, presumably the previous evening. It is DCI Bryce's task, aided by Detective Sergeant Haig and others, to discover the identity of the victim, why he was

killed, and who shot him.

3. For a few months in 1946, a traditional London bus was modified in an experiment to allow passengers to 'Pay-As-You-Board'. Doors were fitted, instead of having the usual open platform. The stairs rose from inside the saloon rather than directly from the platform. On the upper deck, a man is found stabbed to death. None of the passengers can shed any light on the murder, yet the design of this bus meant that no-one could have jumped off the bus unnoticed – one of them must be the murderer. Inspector Bryce, together with colleagues from Leman Street police station, solves one of his earlier cases.

Death At Mistram Manor

In September 1949, a wake is being held at a manor house in Oxfordshire, following the burial of the chatelaine. Over a hundred mourners are present.

Within an hour, the clergyman who conducted the funeral service is taken ill himself. The local doctor, present at the wake, provisionally diagnoses appendicitis, and calls for an ambulance. However, the priest dies soon after being admitted to hospital.

An autopsy reveals that the cause of death was strychnine poisoning.

The circumstances are such that accidental ingestion and suicide are both ruled out. The rector was murdered, and the timing means that the poison must have been taken during the wake.

The local police, faced with a lengthy list of potential suspects, ask Scotland Yard to take on the investigation, and the case is assigned to Detective Chief Inspector Bryce and two colleagues.

Although most of the mourners can easily be eliminated from the enquiry, around eight of them cannot. The experienced London officers have to sift through a number of initially-promising indications, before finally being able to identify the killer.

Machinations Of A Murderer

There are at least two reasons why Robin Whitaker wants to eliminate his wife, Dulcie. He is not allowed to drink any alcohol, nor to gamble.

Dulcie controls his life to an extent that he finds

intolerable. But she is also wealthy, so merely leaving her is not an acceptable option.

In most circumstances Dr Whitaker thinks and acts like the very intelligent and highly-educated man he is. However, he has somehow convinced himself that the action of killing his wife is justified. He is also certain that his innate brainpower will give him a significant edge over any police detectives, and allow him to outwit them with ease.

What are his thoughts? How does he make his decisions? What does he do?

Will he get away with murder?

Future books to be published in
the Philip Bryce series:

This Village is Cursed
The Amateur Detective
Demands with Menaces
Murder in Academe

Printed in Great Britain
by Amazon

29134615R00208